THE GHOST OF A LIE

The Ghost of a Lie

A novel

by

MICHELLE GRAHAM-TAYLOR

Adelaide Books
New York / Lisbon
2021

THE GHOST OF A LIE
A novel
By Michelle Graham-Taylor

Copyright © by Michelle Graham-Taylor
Cover design © 2021 Adelaide Books

Published by Adelaide Books, New York / Lisbon
adelaidebooks.org
Editor-in-Chief
Stevan V. Nikolic

For any information, please address Adelaide Books
at info@adelaidebooks.org
or write to:
Adelaide Books
244 Fifth Ave. Suite D27
New York, NY, 10001

ISBN: 978-1-955196-70-3

Printed in the United States of America

To family, the fuel that inspires us daily

Chapter 1

As he walks from his house into the bright sunlight, Joseph sees a lad sitting amongst the carnage that is now his garden, perched on top of an upturned shiny bucket at the very bottom of the property. The bucket catches the harsh sunlight of a clear Invernesian sky. Joseph uses the flat of his hand it's a poor attempt to shield his eyes. He's annoyed. The young man is the only workman in the garden, despite having hired four of them to sort the mess. The lad waves. From the house, Joseph can make out one skinny arm, held high above his head, as he gesticulates in an over-exaggerated manner. Needing to find out what is going on, where his other workmen have gone off to, Joseph makes his way unhurriedly to where the boy sits.

Spring threatens even this far north. There's lightness in the air, and with it comes a newness that washes the colours and blurs the shape of the landscape. A self-sustaining, self-creating cycle that promises much. What was drab, rain-soaked, and dead is once more on its way to being resplendent and restored. Joseph wants to take the time to notice and appreciate all this, but he can't. His focus is on the young man on the upturned bucket, and the work that still needs finished.

As he nears the lad, Joseph looks about him, seeing dirt and destruction where once there were beautiful lawns. The pungent earthy smell of mud and something decomposing spoils the air. His gaze returns to the lad, his mop of hair is without shape or style, the colour matching perfectly the mud he is sitting in.

Assuming the young man knows who hired him, after all it is Joseph's garden he is sitting in, Joseph forgoes introductions and asks, "Where are the others?"

A few short months ago, as crisp cold air filled their lungs, Joseph had looked out across these grounds, then well tended and well ordered. He'd taken the seat beside his wife, and Mary, sinking back into her coat, had prophesied that Joseph would be "fine" and that he would in time reclaim his prosaic life. "Like the garden, the landscape and the trees," she'd said, "you will remain unchanged.... fine."

He recalls trying and failing to make an acceptable response. Saying "No," and then "I will miss you" Mary had sworn at that, and gone inside. Now he is an unwilling witness to the re-run of that very moment. He sees her. She is there, able to manifest in the soft sunlight beneath a canopy of leaves. Where favoured trees have endured the storm, she now walks in and out of the sunlight. He watches the familiar way she carries herself, conservative in her movements but still graceful in her sulk. The coat gone, replaced by a simple shapeless summer dress that ends at her knees. The pattern faded, washed out by the same light that blurs the scenery. Her shoulder-length hair sways in time with each step she takes. He thinks, "'Fine' is a shitty little word, one that has come to epitomise my life so well."

Fine. It had always been there, hidden in the marriage, anchored to the uneasiness but masked by their respectable middle class roles. The lie that everything was 'fine' had served them both well. Now the apparition of Mary is sulking about the garden, showing her displeasure. She is, he thinks, determined to bring the truth of that lie back to life.

Paunchy and middle-aged; Joseph feels everyone of his 47 years. With button brown eyes, a sore back, and hair cut into the same style since childhood, he is a humourless and aloof workaholic with a dogmatic and tactless approach to situations and people. He worries far too much what others think of him and now tormented by regret for what might have been a wasted and wretched marriage. Disappointment agitates his guts. It fuses with the niggling certainty that he is taking the first hesitant steps into madness, having yet to come up with a plausible explanation for why he is seeing the apparition of his recently deceased wife. It has left him with no choice but to hide himself away and hope that the madness passes.

Mary shows her displeasure with caustic silence and withering glances, Joseph wonders, is it because she's dead or is it born out of frustration at no longer being able to nag at him? Perhaps it's because she was wrong, he thinks. She hated to be wrong.

The storm, when it hit, gusted in from the west, dislodging trees. Branches weighted with snow during the winter months, with roots loosened by heavy rain and waterlogged soil, ripped from the ground. In the days after the storm, Joseph learnt that there's a lot more to a fallen tree than what is noticeable when still rooted in place. The uppermost branches of a beast of a thing just missed the house, but the trunk flattened a good portion of the side wall and the roots scratched a significant scar into what were once linen-smooth lawns. Yes, he thinks, as he looks about that garden, Mary was wrong, neither he nor the landscape has remained unchanged.

The storm and the destruction to his property, along with the persistent and annoying messages still being left on his answerphone by family, close friends and work colleagues who continue to reject the belief that he has cut them all adrift, has led Joseph to the timely realisation that opting out of life, and all aspects of any normal routine, is bloody hard work.

As he stands side on to the young man still seated on his bucket, Joseph is further annoyed that now he has no choice. He is being forced to re-engage with the outside world. He hopes the hiring of workmen to get the mess sorted will only cause a brief slip in his solitude. The four of them had arrived that morning in a flatbed lorry pulling a clapped-out trailer, a complicated looking piece of machinery insecurely tagged on to the back. And now, standing in the wreck of his garden, stumped by the disarray and damage, Joseph wonders how much of an intrusion into his mental meltdown all this will cause. Adding to the rest of the mess that is his garden are the bits of tools and work gear, but only a single loan workman, and even the lad is not using any of the tools. He is just sitting on his bucket as if it were a throne.

Joesph's question has caused the lad to look up, and he squints because of the sun's position high in the cloudless sky just behind Joseph's right shoulder. He then points at the dirt between his feet.

"Look," he says, his head now bowed, dejection sludged into the single word. Perfectly suited to the heaviness of his actions, thinks Joseph.

When Joseph looks to where he is pointing, all he can see is a darker stain of mud. Having asked a question that needs answered, he refuses to ask a further one; an unnatural silence settles between them. When the young man looks up, Joseph sees that expectancy has replaced the despondency of moments before.

"What... am I supposed to be looking at?" Joseph asks, finally giving in. His response, he knows, is huffy, but the young man's silence and the lack of any meaningful work being done to fix the mess tries his patience.

The lad digs the toe of his work boot into the dirt before answering, and when he speaks, his voice surprises Joseph. Soft, only a breathy whisper, the words stutter out in amongst a thick inner-city accent. Even within the silence of the garden, Joseph must strain to hear him whine.

"Ah spilt ma juice."

Joseph's own words and his pattern of speech are more "cleaned up," the result of years of studying away from home the long periods of time helping perfect his skills as a doctor and clear communicator.

"And?" he says, still huffy, his irritability compensating for his not knowing what else to do. The realisation that all is "not right" with this lad forces him to temper his response, but only slightly.

"Ah'm thirsty. Ah've bin working real hard all morning, and now Ah've nae juice."

Joseph would like to challenge "working real hard," but the young man whines on, not giving him a chance too.

"Dae you think it's awe rite tae drink fae the hose?" he says, and he points at the hose as if Joseph doesn't know what one is. The hose is lying in the dirt, clear, fresh water trickles from the mud incrusted end, as if its sole purpose is to torment.

"No. It's covered in mud and you will make yourself ill," Joseph says. To which the lad throws himself backwards off the bucket. He is lying in the dirt, his long skinny limbs elegantly splayed, one arm now dramatically covering his face.

"What are you doing?"

Unprepared for such odd behaviour, Joseph lets his voice reveal his alarm, and the lad, knowing he has centre stage, peers out from underneath his arm, needing to move it just a little so he can see his onlooker better and pouts. This time when he speaks, the words are woeful.

"Ah'm thirsty," is all he says, and straight away Joseph feels a need to make amends. As annoyed as he is with the workmen, and the mess that they've still to sort, and the lad is one of them and therefore also responsible, he wants to put things right for this dirty individual. He looks to be in his early twenties, but his mannerisms are those of someone much younger, more like a stroppy teenager than a young adult.

"Come up to the house and you can fill your bottle from the tap in the kitchen," he offers, but the lad will not have his misery so easily resolved and whines on.

"Ah'm nae allowed," he says. But it is Joseph's garden, and he puts his hands on his hips, backing up this authoritative stance with a statement of equal weight.

"Nonsense," he says before clicking his fingers at the boy still lying in the dirt. Dirt that should be a nice, well-tended stretch of lawn, Joseph reminds himself.

"Get up," he orders, but this increases the young man's attitude, and making no effort to respond, he interrupts Joseph again.

"Ah've tauld you Ah'm nae allowed."

"Who says?"

"Uncle Tony. He says am tae stay here oan this bucket and keep care of the equipment."

"Keep care?" Joseph questions, as this is not a phrase he is familiar with. Sitting up, the lad pulls the bucket which got away from him, back between his legs, and he places his large dirty hands flat on its surface so it looks like he's about to play a drum.

"Keep care of everything while the others gae tae the pub."

And now Joseph understands. They have left the lad behind, he is dirty and more than a little "special" and so not welcome to go along with the rest of the workers when they go off site for lunch. Instead, he has the pointless job of watching the equipment and the added humiliation of sitting on a bucket. Taking his time before he speaks again, Joseph looks about the garden. There is an ominous smell. Something has crapped or died nearby, but shrugging off his revulsion at the smell and still resolved to muster some sympathy for the lad, he tries a softer approach.

"This is my garden, and so I'm in charge here," he explains. "So, if I say it's all right to come up to the house, then it's all right."

Joseph looks briefly back at the lad and then away again as he speaks, but when there's no answer, he must look back down and away from the damaged garden. The lad squints badly into the sun, and so Joseph shuffles round just enough to block out the glare.

"Whit abit staying on the bucket?" the lad asks.

"You're not even on the bucket," Joseph points out.

"Whit abit keeping care of the stuff?"

"You can see it from up at the house. I could see you from up there and you could see me, right?"

"Right," the lad says, leaping to his feet. They stand more or less the same height. "Mister," he says, as they begin the short walk back towards the veranda.

"Yes?"

"Can Ah fill my water bottle, and then drink the water, and then fill it back up? Dae you think it would be awe rite tae dae that, cos Ah'm very thirsty."

Joseph, thinking about Mary and not the person walking beside him, frowns before answering. Everything is a reminder everything triggers unwanted memories of her.

"That would be fine," he tells him, as they reach the steps up to the veranda. Each step marked by a plant in a pot on alternating sides, another prompt, another unpleasing testament left by her. She is waiting for them at the bottom of the steps; or so it appears to Joseph. As he goes to pass her, she lifts her hand to tuck a stray piece of hair behind her ear and the sunlight bounces off her wedding ring. The movement strikes Joseph as a perfect blend of memory and actual happenings.

From the very onset of their union, Mary made no secret of the fact that she intended to be the one to bury a spouse. Younger, fitter and with a far healthier lifestyle lifestyle, Joseph believes that now her persistent presence is in part some ethereal payback because he had the audacity to survive her. It's the debris of disappointment that death has not delivered on its most fundamental promise, and that they have in fact 'not parted', that is upsetting them both. Joseph believes it is reason enough to keep the heat of anger and the spark of madness smouldering. It fires him up, the very sight of her each time she intrudes into his attempts to grieve, reminding him of every deceit, every lie they shared.

Now, careful to avoid even the slightest contact with her presence, he moves past her and on up the steps. Aware that his guest has hesitated and is still standing at the bottom, he forces a laugh, amused at the thought the lad might have stopped because he sees her too!

Now standing in the kitchen, his head tilted slightly to one side, Joseph watches as Mary follows him into the house. The light changing from bright sunshine to the dullness of indoors means her image flickers and readjusts before once more coming into focus. Only when the apparition settles in the stronger light by the open back door does Joseph call to the young man, "If you're thirsty, come on up."

It is then that it occurs to Joseph that he could have taken the bottle and filled it for him. It's not that long a walk, and it

would have meant his madness and his privacy remained unin-
terrupted. To invite him onto the veranda and further into the
kitchen, into his home, he now thinks, is foolish, he doesn't
know this lad, and he doesn't want to get to know him, definitely doesn't want to have to invest any time on this errand.
What he wants, he thinks lamely, is to rewind his now-disman-
tled life and have its wretched normality return, at least the
parts that still suit him such as they were.

But Joseph has made the offer, and although he is now
berating himself as he listens to the heavy tread of work boots
on wooden steps, he does not renege. By the time the young
man stands framed in the doorway, Joseph's eyes have adjusted
to the gloomy light of the kitchen.

"Sink," he says, pointing, and he means that the lad is to use
the tap to fill his water bottle and then go. And understanding
this one word directive, in the heavy work boots, the young man
lumbers to the sink and fills the water bottle before drinking the
entire contents without taking a breath. A little water escapes,
which runs down his chin as he fills the bottle back up.

"Ah sure was thirsty," he says, wiping his mouth with the
back of one large dirty hand; the water mixes and smears the
dirt further across his face.

Being inside and out of the sun's glare means Joseph can
see him better now. His mouth has the corners cut deep, giving
the illusion of a permanent smile; but when he pouts as he is
now, it exaggerates the sulk. It is an attractive face, even covered in dirt. It is still easy to appreciate the fine features, the
delicate press of the cheekbones. The filthy mop of hair frames
the lad's beauty, and whilst it shouldn't add anything, its dirty
untidiness seems to make the fineness of his features and the
perfection of his face even more intense. His eyes are vacant but
not cold, and they hold Joseph's attention. He notes that the

white of the eye and the iris have merged with the limbal ring. The uniform Gainsborough grey hue gives the impression that they are in fact colourless, leaving the only substantive colour to come from the exaggerated blackness of the pupil. There is a striking and empty quality to the young man's stare. If pushed to give a diagnosis, Joseph would consider ocular albinism, even though the lad doesn't show any other traits.

"What's your name?" It's an open question, one Joseph has asked many times in the past but had not intended to ask now. Strike up a conversation, and then… what?

"Nate," the lad says, shuffling his feet around so he turns in a circle as he speaks, getting a good look at the kitchen.

"Nate? Is that short for something?"

Another question? Inside Joseph's head, he lectures himself. Why prolong this? Is he now so desperate for company that he would want to converse with this dirty, monosyllabic youth? 'If it is companionship that you want, he tells himself, phone Lachlan or George' friends he has had since childhood who's phone calls and messages have gone unanswered for weeks. "Or if you're desperate, dad or Kenneth" he laughs to himself at this, at the thought of being so in need of company that he would turn to his father or brother.

"Nathan. Nathan McGillivray," the young man says as he completes the circle and returns to his original position. Having been a GP for many years, Joseph knows most of the locals, but this is not a name that registers with him.

"Are you from around here?"

Joseph looks him up and down as he speaks, trying to put an age to the lanky frame. This is a young man just starting out in life, he thinks, tall and thin. But too thin is Joseph's assessment. There is not an extra ounce of fat on him, but physical work has developed his muscles, every one of which Joseph can see through his ill-fitting and worn clothes.

"Ah'm jist here tae fix the garden," he says, and it's clear he does not understand the question.

"No, do you and your family live local?" Joseph persists.

"Ah live with my dad and Irene."

The lad, standing in the kitchen holding the water bottle, looks lost and uncertain, and perhaps, Joseph thinks, waiting to be dismissed. The disgusting smell from the garden has followed them into the kitchen, and Joseph wonders which one of them has walked in something. He is about to investigate further when the lad says, "Gonnae gie us an apple?" On the kitchen table is a large and lavish fruit bowl, and no doubt the lad registered the contents as he made his inspection of the room.

"Ah'm hungry and thirsty," he says, as if clarifying the request, and Joseph laughs easily at his cheek.

"Let me see your hands." The lad puts down the water bottle and holds up his hands to show that they are empty; Joseph means only to check that they are clean.

"Wash them and you can have an apple," Joseph tells him, and then not convinced that washing has made any difference to the cleanliness of the hands, he chooses the apple for him, tossing it. The lad catches the piece of fruit with ease.

"Thank you," he says.

The kettle boils, and the familiar prolonged sound of water bubbling in a confined space is both comforting and distracting. For a moment, Joseph thinks of nothing other than making a drink. He is on automatic pilot as he asks, "Do you want coffee?"

"Ah have water."

"Don't you drink coffee?"

"Ah dinnae ken. Should Ah go back? Ah think Ah should go back. The stuff might get took'en."

"It might get taken," Joseph says, correcting the boy without thinking, causing the lad to let out a wail and run from the kitchen, dispersing Mary's ethereal image on the way out and dumping the apple and water on the table outside.

"Nathan!" Joseph shouts, making it outside in time to watch him leap from the top step down onto the grass, which is still green and perfect here by the house, un-marred by the mayhem that has occurred further on up the garden.

"Nathan, wait up. The equipment is fine."

"You said its bin took'en."

"No, I meant… Never mind. You can see it's all still there. Come back up to the veranda and you'll see it's fine."

Lumping his way back up the steps, Nathan comes to stand as close as he can to Joseph. It is then Joseph realises the smell has nothing to do with dead animals or scat and everything to do with Nathan.

"See, it's all still there," Joseph says.

"Uncle Tony would skelp me if stuff got took'en."

Deciding against correcting him, Joseph turns his head away from the smell that is getting worse. Their meeting he feels has reached its natural end, "Perhaps you should go back now, before the others return. That way you won't get into any trouble. I don't want you to get into trouble," He says.

It is then that Nathan holds out his hand for Joseph to take. "Thank you fur the water and the apple," he says, and they shake hands.

"You're welcome," Joseph says, and he means it, and with that Nathan takes his things from the table and makes his way back to his bucket.

Joseph watches the lad's journey back to his seat, as he sits back down he uses the very tips of his fingers to wave, it is a much sadder, quieter gesture—a goodbye, not hello.

Chapter 2

Joseph stands at the front window and watches for the workmen to return. He will, he thinks, monitor the work being done. If nothing else, it will be a welcome distraction from the unsettling experience of Mary, of witnessing her mismanagement of light. She is, he tells himself, still new at this, and manifesting as she does must require practice and patience. Neither are qualities she ever possessed in abundance.

Joseph watches as Nathan takes a swig of water every so often. The lad's focus is on the road. He straightens himself out, stretching to peer over the abundance of foliage without raising his backside from the bucket. From his raised vantage point Joseph sees the workmen return before Nathan does. There is something in the way the oldest of the workman walks. In the way his arms hang tight to his sides, Joseph believes his intentions are not good.

With the sun still in his eyes, Nathan cannot see what Joseph sees even as the man nears. The man, without breaking stride, kicks at the bucket and it flies out from under the boy, leaving him sprawled in the dirt. The once-silent garden now ripples with the workmen's amusement at the lad's misfortune. The bucket kicker then holds out a hand. Joseph thinks it's meant as a peace offering. However intended, Nathan, red-faced and with downcast eyes, declines it. Rolling away from the group, he gets himself to his feet unaided.

Once Nathan is upright, the group gathers in a huddle for a brief discussion. Then, as if choreographed, the workmen go about their business, each man with his own task to perform. Two of them shovel debris into a wheelbarrow while Nathan waits patiently until the barrow is full and then heads off to empty it at some pre-designated area that Joseph cannot see. It is the only time Joseph sees Nathan included in the goings-on. The mess that has come to define the garden diligently tackled for the rest of the day, and while the workmen work, Joseph watches.

It was Mary's decision that they would remain childless, that they would settle in the Highlands and live away from other people, turning what had been a four-bed family home into a two-bedroom en-suite extension to the workplace. It was also her idea to turn the second lounge into a home-office and take away the entire north-facing wall in the larger sitting room, replacing the stones with toughened glass so they would have the panoramic splendour of parts of the Great Glen Way to look at. It is from here that Joseph surveys the work being done.

A hint of the original farm with stonework in the traditional style remains. But not unlike its lone occupant, the house gives the impression it has turned its back on the ever-expanding village below the sloping sides of the crag, looking North, choosing instead to appreciate the views of an abundant forest in favour of the manmade abortion that sits behind and beneath it.

For the last two hundred years, the old farm's stone walls and slate roofs have endured high winds, snow and torrential rain, clinging as it has always done to the side of the Ben. In summer, the track leading up to the house is dusty and riddled with potholes; in the winter ice cracks and compromises the bedrock, and snow drifts into the high points, causing humps and bumps to form blocking the way. Joseph loves that. It puts all but those most determined of visitor off making the effort. A small price to pay for having no post delivered or bins emptied.

The wisdom of living in such an isolated place now that Mary is supposedly gone, and the legacy of his own aloneness, causes Joseph to reflect now on whether he will remain here. They'd always loved the property best in winter when the feeling of seclusion, of being cut off from the rest of the world, was born of fact. Trapped by snowdrifts and slick tarmacked roads of black ice, and forced together in a weird, macabre confinement. And whilst the road from the village leading up to the track supports several other properties, they have all settled at a much more acceptable altitude, builders nowadays defeated by the steep blind bends and narrowness of the road. Only Joseph's home and one other property share the track. What was the outbuilding to the original steading is now a holiday home for a retired sedimentologist from Leeds University. Seldom seen and not one to socialise Joseph has only met her a handful of times. It allows him the pretence that now he alone owns the summit.

Nathan sorts bricks from the broken wall on his own, and the bucket kicker has returned to the truck and brings out two chainsaws of differing sizes. Then the three pub-goers don hard-hats with visors and gloves that stop at the elbow and set about the tree. Fascinated, Joseph pulls a chair up to the window and watches from behind the drapes. They use the smaller chainsaw on the spindly branches that need removed before they can tackle the bigger stuff. They cut bits of tree away, and two of them drag, pull, and push the bits of tree into the chipper. Vibrant green-leafed branches are being transformed into yellowed piles of nothingness. Joseph is sad for the tree, which stood for so many years minding itself. Felled by an obstinate wind following behind the snow at an unfortunate angle. Nothing lasts, he thinks, but trouble and dirt, and now the tree is both.

The workmen are swift and efficient; the job progressing nicely, and Joseph has little to complain about. The bucket kicker comes to the back door late on and calls out, "Mr Murphy."

Coming to the door, Joseph finds the workman already back on the bottom step. Saw-dusty from the chipper, each movement he makes agitates delicate crap-clouds of dirt that catch in the sunlight.

"Mr Murphy," he says again.

"Doctor Murphy," Joseph corrects him, deciding on a brief opt back into his life.

"Sorry," the workman says without sounding it. "That's us away."

Joseph, making a point of looking at his watch, says nothing.

"The light's fading fast back there, and Ah don't like tae use the machinery when the light's nae so guid."

Copying Nathan from earlier on in the day, Joseph lets the silence hang between them. Finally the workman says, "We'll be back first thing tae-morrow."

Looking down on the man, Joseph feels he has more than just the moral high ground, and without answering, he turns and goes back inside.

That night his dreams are heavy and muddled, and in attempting to fix and make sense of the nonsense, he tells himself it is just a dream even whilst still immersed within it. Mary is there, her image frozen in time. Only ever an observer to the action, she is in the way. Each time Joseph attempts to reach Nathan, she blocks his path. In the dream, it is clear to Joseph that in death as she was in life Mary is there for one purpose, to stop him from reaching his goal. He sees her face as it was, and it frustrates him, for in the three short months since she passed he has changed and she has not. He tries to sort the facts. Like the men with the tree branches, he wants to tidy the facts away, only he can't work the wood chipper and Mary is sitting on the bucket. Nathan being trapped in the house, and Mary falling from the bucket and being hurt breaks the dream causing Joseph to wake.

Early the next morning, still lethargic from lack of sleep, Joseph needs to hurry getting the daily paper and some fresh milk before the workmen appear. When he returns, sitting on the veranda warding off the chill from a deficient sun, he waits for them to arrive and unpack their equipment. He sees Nathan stowed in the back of the flatbed, no safety belt, no protection, and then Joseph watches as jumping from the vehicle he is given his instructions before setting off to do what he's been told. Two of the men go through the gap in the wall and start work there; the third cranks up the larger of the two chainsaws and attacks the main body of the fallen tree. Joseph would have liked to sit outside and make the most of another fine if still cold day, but the mess, the intrusion of the workmen, and the distraction of the lad are all too much. Even knowing that this brief spell of good weather will not last, the noise drives him indoors.

Trying to silence the disruption, he turns on the sports channel. But last night's muddled dream and Nathan's treatment by the workmen yesterday is in his head and won't leave. He cannot silence the noise of the chainsaw destroying the last remnants of a tree that should have stood firm through all of this, and standing in the faded light of the living room, Mary mirrors his own unhappiness. She paces, stopping only to give him a look of restless disquiet. It is a miserable morning.

As it nears lunchtime, however, he stops his negative contemplations and stands by the drapes, watching the workmen as they load themselves into the van—all but one. The man in charge gets the bucket and sits it down in front of Nathan. Then Nathan sits down, and they exchange a few words that Joseph cannot hear before the men leave.

When Joseph is sure they have gone, he moves from the dull interior of his home out onto the veranda, standing where he knows Nathan can see him. Tilting his head up and shading his eyes so he can appreciate the heat from a roused and warm midday sun on his bare arms, he expects Nathan, on seeing him, to wave. He waits, but the expected gesture never comes. Irritated by the perceived slight, he makes the first move, waving benignly at the lad. Still, the boy does not wave back, which only adds to Joseph's annoyance. As he remembers it, they parted yesterday on good terms. They shook hands. Interested to find out why he is ignoring him, Joseph leaves the veranda and walks down to Nathan and his bucket.

"Hi," he says, but Nathan, squinting into the sunlight, says nothing, "So how's it going today?" Joseph asks. Nathan only shrugs. Exasperated, Joseph snaps, "What's wrong? Why are you not speaking to me today?"

"Uncle Tony said nae tae."

"Your Uncle told you not to speak to me?" Nathan nods, then lets his eyes travel slowly over the length of Joseph's frame.

"Why… why would he do that?"

"He said that you're a crabbit auld bastard, an jist cos your garden's a mess and your wife died disnae mean you can take it out oan heem. And that Ah can gie oan a person's last nerve, and that he disnae need me making the whole sit… situation worse, so Ah'm nae tae bother you, and speaking tae you is bothering you. Ah checked that out."

Joseph believed Nathan to be word perfect.

"The tree didnae fall oan your wife's heed, did it?"

"No."

"Well, thank goodness fae that."

The lad's words are simple, thinks Joseph: no sympathy, no thought laced into them. As refreshing as this is, Joseph will not discuss his wife with him or with anyone. He changes the subject.

"Come have lunch with me," he says, not sure where the invite has come from. It had not been his intention to make such an offer when he left the house.

"Ah'm nae allowed tae move, even more nae allowed than yesterday."

"It worked out all right yesterday. Nothing got taken, and you never got into any trouble, did you?"

"Ah'm hungry," Nathan says, and Joseph supposes that it's possible that this young man with the ill-fitting clothes and no fat reserves to speak of is permanently hungry.

"Well, come on up to the house and you can have chicken salad." The lure of food does the trick. Nathan, bouncing up off the bucket, throws an arm out in a casual hook around Joseph's shoulder, which is more physical contact than he is comfortable with or used to. Space is everything to Joseph, and there is an abundance of it not only in the garden but in his life, and without invite, Nathan is invading that space. Turning together, they walk back towards the house and anchored as they are, side by side, their hips bump. Joseph stares straight ahead, his mouth dry, fighting the realisation that he is both confused and intrigued by the closeness. He tries to steady his heartbeat. The smell from the lad is every bit as bad as it was yesterday, and this alone should be reason enough for Joseph to want to put some distance between them. Instead, he alters his step to keep better time with his companion, and breathing through his mouth to avoid the stench, he appreciates the moment for what it is—company. Acutely aware of how easy it is to give life to a lie, he looks away from Mary who is waiting once more for them at the bottom of the steps.

"Mister, Ah don't think you're a crabbit auld bastard," Nathan says, and as he walks, he drags his feet in his heavy work boots in a kind of rolling gait, weaving from side to side like a skilled deckhand mastering a fitful sea. It pulls Joseph into step, but he doesn't respond straight away, processing the boy's words instead. He believes himself to be a pillar of the community frequently asked to sit on committees, boards, and trusts. They don't ask miserable or crabby bastards. They ask educated men who have given up their working lives to help others. Instead of pointing this out, however, he asks, "How old are you?"

"Twenty an' a bit. How old are you?"

"Too old to answer that."

As they reach the steps up to the veranda, Nathan stands aside to let Joseph go first.

"Go wash your hands," Joseph tells him, ignoring Mary, fixing his gaze on Nathan as he speaks.

"Och aye… Yes, sairr," Nathan says, excited now by the prospect of food.

While he lays out the table, Joseph berates himself. Why has he sought this lad's company again? Why is he willing to entertain this stinking young man, why take such a risk? But while the questions bounce about in Joseph's mind, dishonesty prevents him from finding a fitting answer. Here is a person with whom he cannot have a stimulating conversation, someone who smells as bad, if not worse, than yesterday, a…

"Mister, Ah still have juice left, but if Ah drink it right doon, all of it, can Ah fill up the bottle and then drink that, and then fill the bottle up again? Like Ah did yesterday?"

"Joseph," Joseph says, as Nathan looks blankly back at him.
"Huh?"

"My name is Joseph, Doctor Joseph Murphy, but you can call me Joseph, not mister. And yes, you can fill the bottle up as many times as you want."

"Thanks."

"Thanks what?"

"Thanks very much… fur the water."

"No." Joseph laughs, holding out a plate for him.

"Thanks fur lunch."

"You're welcome, but that's not what I was going for."

"Thanks… Jo-seph."

Nathan sounds out the name in two distinct syllables in his soft, breathy, whispering voice, and Joseph smiles.

Sitting outside making the most of the good weather means the added work of bringing out cutlery and plates from the kitchen, but it is still preferable to having Nathan sit inside. The smell coming off him burns in the back of Joseph's throat.

"Sit," he says, and as he gives the instruction Nathan glances towards the equipment and then takes the offered seat. Joseph watches as he picks up his knife and fork. He holds his knife, so it sticks straight up in the air in a death grip between thumb and fingers. It stays this way throughout the meal, never used. The fork is used to squash, saw, and shovel food into his open mouth. It is like watching clothes tumbling about in a dryer, Joseph thinks. The sight, combined with the smell that every so often accosts his nostrils, makes the whole dining experience horrid.

"Ah like it when it's aw mixed taegether," Nathan says, and Joseph can't link the random sentence to anything.

"Sorry?"

Nathan stands up and looks across the garden to the equipment. Satisfied that it is all still there, he sits back down. He has not explained himself, and so Joseph asks, "What do you mean when it's all mixed'?" The sight of the food going around in his mouth is hypnotising now, as if witnessing a car crash; Joseph doesn't want to look, but he just can't help it.

"Ah like putting the chicken with this stuff and the tomato and some ay that other stuff that Ah dinnae ken, and then tasting it aw at the same time."

Then, whilst Joseph holds his napkin in front of his face, mostly his nose, in a futile attempt at preventing the smell from invading his nostrils, Nathan gives a demonstration.

"That's lettuce and cucumber, and those are green and red peppers," Joseph informs him.

Nathan stands up again and looks across the lawn. "Still thaur," he announces to himself before sitting back down. He does not acknowledge the information given. Nathan's movements have stirred the air.

As a doctor, Joseph knows all too well how disgusting the human body can be, capable of generating horrific smells even when looked after. No one looks after this lad. He does not smell of clean fresh sweat from hard work, but the more musty overbearing smell of dirty hair, pee, and old rancid sweat—and feet.

"Do you like the work you do?" Joseph asks.

"Ah'm lucky tae have a job tis all."

The food continues to churn and tumble, and Joseph tries to time his next question so that Nathan's mouth is almost empty.

"How so?"

"Cos Ah' am a not-right."

The words said around a rather ambitious bite of chicken leave Joesph wondering if he has heard the boy correctly.

"Sorry. You're a what?"

"A not-right," Nathan says again slowly, this time with his mouth almost empty.

Putting the napkin down, Joseph studies the boy. "And what's that exactly?"

Nathan laughs, finding the question somehow amusing. "You ken."

"No, I don't think I do," Joseph tells him, and he can hear an edge in his own voice when he speaks.

"Ah'm slow, stupid. NOT RIGHT in the heed," he says, exaggerating his words for emphasis and speaking slowly, as if Joseph might be the one not right in the head.

"Who says?"

"All fowk. Everyone."

"Everyone?" Joseph repeats the word just to make sure he has it correct.

Nathan stands up again to look down the garden. He nods. "Still thaur," he says.

"Still there," Joseph says, and mirroring him, he nods too. Nathan has finished his meal, and deciding that the smell mixed with the heat from the sun is becoming unbearable, Joseph says, "Perhaps you should go back now, before the others return. We don't want you to get into any trouble."

Standing again, Nathan holds out his hand and they shake on the meal. "Thank you fur the water, and the other water, and thank you fur the chicken salad with aw the lettuce, tomatoes, and peppers—the red and green ones. Ah liked it aw very much, Joseph," he says, which makes Joseph smile. The supposed not-right has taken everything in?

"You are most welcome, and I'm glad you enjoyed it so much. It was nice having company," he says, and he means it.

In this young man, Joseph believes, he might have found someone worse off than he is. Morosity and madness, he thinks, welcome an alliance with someone kindred to suffering.

"Watch out for their return this time, and stand up just before he kicks the bucket," Joseph says. Nathan has turned his back whilst Joseph is still speaking, thinking the conversation is over. Joseph thinks he has embarrassed him, and for a moment he regrets saying anything.

But then Nathan says, "That's jist Uncle Tony funning."

Joseph now feels a further need to point out it wasn't funny. The young man's quirky mannerisms, hesitant speech, and discreet beauty not only have him intrigued but have stirred a protectiveness within Joseph that he'd not realised he possessed.

Chapter 3

Joseph remains inside the house during the morning, coming out only when he is sure the workmen have left for the pub. From the veranda, he waves for Nathan. They spend the hour together over lunch. Mary ventures out onto the veranda to join them, seeking the patches of bright sunlight in preference to the shade. She paces, twisting her faded fingers together as her image, troubled by the shadows, splinters into pieces. Joseph thinks she looks nervous, seeing perhaps something in their future that he cannot. It compels him to glance from one awkward acquaintance to the other, from the illusory image of his wife to the very real presence of the young man seated at his table.

He is grateful that, at least so far, the spectral form of his dead wife has consented to remain silent and contained about their home, suppressed within his own fragmented mind. Still, fear that this madness might somehow seep out and become public knowledge keeps him imprisoned. It has forced him to give up on his career and friendships, so instead of working twelve hours a day and carrying a heap of unresolved work issues back and forth; he hides and hopes the anger and psychosis will pass.

With the meal finished and everything returned to the kitchen, they once more shake hands before Nathan makes his way back to the bucket. He is, Joseph thinks, a welcome distraction and, by choice, his only social interaction now. He tells himself that unlike his normal acceptable and perceptive circle of friends, Nathan is too stupid to see the madness and too down on his own luck to offer a judgement on any part of Joseph's life.

Nathan dances into Joseph's dream. In the dream, he makes his way through all the rooms in the house, even though Joseph knows that this has never happened. The lad has only ever stood in the kitchen. The restlessness of trying to correct the details causes a weighty fatigue and tired, useless limbs impede Joesph's futile attempts to fix the specifics. Mary is ever present, looking miserable, tired and detached, possibly because she's displaced, but Joseph thinks it probably has more to do with Nathan being in their home and the dream. Even though Mary remains silent on the matter, she can still direct her unhappiness at him. He is sure she is jealous of Nathan, of his aliveness and sentience, but her quiet, guarded anger is just for Joseph. Mary might be unhappy with Joseph, but in the dream Nathan is ecstatic.

Joseph, once more deprived of sleep, leaves the bed and goes naked downstairs and out onto the veranda. The night is warm, and except for the incessant strains of insects, silent. Humid air clings to his bare skin, raising bumps, pressing him to rub his hands up and down his arms to stave off the unwelcome feeling. In the darkness, the garden is a changed and unfamiliar landscape. Misshapen trees blend into their own shadows, and the mountains, disguised by the grey night sky, look closer than they are. Joseph fancies he can stretch out his hands and touch the unforgiving stone. Being able to hold something tangible and permanent in defiance of the weird and confusing mess that surrounds him pleases him. His perception of the mountains being closer than they are, close enough to touch fits with the trickery his senses play on him when he sees Mary flicker and form in the sunlight. He is not seeing reality, but what his bereaved and broken brain conjures up to fill in the blanks. Nothing exists he thinks independent of one's own mind. When you are in your right mind, the world exists and shows up to be experienced. But if you lose your mind…. Thoughts tangle inside his head like piles of spaghetti; he has been here, he thinks, too many times before.

As he stands naked on the veranda, he pictures himself still within the dream. The light and the smells of the night are so different from the day that it feels like he should still be asleep and able to fix everything and make Mary happy. There's also the nakedness. It is mischievous to stand in the darkness exposed, even though it is his house, his garden, and his night. Naked in the dark, alone and resolute, Joseph decides that he will not see Nathan tomorrow. He hopes then Mary may quit her insomnious torment and sleep will come without interruption.

It is the sound of the men having already arrived and working in the garden, which finally wakes him. Joseph watches for a while from behind the drapes before committing to the plan he has made the night before. He leaves, his intention is to stay out until the workmen have finished for the day. He will tell Nathan that he has had to work, and then he laughs at this. Why would he need to tell him anything when he intends never to see or speak to him again?

With the work finished, the young man will go. Leaving Joseph alone once more.

"Alone" is now a thing with form. It haunts him like Mary haunts him, but not as memory or regret. Aloneness is like the road he is driving down, endless and uninspiring but taking him somewhere. The thought that 'somewhere' is away from

Nathan twists his insides and causes him to consider stopping the car to throw up. Instead, he makes a U-turn at the first place he finds that is safe to do so and heads home. It is only when he is about to pull into the drive that the realisation that he has nothing to feed Nathan hits him, and he turns around again to sort that.

When he returns home for the second time, he does not go into the house but straight into the garden. Nathan is his priority now. He is ten minutes adrift, and as always, Nathan is there sitting on the bucket. Feeling bad for keeping him waiting, Joseph jogs the last part of the garden, trying to give the impression of making up for lost time.

"I'm sorry," he says, straight off admitting his guilt. Joseph does not lie and say he has had to work, but lifts the bag he is carrying to show him he has brought food. It is a gift for Nathan, something special, and he thinks the lad should understand.

"I bought lunch… take away… to make up for… for keeping you waiting," he says, but Nathan does not move, does not speak, and does not smile.

"You coming?" Joseph asks as he turns to walk towards the house. He takes four steps before realising he is not being followed. Turning then to see Nathan still looking at him, he feels tricked, having shown more of himself than he'd intended to in his strained apology. In Nathan's expression, the cold, hostile honesty of his eyes, and the silence of his voice, Joseph senses a new understanding. Dogmatic and tactless, he might be, but Joseph also considers himself perceptive when it's required.

Dropping his head, Nathan uses one already filthy fingernail to dig into the mud between his feet.

"I bought take away for us, for you, to say sorry. It's not chicken salad, but it will still be good, and I'm sorry. There, I've said it twice."

"Three times," Nathan corrects him, still refusing to look up. "If you dinnae want tae have lunch with me, then fine, dinnae have lunch. Jist say so. Dinnae gae off and leave me waiting… jist sitting here waiting an' hoping."

"You'd just be sitting there waiting anyway, even if I had told you."

"NO." Nathan is obviously angry. His words crack, taper, and then fade, and when he looks up at Joseph his eyes are cold puddles of misery. Now that he has looked up, Joseph wishes he hadn't.

"Not waiting and hoping, jist sitting. Big difference. Ah might sit here oan a bucket, but Ah am nae a bucket." He then goes back to digging with that one dirty fingernail, which Joseph thinks is a beautifully elegant and abused digit at odds with the vexation of mud. One dirty fingernail and now there is one insignificant fingernail-sized hole in the ground.

"Stop that. My garden's a big enough mess already," Joseph snaps, unable to contain himself any longer. His own anger is clear in the harshness of his tone and in the way he holds himself, his feet rooted in place, fists and jaw clenched. Exposed and with nowhere now to hide, it pisses him off. He doesn't owe the lad an apology, any more than he owes him lunch.

"The last thing I need from you, from anyone, is a bloody lecture," he tells him, and the way he says "you" it sounds like a filthy word. Then he retreats, leaving Nathan to his bucket and returning to the house, stopping only to dump the lunch still in its bag in the dustbin. And only when he is safely out of sight of Nathan does he drag in a great lungful of air. Irate but also aroused by the tremors of anger running through him, he finds the sensation oddly pleasing. Nathan's disapproval has ripped into him, setting him afire, and it is good - better than the dull, empty heaviness that he has felt clawing at him for so long. He feels more than a little stupid for overreacting, but he is also grateful to Nathan for finally waking him up.

He paces about the kitchen, the only room that Nathan has stood in, then makes coffee and stands behind the drapes in the lounge, watching as the men come back and work resumes.

"Fix my garden and then get lost," he says out loud, standing in the room, alone and bereft anew. The coffee goes cold in the cup, and the light changes from bright midday to early evening. The workers pack up and go home.

Wednesday arrives hot and dry, the sun breaking through the heavy bedroom drapes, waking Joseph before he is ready. Yesterday's events have stained his dreams. Mary's presence troubles him now whether he is awake or asleep; she plagues all aspects of his life. Accepting that he must sort all the fractured parts—fix the garden, decided on returning to work, re-connect with his friends and possibly his family, piece the splintered parts of his life back together—all he has to do now is work out how. He is drinking coffee and standing in the kitchen in just his underpants when the workmen arrive. They can't see him, but the thought of them, knowing that they are about, is enough to make him shower and dress.

He takes reading materials outside and sits on the veranda in full view of everyone, making it obvious that he is watching the work being done. He has decided that he will not hide anymore. Even when the workmen go for lunch, Joseph continues to sit outside and work. He knows without looking that Nathan is sitting on his bucket down there at the end of the garden with his crummy lunch and a bottle of juice. Joseph half expects him to wave or call out, but he doesn't, and nothing good comes from the standoff.

By the time the workmen leave for the day, he has read a piece of research that has been on his to-do-list for some time, but Nathan has marred the satisfaction gleaned from this achievement. The lad has not caved, has not called out, or better still come up to the house and offered the desired grovelling apology. A measured realisation settles on Joseph as he goes inside: there is something about Nathan that he needs. He'd told himself it was just friendship with someone who also suffers, someone that faces similar struggles. But now it is clear, Nathan might offer more than that, and that thought intrigues and terrifies him.

Thursday Joseph spends the morning concentrating on lunch, and by the time the workmen leave, he has rehearsed what he will do well. He has made himself a sandwich, broken the seal on a bottle of water, and collected his car-cleaning bucket from the garage. He is ready. As the van drives off, he makes his way slowly to the bottom of the garden, walking casually as if he has all the time in the world. Nathan is there, sitting in his usual spot, already halfway through his sandwich. The edges of the "pappy" white bread are dirty where his filthy hands hold it.

"Mind if I join you?" Joseph asks as he sets the bucket down opposite Nathan. Nathan does not speak, but he watches. Joseph's bucket is cheap and plastic and not as stable as his, and as he puts his full weight on it, he feels the bucket object. Joseph must sit still as he unpacks his sandwich and sips the water to avoid tumbling off his seat. He has rehearsed this scene over and over in his head. He takes a bite of his sandwich, another sip of water, looks about the garden, and ponders his next move. Finally, he says, "That was the worst lunch ever."

Still Nathan does not speak.

"How boring is one sandwich?"

That's when Nathan looks away, but he breaks his silence as he does so. "You're making fun ay me?"

"No. I would never. I'm just being like you for the day. I'm seeing what it must be like to be you, eating lunch while sitting on a bucket in some idiot's garden."

The bucket, with prefect Broadway timing, gives way as he says "idiot" and dumps Joseph in the dirt. Falling sideways, the water spills from the bottle over his shirtsleeve. Joseph swears as he sits up, but he does not get up.

"Are you awerite?" Nathan asks, and standing, he retrieves the water bottle and tries to brush the mud from Joseph's shirt. The shirt is already damp between the shoulder blades and under the arms, and the material clings uncomfortably to Joseph's skin. His world is one devoid of all physical contact, but now Joseph feels Nathan's hand running lightly across the barrier of his shirt. Nathan has touched him before, throwing an arm out over his shoulder, and Joseph files that memory with this one to appreciate later.

"Yes, I'm fine. Your bucket is better than mine. This just shows the stupidity of eating lunch sitting on a bucket when I have a perfectly good set of chairs and a table right there," Joseph says, pointing to where he wants them both to be, on the veranda. "But if you won't come up to the veranda, then I guess I have no choice. I think I'd better invest in a stronger bucket."

Nathan nods. He knows about buckets. "Buy a metal one like this. These last forever nae matter how much ye sit oan it," he says, and he bangs the bucket with the flat of his hand to show its strength.

"Will do, but does this mean we have to have lunch here every day now until you finish the work?" Joseph asks.

"You can have lunch wherever you want."

"I want to have it with you."

"Why?"

"Don't ask me that. Just say tomorrow you'll come back up to the house. We can have my Nathan special."

Nathan, sitting back down on the bucket, both hands resting on his knees, leans forward and looks straight at Joseph.

"What's a Nathan special?"

"Chicken salad, of course."

Standing up, Joseph looks at his watch even though he already knows their time is up. He will not risk being seen by the others. He tells himself it is to protect Nathan, knowing full well he is intent on protecting himself.

"I'll come and get you tomorrow. Okay?"

"Mebbe."

"Maybe! Do you have a better offer?"

"No," Nathan says, and he sticks out a dirty calloused finger, the nail edged in mud, and pointing it at Joseph's stomach, he says, "But you might."

"No. I will be here. I will come and get you, I promise."

Nathan does not respond. He looks up and past Joseph, squinting into the sun. Not knowing what else to say or do, Joseph collects the bucket and water bottle. Finally he says, "I will see you tomorrow." He studies the split in the bucket while he waits for an answer.

"Bye," Nathan says, which ends everything, and Joseph nods. He walks back to the veranda, swinging the broken bucket, stopping only to ditch it in the bin on the way up the steps.

Chapter 4

In a moment of reprieve, Joseph caught between the day beginning and the lingering residue of sleep. thinks Mary is still alive. He has had the dream many times, and he knows if he stays within the dream, Mary will stay with him. To awaken and leave will replicate the loss of her, and so he remains in the perfect and painful atrophy of the dream. If he stays asleep, there is still the very real and safe sense that all is well. "Let me dream on," he whispers into the bedding, but the early morning sounds of the day getting started blow the dream and Mary away, causing reality and renewed grief to hit him like a shovel.

As he sits and watches the workmen, whilst still opting out of doing anything more meaningful with his day, Joseph is resolute. He will not let Nathan down, not again. Determined now to be a better person, someone worthy of the lad's 'friendship', he considers how his good intentions can be translated into actions. Nathan is concentrating fully on the work that has been assigned him. He does not stop to chat or laugh with the others, and they in turn disregard him. Joseph ponders this. He too is no longer part of anything, but unlike Nathan, this is now, by choice. Nathan is ostracised because of his real and imagined differences, and the thought, although needlessly unkind, makes Joseph happy. His has been a life of sensed rejection, a mother that already had one son and longed for a daughter. A father that started every sentence of his child-hood with ' I'm disappointed Joseph', to an older brother in whose footsteps he could never hope to emulate. To friends who teased and bullied him into conformity and a wife who was content to settle and chose stability and respectability at the cost of honesty and passion. An imposter in his own life, marriage and family has left Joseph with the awareness that 'Nobody knows me, not the real me. Some of us, he thinks, just don't fit', and the idea that this will be the one thing that serves them both makes him smile.

At lunchtime he stands on the veranda and waves, but Nathan doesn't wave back, nor does he get up from the bucket. So Joseph leaves the veranda and makes the walk once again down to where he is sitting.

"Hi."

"Hi."

"Are you coming? Lunch is ready."

Nathan holds out his hands, showing that he wants to be pulled up off the bucket. Joseph frowns, but playing along, puts both his hands into the lad's pulling him up straight. It is then that Nathan should let go, but he doesn't. Instead, apparently recognising Joseph's own desire for company, he tightens his grip. Then letting go of one of Joseph's hands he keeps hold of the other. Holding hands is, Joseph thinks, unnatural, odd, and yet somehow crucial, eliciting not only forgiveness but also enforcing a bond he wants cultivate between them. Joseph can feel the dustiness of the dirt and hard-calloused skin from all the manual work Nathan does. Reaching the house, he turns Nathan's dirty hands in his own so he can look at them.

"You need to wash these, and try to get the dirt down the sink and not on my towel," he says before letting go. Nathan grins at him as he lets wanting hands fall to his side.

Nathan knows now to take his allotted seat at the table.

"How's it going down there today? I went down there last night when you had all gone home, and it looks like things are getting sorted," Joseph says, all the while trying hard not to react to the smell that still tattoos the lad.

"Yep."

"Has Uncle Tony said how long he thinks the job will take?" Joseph no longer asks because he wants rid of the intrusion.

"He thinks we will be dain by the end ay next week, if the weather stays guid. If nae, then the week efter. We have tae get a move oan because there is awreddy another job waiting." Nathan eats as he speaks, the words cluttered with food.

Joseph looks about the garden and then studies the distressed-by-design marks in the wooden table so he doesn't have to watch the tumble of food. One week and then gone, if the good weather holds. Should he pray for rain?

"What shall we have for lunch tomorrow?"

"Nae here tae-morrow."

"What?"

Joseph's voice is too loud, the question asked too quickly. Nathan, with food frozen in his mouth, looks concerned.

"It's days aff tae-morrow, and the next day, like always."

Joseph has lost track of the days. The weekend is upon him and he has not noticed. All the days now run together, nothing distinguishing them, no one day more pleasant or more important than any other. In the past, keeping track of time, being punctual and the marking of each day, each week, and the passing of each season were central to his life and his work. Now it concerns him that something so important has been so easily neglected. He recovers with another question.

"So you get two days off? What do you do with yourself on your days off?"

"Ah ride my bike."

"And what else?"

"Neathing."

Joseph raises an eyebrow at this. Looking straight at the boy, he wills him to elaborate.

"After Irene makes my cornflakes, then my dad says 'now fuck aff till it's dark'. So Ah gae git my bike from the shed an Ah ride aroond all ower the place till my watch beeps." Nathan shows Joseph the watch, which is cheap plastic and digital.

"Then Ah gae tae Fusion fur my lunch, then Ah ride aroond until it's almost dark, then Ah gae hame and Irene has my tea ready. Then it's bedtime."

"Irene?" Joseph questions, wanting Nathan's story to make more sense.

"Aye, Dad's girlfriend."

"What if the weather's bad?"

"It's like sitting oan the bucket. If Ah'm tauld tae dae something, Ah hud jist better dae it, no matter the weather or if Ah want tae or no."

Words fail Joseph, and because he doesn't answer, Nathan fixes him with a look Joseph is hard-pressed to define. His weird eyes that have no discernible colour pin him to his seat.

"Maw says it's cos Ah'm hard work, nae cos Ah'm bad or naething. Jist being nae right, Ah guess. Ah don't mind, nea so much. Ah get it. My dad jist cannae be bothered with me, that's all."

The time has run away from them, the faint sound of a van pulling into the driveway alerts them both that the workmen are returning. Nathan, jumping to his feet with eyes wide, knocks his chair to the floor in his haste. He runs headlong for the bucket as fast as he can, making it by the narrowest of margins; and Joseph, a spectator to the drama, stands on the veranda holding his breath as he tries to plan a plausible story in case they are caught. Raising his hand to shield his eyes, he sees Nathan gather the bucket beneath him just as the workman get out of the van. Taken by surprise with no time for goodbyes, no time to make plans for next week, Joseph's only consolation is that Nathan is safe.

"Thank God," Joseph whispers before going indoors and staying there until everyone has left.

Mary isn't in his dream, just Nathan. The night is warm and close, and the air hangs heavy in the bedroom. Even in the heat, in the dense airless room, Joseph sleeps untroubled. In the dream he watches, and from this distance, from this other level of consciousness, sees Nathan walk through all the rooms in the house, turning in childlike circles in each of them, marking his territory and defiantly making his presence known.

The weather holds good and dry, but Joseph knows that inevitability hangs in the air. The rains will come at some point soon. Left alone with Mary, her intrusive wanderings and his own thoughts, the prickly panic of madness is never far from his mind. Somewhere in his future he hopes to have a different life, one that he can feel comfortable in, but the how and the when still lie beyond his dreams. His last words spoken aloud were to Nathan on Friday afternoon, and he hasn't seen a living soul since. His world has turned from constant human contact and chatter to silence. It leaves Joseph with the terrible feeling that turning his back on the world, and trusting that time out will mend his fractured lucidity, is not the answer. It is clear it is not working.

Arriving at the bottom of the garden, Joseph holds out his hand to him now. And looking up at him from his subordinate position, Nathan wordlessly takes what is offered.

"How was your weekend?" Joseph asks, and as he speaks these first words, he squeezes Nathan's hand in his own, an unspoken acknowledgement of how much it means to have company.

"Guid. How was yours?"

Looking back at him before he answers, Joseph wonders what has been good about it. The weather? That he has stayed out of trouble?

"Quiet."

"You like quiet."

It is not a question but a statement, one that makes Joseph frown in embarrassment. They've reached the steps. Stalling for time, he places his hand over the top of the Nathan's, sandwiching it now between his own. He smiles, but instead of looking at him, Joseph stares down at their hands to shield his smile. It is not meant for Nathan, not yet.

"Quiet is losing its appeal," he says.

"What's appeal?"

"Here, its charm. I liked quiet, but now I don't. Not so much, anyway."

"Why?"

"Why!"

Joseph thinks about the question. He tastes the words, trying them out before he forms an answer he thinks will do.

"Why, why, why? Well, Nathan, I think it's all to do with you."

"How?"

"Don't ask me that."

Nathan laughs, delighted by the answer, and lifting hands still trapped together, he brushes mischievous lips across Joseph's knuckles. Then he giggles, apparently knowing he is doing something naughty, and together they let go. Taking his normal seat at the table, Nathan stares down at the plate Joseph has offered.

"What's this?" he asks.

"Joseph special."

"Oh." It's all he says. Putting aside the brush of lips against knuckles, the acknowledged pleasure of meeting up again after the forced interruption, Nathan lifts his knife into the air in his usual way, and with his fork, he begins an assault on the food.

"Stir-fry," Joseph says, and is rewarded with a grin, accomplished despite a mouthful of food.

"Ah need tae hurry. Ah only jist made it back last time, and Uncle Tony will be as mad as he can git if he finds me haur with you."

"Why would it bother him?"

"Because he tauld me tae stay away, and when he tells me tae dae something, Ah jist better git and dae it."

"Oh, yes. I remember, something about me being a miserable bastard."

"He disnae ken you, no like Ah do."

"You think you know me?"

Nathan doesn't answer, but instead continues to shovel more food into his mouth before grinning and then making the announcement. "Ah like stir-fry."

Knowing every day now is precious, Joseph puts great thought into what he will prepare for lunch. And each day he waits for the van to leave before going down to collect Nathan, now a ritual. He no longer waves to encourage him to make his own way up the garden because going to collect him means there is the fleeting opportunity for physical contact.

But the distance from boy and bucket to the veranda is as short as the week, and all too soon Joseph is thinking Nathan will be lost to him, gone forever. The garden will soon be restored to what it was before the storm, and the workmen are making plans to move on to their next job. Nathan, smiling between mouthfuls of food, seems not to care that he will go back to eating lunch alone, a single sandwich upon a silver bucket.

Joseph voices the nearing of the end of their time together. "I will miss you next week. Lunch will not be the same," he says, and Nathan pulls a face. Joseph is used to this now. The boy has a whole range of facial expressions that he uses to replace words. His vocabulary is limited, his mannerisms less so.

"Ah'm gonnae miss you tay," he says, and to Joseph the words are bland, insipid. He wants, is expecting, more from him. He wants Nathan to show some sadness. He needs to know that the end of their time together will be as upsetting for him as it is for Joseph. He wants to know that, in some small way, he means more to the boy than just a free lunch and someone to talk to.

"Maybe you could come visit?" he offers, pushing him to make more of a commitment.

"When?"

"Whenever you have some free time."

"Like oan days aff? Ah can ride my bike up haur insteid ay the other places Ah go."

"It's a long way, and that hill is very steep."

"Ah can make the hill, nae bother," Nathan brags before fixing Joseph with his best look. "Say now if you dinnae want me tae. Dinnae be blaming the hill and how far it is. Ah ride further than this oan my bike all the time. But if you dinnae want me here, then say and Ah wulnae come."

"I want you to come."

"Why?"

"You know not to ask me that," Joseph says, causing Nathan to smirk. Joseph stands then to indicate that the meal is over and that he should go back to his bucket.

"Tomorrow I'm going to make my Nathan special because the garden will be finished and the workmen gone for good. I was going to make it for you to say goodbye and thanks very much for everything; but if you're coming back to visit, then it will just be goodbye to the others and not to you."

"That's better then," Nathan says, and he hugs Joseph before retreating to the bottom of the garden. He is sitting all innocent on the bucket when the others return.

Chapter 5

The first day Nathan is not working in the garden and breaking into Joseph's apathetic routine, drags. Trying to lay some meaningful weight into the empty hours and empty rooms, Joseph reflects on how the passage of time is no longer the same. Events hurried by when spent with Mary, weeks merging into months that passed in a hasty procession of social engagements, downtime, and demanding work. Then, with the forced hiatus with Mary becoming sick, time had not slowed but paused as if, like them, it held its breath and waited.

That point, from the beginning of her illness until her premature end, had not been marked in hours or passing days but had been broken down into single sentences, bitter glances, and silence. When Joseph thinks of Mary now, it is the shared hurt they caused each other over those last days that haunts him the most. Memories of his his many fuck ups during that time will never be erased. He'd tried to put everything right, tried to tell her honestly what their marriage had meant to him, wanted to acknowledge the lies, but also the many truths, stuttering and stammering over the words while Mary had done everything she could to silence him. Even now alone with just her apparition he cannot find the proper words.

Mary is standing at the window now, her arms wrapped about her neat waist. She faces out towards the wider world and away from Joseph.

"I'm losing it," he says, and his voice resonate in the emptiness of the room as it repeats over and over in his head. Watching this faded version of her sparks a memory that throws Joseph into their past. He recalls a particular winter break and looking forward to it. The downtime would be a welcome interruption to exams, lectures, books, and study.

He is not sure why it should be this memory plucked from all the others, that now intrudes into his thoughts. He is twenty-one and has received in the post a selection of underwear and a fountain pen from his mother. The card says: "Happy birthday, Mum and Dad." There is no "Love," no crosses to represent kisses. It is one of many insensitive gifts and slights that have been building gradually into a black pit of animosity that he has carried inside him. He does not want to go home for the holidays, but he does not want to stay "in halls" and be alone. Joseph remembers the hurt; somethings, he thinks, will always stay with you. He has offered to give a girl a lift. She is only going as far as Aviemore, but he is glad of the company. She is the friend of a friend, a chance meeting that could have easily led to nothing. But the girl is easy to talk to. She makes a joke about their names, Joseph and Mary, and travelling together at this time of year. He groans at her joke. She flirts and bathes his wounds in compliments. His journey becomes their journey, and it starts and ends at Aviemore. It is the first time he spends Christmas away from his family. His twenty-one year-old self is a coward, and he phones his brother, not his parents,

"I've had a better offer," he tells him.

"It will upset them."

"Doubtful."

"They have news."

Joseph thinks the news is about his brother, and he is not interested. "Tell her to put it in a letter," he says. He refuses to give his mother her title. He is still hurting. The card and yet another apathetic gift has deepened the wound.

He recalls now the slow, dishonest build up to his family's departure. He is told when everything is finalised that they are leaving for Australia? His childhood home, his base, will now be someone else's home. A new family will close the front door and shut the world out at night. Young children will once more play in the back garden and use the spindly trees by the back wall to build dens to hide in, but they will not be his or his brother's children. They will be strangers' children. He can remember his father placing cardboard packing boxes in his bedroom and asking if there is anything he wants from the house. He is insolent, hurting from what he sees as their insensitive treatment of him, and he declines to take a single memento. Now he could list books, ornaments, and furniture that he wishes were still in his possession; but it would have been pointless, he thinks. Mary would have found a way to dispose of any keepsakes—a part of him knows this. She used his situation to her own advantage. Back then, she solved each problem as it arose, found them a place to live and filled it with new keepsakes that had meaning to them and only them. Every time he stumbled, she offered him unwavering support. When everything else had tipped, changed on him, Mary was the one constant and he loved her for that. It had been easy to settle, to go along with her plan. But what felt easy never felt right. Not then and not now. It is he thinks, when the lie that haunted their marriage first took hold.

He sits in his office walled in by paperwork, the laptop open. Feeling quasi-content in the warm air, in the sunshine with a cold cup of coffee, he pushes the unwanted thoughts away and forces himself to re-read papers. He concentrates on the same sentence over and over until the information finally sinks in. It stifles the unwelcome memories of indifferent parents, of letting his wife down and her resigned acceptance to it all. Memories of them both devoting so much time to work that there was little time left for each other invade his peace. He push them aside replacing them with new ones, of Nathan and fantasy images of idling away the days in his company. He thinks of Nathan possibly visiting at the weekend, and these thoughts are the ones that feel safe. These are the images he believes will stave off insanity and save him.

The young man is an enigma, his eyes that squint into the world and see far more than they let on are balanced by the practised, halted pattern of speech that changes in accordance with the demands he is trying to illicit, especially from Joseph. The whining, sulky teenager act of Nathan's is losing its clout, but it is no longer needed. That con has been replaced with the promise of companionship and of snatched moments of physical contact. The more Joseph learns about Nathan, his diagnosis and motives, the easier he finds it to accept that, even though they are so different in their outlooks and sensibilities, even though they should not have found any common ground, they have. There is the shared sense of being slightly out of it and of wanting to remain there on the fringe, both happy in their forced, self-inflicted isolation. He has watched Nathan while working in the garden, keeping himself away from the others and making no attempt to fit in, and all by choice, just as Joseph has done with his own work colleagues and friends. Their differences have become in themselves notes of interest.

Now every time Joseph leaves the house, he hopes to glimpse Nathan weaving his way dangerously in and out of the traffic, no doubt a nuisance. But he has yet to see him on any of his forays.

Chapter 6

Walking out of his house early Saturday morning, heading to the local shop for the daily and fresh milk, Joseph falls over Nathan sitting inside his front porch. The lad has his knees drawn up under him and appears mesmerised by a slither of light that has found its way in through the weathered wood.

"What the hell?" Joseph says, regaining his balance as he looks back at the lad.

"You said Ah could come." Nathan's words are said in a mumbled whisper.

"Jeez, what time did you get up this morning?" Joseph asks. Nathan pauses before answering, perhaps thinking his answer may affect the outcome of the day and being able to stay.

"Same time as always."

"Why didn't you knock or ring the bell?"

"Ah didnae want tae disturb you."

"I'm away to get milk."

"Ah'll wait."

Joseph looks down at Nathan, whom he'd been half expecting, but he is nevertheless caught off guard. He thinks for a moment before saying, "Well, okay. I'll be back shortly. Just wait here." The smell in the porch is bad, and he doesn't want Nathan in the house. When he'd made the offer, suggesting he visit, he had not considered this, and now looking at his watch, he again stalls for time.

"I won't be long," he says, and then committing once more to the task at hand, he hurries now to do a job that for weeks has been the leisurely high point of his day.

Twenty minutes is all it takes, but even so Nathan hasn't moved, and on his return, Joseph realises that the porch now replaces the bucket. By insisting that he remain there, perhaps Joseph is unwittingly replacing Uncle Tony.

"Come in," he says, opening the front door, and then he marches the boy straight through the house and out into the kitchen. The back door is still closed and locked, and that is the first thing that Joseph sorts. With the door open, a subtle but cold draft brings the smell of outdoors in to fuse with the now spoilt air of the room. Putting the kettle on for a much needed first cup of the day, Joseph says, "You've caught me by surprise. I was expecting you, just not so early."

Nathan mumbles, "Sorry. Will Ah gae and come back?"

"No, no. You're here now. Do you want coffee?"

"No," the boy whispers.

"What about breakfast? Do you want breakfast?"

"Ah've had breakfast… cornflakes," he says, and realising that the ease with which they previously conversed is missing. Joseph worries that being inside has altered the dynamics, he thinks the change in routine and placement has caused an upset in how they speak, how they will get on, and it is not the only problem. The smell is bad, and now Joseph has no idea what he will do with his foosty guest all day.

"Do you always have cornflakes?" he asks, working hard to try to ease Nathan's obvious discomfort.

"Yep."

"Well, how about a second breakfast? Eggs on toast, that's what I'm having."

Joseph is rewarded with a slightly more enthusiastic, "Awerite."

Although it feels like he might get somewhere, Joseph knows the situation still requires discretion. Nathan is, after all, in his home by invitation, but even with the back door open the smell is not improving and is in fact getting worse.

"Nathan, it's good to see you, it really is… but there's a problem," Joseph tells him.

Which prompts Nathan to ask, "You busy?"

"What? No."

"You want Ah should go?"

"No, I want you to stay. I very much want you to stay, but I also want you to take a shower," Joseph say this whilst looking away, preferring now to study the disgusting but colourful contents of the sink strainer in preference to meeting what he thinks will be Nathan's hurt gaze.

"It's nae Sunday," he says, and rather than be offended, something Joseph is still working hard to avoid, he just looks utterly confused. He peers out from behind his greasy fringe, and his eyes flicker from side to side. Joseph, feeling somewhat buoyant by the lack of upset caused by his words, now watches Nathan as Nathan watches him. He imagines he's trying to decipher the meaning behind his words, and so he makes it clear. Simple, brutal, honest: "You smell bad, Nathan, you really do, and if you want to spend time with me in my home, then you need to shower… and smell better."

"Ah dae shower, every Sunday. Irene makes it fur me. Ah'm nae allowed tae gae haem and shower and then come back. It's nae Sunday and, it's nae nighttime," he says.

"No, see… You don't have to go home. You can shower here," Joseph offers, and moving from the sink to the open back door, he looks out at the garden. The early morning sun has back-lit a low-lying cloud cover turning the misty edges a soft smoky pink. He takes a deep breath of fresh air, then turns around, startled to see Nathan already naked.

Standing in the kitchen, in the draft from the open door, goose bumps forming on his unprotected arms and thighs, Nathan shudders and hunches his shoulders. He looks cold, a combination perhaps of waiting in the porch in just a thin t-shirt and grimy threadbare jeans and now standing naked in the frigid kitchen, Joseph thinks. Nathan clenches his teeth as he says, "You have tae make it fur me, cos Ah might gie it all wrang."

Joseph is no longer concentrating on what Nathan is saying. Instead, he considers the simple beauty of the young man's innocently exposed and trembling form. It both charms and changes him. The apathy that he has fostered towards all naked human forms for so long dissipates. Puzzled, he finds he is captivated anew, but still this is territory that scares and excites him and he will not comment on Nathan's state of undress.

"Make it?" he questions instead, still distracted by Nathan's nudity, the lad is now shivering.

"Make the shower. Ah cannae dae that," Nathan says, and the cold words trip out over themselves.

"Right… Yes, this way," Joseph says, and he beckons with one overly excited hand for him to follow.

Without his work boots on, Nathan no longer makes a noise. He follows close behind Joseph as they leave the kitchen and walk the length of the hallway. Joseph feels him now, a soundless adherent to his every move. As one, they both hesitate at the bottom of the stairs. Joseph pauses because he knows that he is about to allow this naked lad into his most private space, a thought that is weighted by a significance that only he can place on such a non-event. Nathan waits because he mirrors Joseph's actions, although doubtless not his thoughts.

The bedroom is essentially unchanged. Joseph has cleared some of Mary's things—perfumes, creams, and trinkets—from the dressing table. He also removed a large amount of her redundant crap from the bathroom, meaning there is now emptiness where once there was clutter. But her clothes still wait in the cupboards and drawers out of sight. Her presence is still, Joseph knows, imbued into every space.

Now he feels and sees her try to blend with Nathan. The early morning light causes her form to flicker and fade as she moves towards the boy, and keen to keep them apart, Joseph hurries into the bathroom. He turns on the shower, all the while wondering how Nathan can get this wrong, turning on a shower. He keeps a practised hand under the water until it runs warm to ensure the temperature is right, then turns, and shaking his hand dry, says, "There you go."

With shoulders hunched, Nathan peeks from underneath the mess of dirty, defiant hair. He doesn't move, and because he doesn't move, Joseph feels there is a need for further instruction.

"Get in," he says, and he places one hand low on his back, just above his buttocks, so he is better able to push the bare boy in under the water. His intentions are then to give him some privacy and leave him to it, thinking he will now get on with the business of washing. Instead, Joseph hesitates. He watches as Nathan, standing under the spray, every bone in his back sticking out, now tries to dodge the flow of water onto his body. The patches of skin where the sun reaches are a dirty, bruised, and yellowish brown. In contrast, everywhere the clothes cover is white. In the confused and watery light of the shower cubicle, the lad looks translucent blue. Stooped over, skinny and naked, to Joseph he represents the very essence of fragility and cold. Wanting desperately to get to the end result, he places his hand back on him, this time at the base of his neck. It is easier now to steer him back into the spray. In such a restricted space, the water tracks back up Joseph's arm, soaking his sleeve before dripping onto the mat outside the shower.

"Use soap and wash," he says, irritated now because of the wet sleeve.

"Ach man," is the reply, as Nathan's voice battles up from somewhere under the water, his head still bent low in the spray. Joseph watches, now fascinated. Without grace or ease of movement, Nathan has started the process of washing himself, and straightaway it is clear he has no routine. Joseph assumes his unrehearsed movements show a lack of practice. He gives instructions, but exasperated with Nathan's nonsense, he then involves himself fully in the task, ending with washing his hair, something he has never imagined doing for someone else. Nathan, compliant throughout, follows the directives being given without protest. Only when he is washed to Joseph's satisfaction does he let him out of the cubicle.

Wrapping towels around his frail frame, Joseph then coaxes Nathan from the warm bathroom to the much cooler bedroom. Once there, he stands statue-like, making no attempt to get dry. Only his eyes move to take in the room.

"Get dry and I will find you some clothes to put on," Joseph says, and the boy says, "My clase are still doonstairs."

"There's little point in putting dirty clothes back on a clean body, is there?"

"Whit will Ah wear?"

"I'll find you something," Joseph tells him, and he goes to look for a t-shirt that he has never liked, thinking the style too young for him, and an old pair of jeans, faded and with the back pocket worn away by his wallet.

"Dry yourself," he says again, bringing the clothes and clean underwear over and placing them down on the bed. He watches as Nathan half-heartedly rubs the towel down the length of one arm before screwing it up into a ball to drag across his thigh. His eyes no longer scan the room but are fixed on Joseph.

"You're useless," Joseph tells him, and he takes the towel. "At your age surely you're able to wash and dry yourself."

"Ah am," Nathan says, but the first signs of laughter break in his voice and give him away. Joseph thinks then that he is blatantly trying to trick him into offering more help than he needs. Even so, he plays along and dries Nathan's back and, crouching down, does his legs before moving back up to do his hair. The hair that has always been the colour of wet sand is now white-blond, and a wild, soft and fluffy mess sticking out at all angles from his head. Joseph tries to calm it with his hands, patting it down at the sides. But the hair, is defiant and will not be controlled.

Chapter 7

Spending the day with Nathan is not the difficult task that Joseph had first expected. Funny and energetic, he dives from one thing to another, interested in everything whilst concentrating on nothing. He eats the eggs on toast, and then he watches with interest as his clothes wash and spin in the machine before hanging them out on the line. Then, standing with his hands on his hips and squinting at Joseph, already finding the early morning sun too bright for his sensitive eyes, he asks, "What's next?"

The borrowed jeans hang low on his hips, too low to be deemed decent. So Joseph goes in search of a belt.

"Ah like your clase," Nathan says, and, smiling, Joseph pulls the jeans up on to the lad's wanting waist. He says nothing about the clothes.

"Shall we go for a ride in the car?" Joseph suggests, thinking it will be an easy way of entertaining him for a few hours.

"Can Ah sit up in front, next tae you?" Nathan asks, and because it excites him, the words struggle and stutter to form.

"If you calm down."

He settles, and Joseph thinks it is a shame to dampen such a lively spirit. But, like his hair, Nathan cannot be subdued for long. In the car he sits with his shoulders hunched, his hands balled into fists stuffed into his crotch. He is bent forward, away from the seat.

"Are you alright?"

"I love your car," he says, and he rocks in his seat with delight.

"Right. Where shall we go?"

"Aw ower the place."

"Everywhere! Well, that narrows it down. Right. Let's go everywhere and then we might just end up somewhere. Do you go out in cars much?" Joseph asks, taking a first tentative step into Nathan's other life.

"Ah gae in the back of Uncle Tony's truck fur work, but Ah like sitting up front and watching, Ah don't normally gie tae dae that. Tell me whit you're daeing and why?"

In response to the request, Joseph begins a simple explanation for how to drive a car, and Nathan watches and listens. But no more than half an hour into the ride, he starts to turn an unpromising shade of green, all the while swallowing repeatedly.

"Are you alright?"

"Ah feel sick. Ah'm gonnae boak."

In a panic, Joseph stops the car at the first available place he finds and pulls Nathan out by the t-shirt, ignoring his protests that he needs to first undo the seat belt. Not wanting him being sick in the car, or even being sick *near* the car, Joseph puts a now practised hand on the back of Nathan's neck and marches him away from the vehicle.

"Take deep breaths," he tells him.

"Awerite."

"Don't just say it. Do it."

"Awerite," Nathan says again, but still he does not breathe as instructed. He stands with his head bowed because Joseph's hand is still resting on his neck.

"Like this," Joseph says, turning him again by the neck so that they are now standing face-to-face. Joseph inhales, filling his lungs. Then he takes Nathan's hand and puts it against his own chest so that the boy can feel him take in deep, slow, and even breaths, encouraging him to copy him.

"Better?"

"Aye."

It had been Joseph's intention to drive around the Loch Shore road. Now, because of Nathan's dramatics, he has had to pull off into one of the many lay-bys. Sightseers are known to cause more accidents on this road than the drunk, hasty, and in Joseph's opinion, disgracefully reckless locals. Lay-bys are the council's inadequate solution.

"Let's walk. We can go down to the water where there's a path. You need some fresh air. I think you get travel sick."

"Can Ah gae back in the car?"

"When you've turned a better colour." Nathan is the colour of the seaweed dried out and rotting on the shoreline, but that doesn't stop him from jumping from rock to rock. Joseph feels the need to say encouraging words to make him stop and be sensible. Nathan's age makes him fearless; Joseph's makes him worry. Nathan's compromise is to stand still, balanced now on a rock in front of Joseph, he drags him up onto the rock as well. Twisting his own arms about Joseph's waist, he ensures that they either fall or are both safe. It's clear he doesn't understand issues of personal space, and deliberating on Nathan's tactility, Joseph first scans the landscape to see if there is anyone about.

"Ah like it haur. Ah don't think Ah have ever bin haur afair. Ah might come here oan my bike," Nathan says, but then he thinks about it some more. "No. Ah willnae."

"Why? Is it too far?" Joseph asks. His arms, as if spare parts, hang loose at his sides.

"No. Ah don't think Ah would like tae come haur without you. Ah would miss you, and that would make me sad like this."

Standing toe-to-toe, chest-to-chest. Nathan's arms tightly wound around Joseph's waist, he pulls an exaggerated sad face, and Joseph laughs. Caught in his arms, Joseph can't easily move away, not without risking slipping from the edgy precipice they share.

"We need to be careful," he tells Nathan.

"You hauld me and Ah'll hauld you. We willnae fall," Nathan says, and slowly, carefully, Joseph moves his arms to hold the boy more tightly.

In the car on the way home, Joseph keeps a wary eye on Nathan's colour. The air-con is on and blowing full into his face, and so far he is fine, but Nathan is quiet. Joseph asks, "Are you alright?"

"Yeah," he says, "but it's nearly time tae gae hame." There is a sullen honesty in the pronouncement of the words that Joseph shares.

"So, come back tomorrow," Joseph offers, and Nathan brightens at this.

"You sure?"

"If you're allowed."

"Ah'm allowed."

"Okay, then."

"Okay, then."

Nathan is obviously a mimic, and Joseph hopes that in time he will copy some of his better habits. Pulling into the driveway, they are already making plans to eat outside. Taking advantage of the early evening sunshine once more and sitting in their designated seats, it is a much more pleasant event, now that the smell is sorted. The food still churns in Nathan's mouth, however, and Joseph still watches it. The more time he spends in his company, the more Joseph feels equipped to deal with and manage the nonsense. When Nathan's brat-ish, impatient, self-centred side emerges, Joseph is quick to call a stop to such silliness. But he is careful in his choice of words because Nathan is sensitive and easily shamed. The wrong word or an ill-judged comment can destroy the boy's peace, and then Joseph has to spend considerable time putting things right. He sees promise in the lad. He might be silly and excitable, but he's not stupid. A little impulsive and at times childish perhaps, but he is not reckless or mean. So, using his own biased judgement as a yard-stick, Joseph intends to improve him, smooth off the rough edges, and even though he has not been asked he is prepared to labour at this on Nathan's behalf.

"What shall we do tomorrow?" Joseph asks.

"Same as tae-day."

"Not exactly the same or you will get bored."

"No, nae me. Ah'm ne'er fed up. When Ah ride my bike, Ah sometimes gae tae the same place, but Ah'm nae fed up."

"Okay. Then I'll get bored."

"Nae with me, you wulnae. Ah willnae let you gie fed up, and Ah willnae let you be boring either." Joseph still fixated with his own moral undertakings, too busy working on a plan to fix this lad and tease out the more desired, more mature side of him, misses Nathan's prophesying of his own character.

Chapter 8

The repetitious sound of the alarm hurts all the more because it's Sunday and set it for an hour earlier than normal. It forces Joseph from a dream he is not ready to leave, and just as abruptly as he has awakened, the dream is gone and forgotten. It leaves Joseph with the lingering impression that it was pleasing and that he had wanted to remain secure within it.

As he knew he would be, Nathan is already in the porch, sitting hunched over and wearing the same washed out and worn clothes from the day before.

"Did you even go home last night?" Joseph asks, a tease, and as he says the words, he beckons the boy inside.

"Aye. Ah went hame, had tea, and went tae bed, and noo Ah'm back. You said that Ah could come back, and haur Ah am…back."

Joseph forces a measured lightness into his words, trying to belie the relief he feels. Yesterday he did not bore Nathan into declining any future visits with him.

"Haven't you heard of a long-lie? Especially on a Sunday?" he asks.

"No."

"Don't you ever lie in bed?"

"Ah would if Ah were boak, but Ah'm nae ever sick. Maw say's life's too short tae waste it, and she would ken. And lying in bed is jist that, a waste, a waste of a guid day."

Joseph has not work out the complexities of Nathan's family. From the little he has gleaned, he has assumed that, like so many, this family is fractured. He could ask, knowing that Nathan will tell him everything for, similar to the issue with personal space, he appears to have no margins with private information. A trait of whatever learning or behavioural disorders he carries perhaps, Joseph thinks, but he isn't interested in that part of Nathan's life, in those people and their claim on him. He wants them to have no part in their time together. So he hasn't, and he knows that he won't, enquire what they know or think about Nathan visiting him.

Nathan, feeling at home now, has wandered off. Joseph, thinking he has gone in search of food, is surprised to find him naked with his clothes in a heap about his feet, nonchalantly studying the kitchen as if it were a room he has never seen before.

"Make the shower," he says, and Joseph realises that his guest is looking to replicate the previous day. Once in the shower, Nathan tries in vain to provoke the same responses from Joseph and ensure that he says and does the same as yesterday.

He is quickly and firmly told, "You're at it," and this time Joseph leaves him to it. And with no need for further intervention, Nathan washes and dress without help or protest.

Returning to the kitchen wearing the same borrowed clothes and striding in with an air of confidence that he did not show yesterday, Nathan affirms his want for eggs on toast, disregarding the fact that Joseph has catered for a full Scottish breakfast. He seems unable, or at least is unwilling, to deviate from yesterday's plan, even when offered tattie scones, black pudding, and link sausages. Joseph then realises that the secret to keeping Nathan compliant is to tell him their plans in advance.

"Next week, if you come to visit, we will do different things, and we will eat different things, alright?"

"Aye awerite."

Next week, Joseph knows, Nathan may or may not come back, and he may or may not accept a new plan, but today he wants to be taken back out in the car "just like yesterday." Not wanting to rock the boat too much, and seeing a drive as still his easiest option, Joseph is happy enough to oblige. With no specific destination in mind, he takes the A82 out of Drumnadrochit down towards Fort William.

As a local, he knows the only time to drive this route is when you have plenty of time on your hands. Cyclists, logging lorries, and camper vans convoy along the constricted and coiling road, offering no chance of getting above 40 miles an hour.

Whilst Nathan is content to listen to a CD and admire the ever changing scenery, as it eases from soft green sheep pastures and dense woodlands that cling to the very edge of the road to the frieze of rock that frames the route, Joseph watches his colour and the oncoming traffic. At Oich they are delayed because the swing bridge is up to allow boats through on their way up the Caledonian Canal, where they will eventually merge with the deep black waters of Loch Ness. It is here that Nathan leaves the car to stand on the bank and wave along with a group of camera-clutching tourists. Joseph remains with the car and watches as Nathan chats with the group. He wonders where the lad from yesterday who whispered and stuttered his way through the day has gone.

Bypassing Fort William and the dark grey moisture-laden clouds that cling to the town, they head back into sparklingly bright sunshine. Joseph's plan is to follow the course of tourists and share in their appreciation of a landscape he is in danger of becoming complacent about. Glencoe beckons, and they pull in along with a tourist bus to the strains of a lone piper waiting in the car park. Standing in the shadows of the towering peaks and ridges of the Glencoe massif, they admire the summit which is still holding on to a light sprinkling of snow in contrast to the good weather being enjoyed below.

"Ah could climb that," Nathan says.

The edifice looms above Joseph, making him feel small and insignificant.

"Yes, and… I would watch you."

"How long would it take me?"

"All day and most of tomorrow," he guesses.

"What's it called?"

"Glen Coe."

"Nae the whole thing, jist that bit," Nathan says, and he waves his arm in the direction of the mountain that has ripped itself from the ground in front of them and reaches up to scratch at the sky.

"I don't know," Joseph says, dismissing the question, but then looking away from the view and back at Nathan, he sees the disappointment. The expectation that Joseph has all the answers is there in the lad's puzzled expression. Determined to keep the truth from Nathan, Joseph says, "I mean…I know there's the Three Sisters and the Devil's Staircase, but I'm not sure exactly which are which because they all look the same from here.

"So name more."

"Umm… Aonach Mor and Aonach Beag are about here, I think."

"What else?"

Joseph hadn't envisaged having to pluck long-forgotten fragments of Scottish history from his memory banks, and it is clear Nathan is becoming impatient with his measured response.

"What about the massacre in 1692, Joseph?" he asks, and then not waiting for a response, proceeds to rattle off the salient points of a treachery that can still be felt lingering in the misery of the grey crags, ridges, and peaks before them.

"Let's go as far as Rannoch Moor?" Nathan then suggests. And Joseph, thrown by Nathan's surprising knowledge, and not being able to think of a reason why not, nods his assent. Then he turns and begins the walk back towards the car. He is expecting to be followed, but Nathan walks off in the opposite direction, further towards the edge of the car park, nearer to the imposing landscape. Centred now between the mountains and Joseph, Nathan looks to belong more to the landscape than to him. Joseph watches as he climbs onto a boulder to gain what is a very insignificant advantage in height. There is no danger, the rock's only purpose is to establish an obvious boundary.

"Guid job, God. Well done. Awesome mountains," Nathan shouts. His voice echoes across the car park, silencing the piper and everyone else. He then claps his hands in ecstatic applause before jumping down and jogging back to where Joseph waits. Now, with no way of pretending that they are not together, Joseph feels the heat of embarrassment stain his cheeks. Before scrabbling back into the car to hide, he manages only to mumble, "What the fuck?"

"What was that all about?" he asks. Turning away and refusing to look at Nathan, he imagines instead Mary's face. She is drawing in her breath, narrowing her eyes. He feels her disapproval. Even here, in such a stark and empty landscape, her presence plagues him. Needing to get away, he hastily turns the car and leaves behind perplexed bystanders, but not his anger and embarrassment.

"Ah like tae show my appreciation for God's work," Nathan says, and then he adds,

"*Fur behold, he who forms the mountains an' creates the wind, and declares tae man whit is his thought, who makes the morning darkness, and treads oan the heights of the earth—the LORD, the God of hosts, is his name*! That's in the bible."

"Very good," Joseph says, trying and failing to keep his voice even. He is stunned by this different and unnerving version of a lad he thought he knew. The idea that there are hidden depths of knowledge and confidence in Nathan that might challenge his own authority is scary, any change in the dynamics of their relationship definitely unwelcome.

"You know, when you carry on like that, shouting things out in public, people think you're an idiot."

"What dae Ah care what fowk think?"

"You should."

"Why?"

Joseph does not respond, believing the answer too obvious to need stating.

"Ah ken Ah'm nae an eejit, and those fowk are strangers that Ah will most likely na'er see again, so what do Ah care?"

"I care," Joseph says, meaning he cares what others think about Nathan.

But then Nathan asks, "Why? Why would you care what they think of you? Just because you're wit' me! Why care about something so silly? That's jist bonkers." Silence settles in the car, and Joseph is happy to let it last. In his head he is still dissecting everything that has been said. He's always hated his obsession with what people might think of him, and now, Nathan is pointing out that very defect in his character. Wishing he could be more cavalier about things, Joseph grasps the simple fact that it is not Nathan who needs to be more like him. He needs to be more like the boy.

"We are going tae eat, aren't we?" Nathan asks, and Joseph is pleased. The question offers him an easy way out of the situation.

"Sure. keep an eye out for somewhere to eat and I'll pull in."

Eating places are plentiful along their chosen route, lying in wait to prey on hungry tourists and locals alike, and it is not long before they find somewhere that they both like the look of.

"Ah'm going tae have macaroni cheese and chips. That's whit Ah fancy," Nathan says, half falling out of the car in his haste to get food.

"That sounds great. A good choice. I think I will have the same."

"Nae bad then…fae an eejit?" Nathan says, letting it be known that the issue is not resolved.

"I never said you were an idiot," Joseph clarifies. "I said you carried on like one." It is important to Joseph that Nathan understands the difference.

All too soon it's late evening and Nathan is sitting astride his bike facing down the hill. Here there is still no sign of rain, but they have passed in and out of thunderstorms all day. The smell of baked earth floats in the air, and Joseph is subdued.

"Ah have tae gae now so Ah can be hame afair it gets dark," Nathan says.

"Go careful. I hope I see you next Saturday."

Joseph watches him depart. The hill is too steep to be tackled with just one hand on the handlebars, but Nathan insists on waving.

"Cheers fur having me. See you next days aff," he shouts at Joseph as he pushes off.

Chapter 9

Big fat lambs, slowly being rejected by their mothers, amble in the fields below Joseph's house. Even though the height of summer is still a way off, the days are long and the weather promises good things to come.

Filling in the time between Nathan's visits, and feeling guilty that he is still shunning a normal well-ordered and appropriate lifestyle, Joseph has decided to attend to the unfinished business of Mary's possessions. Her things are still taking up space at her former place of work, and the items she had with her at the hospice need to be collected. Then there are her clothes still in the cupboards in the bedroom that need disposed of. Planning move by move how he will achieve this unpleasant task, he is distracted, and upon leaving the house with his arms full, Joseph does not notice the boy-sized lump tucked into the corner of his porch that sobs but doesn't speak.

"Bugger," he says.

Not expecting to meet anything, he is at full pace when he makes contact with the sobbing obstruction. The collision causes him to end up on his hands and knees. Not how he anticipated starting his day.

"Nathan, what the hell?" he says. He moves so he can see him better, but it is not the happy Nathan of yesterday, gone is the beautiful boy he waved goodbye to the night before, all smiles and a mess of wild white-blond hair. Here is a broken person, his face bloodied, swollen, and bruised—an almost unrecognisable mask. The eyes have puffed into narrow slits, which struggle to open forcing him to peer out from behind a bloated curtain of port-wine dark skin.

During his working life, Joseph has been called on to attend to many a battered soul looking for help with his or her wounds, but never one who has intruded so markedly into his own private peace. Suddenly he understands how much Nathan means to him. His injuries and obvious pain prompts this epiphany. Nathan doesn't speak even when Joseph feels obligated to ask questions that sound, even in his own head, unnecessary and annoying: "Are you alright? What happened?" Then, not getting a response, he follows with a trite, "Stay there." Joseph gets to his feet and leaves to find what he hopes will be a quick-fix solution to a myriad of problems—a blanket to warm him and perhaps offer Nathan a small amount of comfort.

As he retraces his steps back into the house, Joseph's thoughts are odd, and they are not with Nathan. Even amidst the early morning drama of it all, he thinks only of Mary and how he'd wanted so much to be allowed to care for her. Why had she rejected him at the very moment when she should have wanted him most? Both she and the question haunt him now.

Grabbing the first thing that comes to hand, the throw that lies along the back of the sofa and under which Mary and he were meant to snuggle on cold evenings, he hurries to return to Nathan. The throw which was ridiculously expensive and always redundant, has never been used, he remembers, as he drags the thing around Nathan to warm him. The lad snivels in pain, and it is becoming all too clear that the facial injuries that are so evident are not the worst that he carries. His hands rest in a permanent clutch against his ribs, and his breathing comes in shallow, painful pants. Broken breaths are possible evidence of broken ribs.

Moving Nathan inside from the porch is an agonising journey, and Joseph wishes for his own, as much as the lad's sake, that the hurting will go beyond pain to that dull ache that the body achieves when past what the mind can endure. The only consolation Joseph thinks is that Nathan's swollen face hides some of his agony.

Seating him at the kitchen table, Joseph presses once more for information on what has happened. He thinks knowing the details will ease some of his own anxieties, but Nathan sobs and cries, and crying makes his nose run and bleed. He abuses the throw, using it to mop up the fluids. Blood, snot, and tears now sully its weave. So it finally has a purpose, thinks Joseph.

Nathan, his eyes now closed, the strain of keeping the swollen slits open beating him, lists to the left, and Joseph uses his own body as a support. He still wants to know what has happened, wants and needs to know so he can arm himself with the belief that he is not to blame for this, but first he knows he must make sure the boy isn't in any real danger. He runs through the checks first in his head: memory test, reflexes, co-ordination, vision, balance. Then he quizzes Nathan.

"What did you have to eat last night?"

"What?"

"Just answer the question."

"Why?"

He takes a deep breath. "Nathan, just answer the bloody question."

"Spaghetti, same as you."

"Have you been sick? Do you feel sick?"

"Because of the spaghetti? No, it was fine…"

"This has nothing to do with spaghetti…"

"Then why dae you keep oan aboot it?"

"I'm trying to assess how badly hurt you are."

"Ah'm fine."

"Did you fall off your bike? Did someone run into you?"

"Ah'm fine," Nathan says again, but his voice, tired and croaky, trails off.

"Were you in a fight? Tell me what happened."

Now each question is met with silence. Exhausted, Joseph thinks Nathan might have fallen asleep, but his breathing is still coming in irregular pants that don't marry.

"Come on," Joseph says, and he tries to get him to sip water. But a split in his bottom lip causes him more discomfort, and he objects to the drink by dropping his head to hide it against Joseph's waist.

"You need to go to the hospital," Joseph tells him, and he strokes the back of Nathan's bent head to console him; but he has lost some valuable skin at the base of his skull, and blood has dried and matted in his hair. It takes a minute for Joseph to realise that his stroking is causing Nathan more pain than comfort.

"No," he says, and Nathan's one word answer, whilst mumbled and faint, indicates he is not prepared to compromise.

"You need a doctor to look at you," Joseph reasons, and even with swollen slits for eyes, he can see the look of disbelief on Nathan's face.

"I know I'm a doctor, but you need X-rays. Bones might be broken, and you might have a concussion. I can't assess any of this properly here in my kitchen."

"No," Nathan says again, and it takes all his energy to punctuate his words with a sob. Then he adds, "You have tae keep care of me. I jist want you tae keep care of me, jist you."

"What happened?" Joseph asks again, still believing that knowing the circumstances will somehow make dealing with the aftermath that much easier.

"Dinnae ask me that," Nathan says.

And recalling his own reluctance to answer awkward questions, knowing he has used the same phrase on Nathan—many times now—with Nathan always obliging him, Joseph stands a little straighter and breathes a little heavier. He accepts Nathan has every right to his privacy, but he also realises that this is a defining moment and he has to consider the implications at play here if he is going to help him.

"I need to know if you're in trouble, if you've done anything wrong."

"No."

"Is anyone looking for you? Will they be worried?"

"Doubt it."

"Are you telling me the truth?"

"Aye."

Joseph considers manhandling Nathan into his car, that or filling him full of painkillers and letting him rest. When he needs to be, Nathan seems alert and capable of making his feelings clear. Joseph is the one that is dithering over two woefully inadequate options. He scans the kitchen for inspiration. Mary is there, a remnant of his once orderly life flickering in and out of the sunlight, her gauzy hands on her hips, head bent to one side as she always did when deep in thought. He feels her silently judging his lack of clarity and action. He will not, he thinks, allow her presence to sidetrack him from Nathan's situation. Turning his back on her, he concentrate instead on the injured lad and he once more insists, "You should go to the hospital."

"Ah cannae be bothered."

"I'm not asking you to walk there," Joseph says, stunned at Nathan's apathy towards his own wellbeing.

"They'll ask even stupider questions than you."

The thought of awkward questions being asked degrades Joseph's eagerness to take Nathan anywhere. He is right. Just like Joseph, the hospital staff will want to know the details, and depending on Nathan's attitude, they may involve the police. They will also want to know what Joseph's part is in all this.

"Fine. If you won't go, then the best thing is to get you upstairs and into bed. You can rest and get warm. It will help… a little."

Other than painkillers, there is not much Joseph can offer. He is reluctant to even offer this. Nathan was only ever meant to be a harmless, selfish diversion, someone to distract him from his self-inflicted boredom, the loneliness of grief and the slow onset of insanity. It had never crossed his mind that he might end up having to take care of him, that spending time together, would end in this mess. Responsibility was something Joseph had walked away from, relinquishing all his previous obligations and duties for a new life of opting out, he is now loath to be pulled back in.

Nathan's reluctance to comply with any of Joseph's previous requests changes abruptly, and confusingly, he now appears willing to go along with Joseph's suggestion of resting upstairs. He is about to struggle back to his feet when the doorbell rings. Synchronised in their surprise at the sound intruding into the quiet of the house, they both jump, which irritates Joseph and pains Nathan.

"Hide," Nathan says, and Joseph, steadying the lad once more, frowns.

"You said you weren't in any trouble."

"Ah'm not. Ah jist cannae be bothered tae see anyone right now."

"I will not hide," Joseph tells him, and sure that he is once more balanced, he leaves to confront the caller.

The walk from the kitchen to the front door gives Joseph some much needed time to focus his thinking and to risk assess the situation. His concerns for who and what might be at the door are amplified by Nathan's refusal to fill in the details. So opening the door with the security chain on, just in case, Joseph peers through the gap. Uncle Tony is a few inches shorter than Joseph, but solid set and flushed.

He comes quickly to the point, his tone curt. "Is Nate here?" And as Joseph removes the chain, he pushes his way past him to stand uninvited in the hallway.

Given more time to prepare himself for this second intrusion into his day, Joseph might have considered his next move more carefully. But Nathan does not belong to him, he reasons. He belongs to others, unknown and still unjudged; and so he says, "Kitchen."

Uncle Tony nods. He is the best part down the hallway before Joseph feels inclined to give him further instructions. "Straight ahead, first door."

The uncle then walks through Mary and the doorway into the kitchen where he greets Nathan with, "You have tae be dumber than dirt."

His voice, whilst not raised or angry in tone, still has a levelled calmness about it that hints at an underlying animosity. Nathan, having invested all his energy in keeping one eye slightly open, rests one arm on the tabletop to prop him up whilst the other clutches his torso. He is obviously spent. He offers no response to his uncle's opening remark, and none, it seems, is expected.

"Git up, we're leaving," his uncle says.

Nathan, attempting to comply, shuffles his skinny legs tucked into heavy work boots round to prepare for the move.

"No, wait. Hang on," Joseph interjects, and he is considering his own follow-up when the uncle turns his attention from Nathan back to him. The situation feels like it is getting away from Joseph, and an image of the lad falling from the bucket fills the gap between them. He cannot work out how the uncle would know Nathan would come here, to Joseph, of all people. And Joseph cannot and will not forget that this is the bucket kicker, and therefore the most likely inflictor of Nathan's current injuries. It is obvious he already knew that the boy was hurt before he entered the house and saw him. Joseph is then further surprised by the man's reply.

"This has naething tae dae with you."

It raises Joseph's eyebrows and his hackles. Given that they are all in his kitchen, he is taken aback by the uncle's assertion, and he answers with an overly loud, edgy, abrasive command: "Out!" And then, deciding he has to clarify, he adds, "You!" He is pointing at the uncle as he further explains, "Not you, Nathan. You're staying here."

"Eejit," the uncle says, which leaves Joseph wondering which of them he is addressing. Worrying now that there will be a standoff, he thinks he might have to sacrifice Nathan after all so he and his property remain unscathed. Joseph is certain now that the uncle is wholly responsible for Nathan's condition and berates himself. Why has he allowed this thug access to him once more? Uncle Tony, standing with his hands on his hips, feet firmly planted, and the same blank stare that Joseph often gets from Nathan, doesn't look like a person who is easily moved.

"Let me explain something tae you," the uncle says, his tone patronising.

Joseph nods. "Yes, but outside," he says, making a wimpy shooing motion with his fingers that would not, if tested, deter an errant fly let alone an irate uncle. Much to Joseph's surprise and relief, Uncle Tony retraces his steps from the kitchen, back through the door and Mary, who is standing in judgement of them all. Her lips pushed tight together, arms crossed and brow furrowed, she appears even more annoyed at being displaced once more by Uncle Tony as he heads out onto the front steps of the house than she is about the chaos in their home. Tempted as he is to now shut the door in his face and adopt Nathan's original plan of hiding, Joseph realises, with its missing north-facing wall and splendid panoramic views, his home doesn't lend itself to being a very good hiding place.

"He's at it," the uncle says. "He's playing you fur a fool. He sees you as a soft touch."

"Can you give me his mother's contact details?"

"Huh?"

"His mother, so I can get in touch with her." Joseph now has a plan.

"She's deid."

Joseph is stunned, his plan wrecked so soon after it occurred to him.

"I didn't know. He never said..."

"Been deid since he was eight."

Joseph, finding the uncle's statement blunt to the point of cruelty, looks away. The information leaves him distraught on Nathan's behalf. He has always referenced his mother as if she were still very much with them. Never in the past tense. Never absent from his life. And Joseph is suddenly sidetracked into thinking about how difficult it still is to acknowledge out loud that Mary is gone and that she too belongs in the past.

"Dae you want tae ken way his auld man kicked the living shit out ay heem?"

"No." Surprised as Joseph is at finding out the father and not the uncle is responsible for Nathan's injuries, knowing that somehow the thug of an uncle will try to justify the actions of the thug of a father, overrides any wish he has to know the details. Unable to forget that Nathan has turned up at his door dirty and hungry just adds weight to his convictions. He cannot comprehend how one human being can inflict such damage on another, related or otherwise, or how a man can justify that act by another. He wants the man on his doorstep gone.

"Bad enough tae have a not-right fur a son, but a fecking faggot too jist pit him rite ower the edge."

The words send a sharp painful spasm of fear throughout Joseph's body, and fighting to remain composed, Joseph prepares to close the front door. He is done now with the man, done with this family drama that he never signed on for, but the uncle has one more bomb to drop.

"He tauld his auld man that he loves you."

Joseph pauses then, with a sufficient gap in the door for both men to eyeball each other.

"Deid wife and all, Ah jist thought you've got enough tae deal with. Can't see you wanting tae put up with the lad's shite."

"I'll explain to Nathan why saying what he did to his father was inappropriate... wrong. I will clarify the situation to him... to Nathan and tell him he has misinterpreted my actions... my friendship. I only meant to offer him advice and guidance and to help him better himself. He has read more into my kindness, my good intentions, than I intended. And you have my assurance that, when I do speak to him, it will be done in such a way as to not cause further detriment to his welfare."

"Huh?"

"I don't advocate violence as a solution," he tells the uncle, and closing the door, he gives him no opportunity to pursue the conversation further. Muttering, "I am going to kill him." Joseph then walks back to the kitchen.

Mary, having been dispersed by the uncle twice, still looks less than thrilled by the experience. In trying to piece herself back together, she is taking up much of the hallway, forcing Joseph to flatten himself against the wall to pass her.

"Are you wise?" he asks, aware that he might be shadowing the tone and stance of the uncle moments before. His words cause Nathan to jerk upwards, the movement adding to his troubles, but he remains silent. Joseph takes this as confirmation of his guilt. Prejudiced now by the uncle's version of events and burning with embarrassment that his imagined indiscretions are public gossip, he does not want Nathan to offer an explanation. He only wants to secure an out for himself. Just as he has sent the uncle away, Nathan must go too in order to preserve Joseph's standing in the community. Where the boy goes is of no never mind to Joseph.

"I do not deserve this. I have been nothing but kind and generous to you. What were you thinking? Why would you say that?"

Nathan is still not expected to respond. Joseph, thumbing his digit over his shoulder towards where the uncle has departed, lectures on. "He told me what you said. I know you're not stupid. I know you're not *that* stupid leastways. What the hell were you thinking?"

The phone ringing interrupts Joseph's diatribe, the one-sided conversation halted. Waiting for it to ring off gives him time to draw breath.

"Being a local GP, it's important—my reputation. I intend to… Well, I might go back to work at some point. I don't need you or your depraved relatives jeopardising my good name, and…and discussing me."

The phone rings again, and deciding now that it sounds urgent and wanting out of his own monolog, Joseph says, "I need to get that, but we are not done. I am not happy with you, not happy at all. I will take this call, and then you're leaving. I will take you to the hospital where you can get the treatment you need. That's all I can do."

Leaving Nathan where he is, Joseph's intention is to take the call, calm down, and then go back to him in a more composed manner. But missing the call for a second time, he sits in his office with the door closed, heated with embarrassment, anger, and shame. He knows he has not handled any part of today's drama well. Nathan is, hurt, and still he has made the difficult journey to Joseph's home and seek his help before anyone else's. But instead of support and care, Joseph has subjected him to further accusations, anger and resentment. His treatment of Nathan makes him squirm in his desk chair with guilt. But then muddled in amongst his thoughts is still the very real fear of his personal life being talked about in the local community. Joseph's imagination has no difficulty in drumming up scenarios of how such conversations might go, and it only serves to unbalance him further. Dread of what others might think of him, he knows, is self-regarding and unacceptable compared to the very real issues Nathan is dealing with, but still, his reputation is everything.

Embarrassment for what might happen roots Joseph in his chair. He glances at the clock and is dismayed to see it is just after eight. There is still a lot of the day left to endure

Chapter 10

Only ten minutes has passed since Joseph fled the kitchen, but bike, boots, and boy are all missing. The blanket has been discarded on the floor. Joseph's perfected sulk, sitting in his office with the door closed, had ended abruptly as the need for coffee and some concern for Nathan necessitated his return to the kitchen. Only Nathan isn't there, and a cursory check of the downstairs confirms he has chosen flight over fight. "How dare he?" Joseph says aloud. He is happy enough to see him gone, but the mental image of Nathan freewheeling his way down the hill without a helmet, clutching his ribs with one hand and the handlebars with the other, and coming to grief near the main road, would be bad news for both of them, he thinks.

Waiving the need now for coffee, and thinking Nathan with his ten-minute's head start will have put a fair distance between them, Joseph is careless in his haste. Backing the car out of the driveway and cursing aloud, he ignores the potholes in his rush to get down the hill. His mental picture needs instantly revised, however, as Nathan hasn't gone more than two hundred yards. He isn't on the bike but leaning his whole weight against it so he can use it as a mobile crutch. As he walks, he shuffles from side to side in clear discomfort, his progress agonisingly slow.

Joseph has to drive a good distance past Nathan to find somewhere safe on the narrow road to leave the car which means to help Nathan, he must first walk back up the hill to where he is and assess the situation.

Nathan is concentrating on putting one foot in front of the other and making the arduous journey to wherever he thinks he is going. The hill is steep, the distance considerable, and Joseph thinks, the hour too early for such strenuous shit as this. By the time he reaches Nathan, the inconvenience of it all makes Joseph angrier than he has ever felt towards another human being. Now his own discomfort negates any small amount of sympathy he might have been feeling towards Nathan and his injuries. Caught up as he is in his own narcissism and way past struggling to comprehend how someone can be physically violent, Joseph imagines the many ways he can choke the last lingering breaths from Nathan without being caught.

His first words are a breathless grunt, and then he says, "Shit, I'm old." He bends double and clutches at his right side. Black spots swim in front of his eyes and the pain of a stitch causes him to study the ground. He needs to catch his breath and slowly stand upright before he can speak again.

"So, what? No goodbye? No thanks for everything? You just up and leave without a word? That's the thanks I get? You have to be the most ungrateful… shit…"

Nathan doesn't answer but looks away into the distance. Joseph thinks he is working out how he is going to get wherever he is going. But it is clear Nathan has already "left." He just needs his broken body to catch up with where his head is at. Forced once more to bend double, Joseph puts his hands on his knees and sucks in great lungfuls of air. A combination of being unfit, the steepness of the hill, and the energy wasted on a lot of misplaced anger is causing him considerable difficulties. He pants out. "Bloody hell."

"Joseph?" Nathan says, and Joseph is shaken by the pained and puzzled expression on Nathan's face when he straightens. It does not help his mood.

"Yes, Joseph. Who the fuck do you think?"

"Thanks fur everything and goodbye," Nathan says, able still to filter the abuse from the salient points and take out what he needs from Joseph's catalogue of unkind words. Again, looking away, with his one good eye, down the hill, a clear longing is etched into his bruised and swollen face for what is ahead and not for what has occurred behind.

"What is your fucking problem?" Joseph asks. The sadness and pain that emanate from Nathan has thrown him. Caught in the issues and uncertainties of the day, Joseph reverts now to his default position of anger to manage what he is finding unmanageable.

"Ah got the shit kicked out ay me and it hurts. What's your fecking problem?"

Nathan's retaliation, like the stitch, takes the words and air from Joseph's empty lungs and he makes an *aggghhh* sound before bending over again. Bending and stretching several times downgrades the pain of the stitch from considerable to manageable. Now able to stand semi-upright, he plans to address Nathan again, but he struggles for something profound to say. With minimal effort and in more pain, Joseph notes, Nathan is winning the argument.

In the silence, and misreading the lack of a response, believing they are done, Nathan goes to leave. Refusing to accept that he is beaten, and still bent slightly over, Joseph grabs the back of the bike as it passes. Ignorant of this, Nathan carries on walking and the bike pulls up short, yanking him hard backwards. He lets out a pitiful wail,

"Let go," he says, the angry demand knotted into a sob.

Joseph stands a little straighter, but feeling no better, he stutters, "Sorry. I didn't mean that." It is not his intention to add to Nathan's physical discomfort, even if he is giving very little attention to his mental health.

"Let go."

"Tell me where you think you are going."

A tug of war over a bike is not what Joseph had planned for his morning, but somewhere deep in his mind he understands that the bike represents something they both believe is worth fighting for. As Nathan attempts to pull the bike towards him once more in an impressive show of ownership, Joseph, done with trying to appease the lad, wrenches the bike back even harder. In his weakened condition, Nathan loses his balance and the momentum of the pull on the bike causes him to fall forward. If Joseph were standing one step closer to Nathan, his knee would have made contact with the soft mud and grass on the verge. But he is a good foot away, and the boy tumbles towards him, tangled in amongst bits of bike. The result is pure luck and no judgement on Joseph's part, and he catches Nathan. They both go down, Nathan falling forward hard and heavy into Joseph, who collapses under the dead weight of him. They fall to one side, Joseph's right knee cracking hard onto the asphalt road. The sensation now of real and not imagined pain rumbles within the joint and settles to a steady thump.

Nathan's arms are limp at his sides, his face squashed against Joseph's chest. One leg is crunched up underneath him and the other splayed out at an awkward angle, looking like it belongs some place else. Completing the fall and going right over, Joseph's movements cause Nathan's head to fall backwards and his eyes to roll and then disappear into the back of his head.

"Don't you dare," Joseph says, jogging him back into position cradled against his chest. The tone of his voice shows concern where his words have failed.

"I'm not carrying you back up this hill," he says, and Nathan makes a strange *urp* sound, as if he is undecided perhaps whether to vomit. Joseph can smell the blood on his breath, and it stains his gums and has dried thick and black around his left nostril. He watches as Nathan's eyes flutter and roll and then settle.

"Are you with me?" Joseph asks him.

"It's me," Nathan says, and the conversation is suited to the day with its absence of sense or logic.

He knows it doesn't need saying, but Joseph says it anyway. "This is shaping up to be a shit day."

"Aye," the boy says.

Chapter 11

Joseph can't easily unwind himself from the tangle, and so, sitting in the gravel, he marvels at the complexity of "stuff" that makes up the road. Loose stones, tarmac, dust and chippings are piled into potholes, and mud frames the grassy fringe. His knee hurts and it intrigues him to find out how badly bruised it is. It will have to wait. They have narrowly missed falling into a vile clump of nettles, and where they sit the grass is long and leans in towards them, heavy still with morning dew. Nathan is lying half in the road and half on Joseph, his face pressed in against the soft pudgy part of Joseph's stomach. He can feel Nathan's fingers making tight fists clutching his shirt, holding on to the material as if he is unaware that it is not possible to fall any further.

The car is down the hill; The house is up, and Nathan is lying prone at a point nicely in the middle. Joseph judges the distance to either the car or the house to be about three hundred yards. All in all, not far, but it is his Everest. He has no idea how he will get them both back to the house. While waiting for inspiration, he marvels at the work of spiders, their webs lace the heather and gorse bushes.

Joseph realises he is fighting the first edgy stirrings of panic. Never good in a crisis, his worst nightmare and greatest fantasy is to be called on in an emergency. Shamelessly, he is relieved and grateful that members of the public have so far declined to stroke out, collapse, have a fit, or attempt to expire in his vicinity when he's been off duty and away from the safety of his practice. Still, within him is the longing to be a hero, even if there is no desire to put these musings into action in any meaningful way.

Nathan is testing those contradictory daydreams now with this real-life drama. Joseph knows there will be no convenient passing of a car with a compliant neighbour to offer help.

"Nathan," he says. "We will have to move. I've lost all feeling in my right arse cheek and we're attracting flies."

The insect world has discovered them, and their attentions will only get worse the longer they stay.

"Go hame," Nathan says, as he carefully slides himself off Joseph and curls up into the foetal position on the road.

"That cannot be comfortable."

"Leave me alone."

"I'm trying to help."

Joseph knows as he says the words he is asking for trouble for what he said is not true. Nothing he has done so far can be construed in any way by Nathan as helping.

"Go-a-way," Nathan says again, dragging out the words. Lying curled in a ball on the road, he cannot get any energy or heat into his voice. This, Joseph thinks, is Nathan's way of sounding angry.

"I'm worried about the damage to your head. Let's not add to your problems. You might have a concussion or a blood clot… or something. I still think we should get you X-rayed."

"No." The single word has a little more heat in it. Nathan, with his arms tight to his waist to protect his damaged ribs, sobs. Joseph knows it is painful for the boy to partake in such emotion, but it is equally so for Joseph to watch. Because he is a contributor in no small way to the dreadful circumstances Nathan finds himself caught in, Joseph's guilt now casts a nasty shadow.

"It will be okay," he tells the boy, but he is not sure how.

Nathan's crying breaks Joseph's scared and damaged heart, hurts him more than he is prepared for. Egotistical, selfish, and morose: these are his finest qualities, he tells himself. Yet sitting in the road, now free of the lad, he feels devalued and worthless. Nathan's crying is wretched, and the truth of it all is like a physical smack hitting him squarely between the eyes. Here is someone dealing with serious problems. The worst that can happen, Joseph supposes, has happened to him already; but Nathan, lying as he is curled up in the road, is still in the midst of his breakdown.

"I will get the car. Then I will help you get in the car. Then I will put the bike in the back of the car. Then... Well, that's as far as my planning has got. Stay here," Joseph tells him.

The hill is no easier to walk down than up because the steepness pushes his knees into his shins and his shins into his ankles. To add to Joseph's ailments and misery, his left hip has decided to ache. He has an idea to exercise more before it's too late.

Joseph parks the car as close as he can to Nathan's prone form. He is careful not to park on him. He checks and rechecks the handbrake. He has revised his plan, and he puts the bike into the car before Nathan. Nathan made it himself at a build-a-bike workshop, part of a college scheme he was on. Joseph recalls now Nathan's bragging as he told the story, showing off the finer points of the bike and how he'd chosen that course instead of the joinery class his father wanted him to take. The bike is Nathan's pride and joy, and Joseph thinks, if he has the bike, then Nathan will follow. He is not happy about the bike being in the car which is new, the soft leather upholstery immaculate. There are a lot of things he is not happy about, but Nathan is calling the shots. Joseph is learning the hard way to once more go with the flow, after all it had been this way with Mary, he thinks. Nathan is still crying. "Ah'm sorry," he says.

"I'm sorry too," Joseph says whilst trying to uncurl him. His response is off the cuff, but Nathan's is thought-out and deliberate. There is an outpouring of words, but Joseph can only make out some of them amongst Nathan's need to draw in air and breath through the build-up of crusted blood and snot caked to his nose. As Joseph gets him upright, Nathan is talking about days off, then wails on about their friendship now being ruined. The situation would be funny, Joseph thinks, if not for the fact that Nathan is injured and distraught. Crying depletes what little energy he has, and when he makes it to the car, his legs give way.

There is a need to be a lot more careful on the return journey, sharp bits of the bike rest against the soft upholstery and neither of them have seat belts on. Nathan is slumped sideways in the front seat, his head bouncing every so often off the side window. Joseph is concerned that an appendage on the bike will rip the leather. Nathan seems unaware of his own discomfort. He is crying because of Joseph's actions and not those of his father, Joseph thinks. He knows beyond doubt he has hurt Nathan more.

When they get to the house, he leaves Nathan in the car while he thinks through the best way to get him inside and settled. If he can make this much noise crying and carrying on, then he is surely not as badly injured as Joseph first assessed. Pausing long enough to down a pint glass of water, he takes a kitchen chair out into the hallway next to the staircase.

Then returning to the car, Joseph says, "So far nothing has gone to plan. We have to get you inside where you can rest. So, I need you to stop crying and focus."

Nathan sniffles but downgrades his fuss and bother. "Awerite," he says, and he is back to being compliant. They shuffle quietly into the house and he makes it to the seat.

"Now, listen. We've gone about this the hard way, but we're back to the original plan. Let's get you upstairs where you can rest on the bed and feel better." Joseph tells him, as he takes Nathan's boots off. He "admires," the holes in his socks, which are bright orange and none too clean.

The stairs are Nathan's Everest now, but Joseph is carrying the greater percentage of weight by the time they get to the bedroom. Nathan lets Joseph remove his jeans but refuses to take off any other clothing. He whines that he is cold, even though his hair is now slicked to the sides of his head with sweat and curled at the nape. He feels clammy to the touch, and Joseph has not ruled out the possibility that he is a lot more injured than he is willing to let on.

Nathan folds himself back into the foetal position and Joseph tucks the duvet around him. The fear that Nathan might be seriously injured muddles itself in with the memory of being denied the chance to look after Mary.

"I can do this," he says out loud but to himself. It is now just after ten, and the heat in the bedroom is already stifling. Joseph would like to open the windows a little more, but Mary has taken up a monitoring position there, passing in and out of the sunlight streaming in. The image of her flickers and readjusts. Nathan, underneath the bedclothes, shudders; And Joseph knows it has nothing to do with cold and everything to do with pain and exhaustion. He runs through the litany of symptoms and causes, going over in his head what to look for, what to do.

He knows Nathan might be in shock, and there could be internal bleeding, concussion, or some other internal damage.

Nathan, not yet asleep, is still holding a one-sided conversation. He says he is sorry: sorry about what he said, sorry about coming, sorry about Uncle Tony, and so it goes on.

"Shush," Joseph tells him. He wants to comfort him, but because Nathan is riddled with physical damage, any contact is a dicey option. Joseph's shirt is damp around the collar and under the arms, and he feels grimy from sitting in the road. He lets Nathan run out of words and energy, watches as, finally defeated, sleep takes hold. Against his better judgement, he will not give up the care of the boy. The fear of what might happen is quashed by the more terrifying possibility that somebody else could care for Nathan and do it better.

Chapter 12

The warm water of a shower erases the grime from the road but not the tiredness Joseph feels in his limbs. He lies down beside Nathan, who is cool to the touch even though he is curled up under the covers. After sorting the pillows, Joseph stays on top of the bed in just shorts, and the warm mid-morning air in the room is already causing his freshly showered skin to sweat. Like Mary, he feels the need to monitor the sleeping lad closely. He will need to make sure that he can awaken Nathan normally in a few hours and none of his symptoms worsen. To pass the time, he reads a book he put down some months ago and is now struggling to recover the gist of. Book, heat, and boredom take their toll, and he falls asleep still sitting upright. He awakens an hour later because a persistent fly has made its way into the room to torment him.

Caught by the heat of the room, the unnaturalness of sleeping during the day and thirst, Joseph's head aches. He splashes water on his face at the sink in the bathroom and glances at his reflection in the mirror. He does not like the person he sees. To Joseph's mind, the image is wrong. He is confused by the sullenness of the eyes, the tiredness of the face, the disappointment that is etched into his features. He thinks he should look different, but he is not sure how.

The phone is ringing again and, concerned now that it might disturb Nathan, he is motivated to answer it. Even so, he is unhurried as he makes his way downstairs and into his office.

"Can I speak to Doctor Murphy please?"

"Speaking."

"Uh… no Doctor Mary Murphy… please."

"She's not here."

"When will she be back?"

The woman's persistent politeness coupled with the headache and general unhappiness with the day irritates Joseph and he snaps, "She won't be back. What can I help you with?"

The woman stutters over her words, her well-rehearsed pitch thrown by Joseph's shortness. He catches the abbreviations for a charity and a hurried, disjointed explanation about raffle tickets that should have been sent back by now.

"My wife died, and I don't want your raffle tickets. Stop phoning and leave me alone." His voice rises steadily, and by the end of the brief conversation, he is shouting.

There is a stuttered, "Oh I'm so sorry to…" But he cuts the woman off before she can complete her apology. Straight away he regrets his outburst, and he carefully replaces the phone in its stand.

Mary has joined him; Following him about as his constant shadow. Her broken sense of self, her being this way, dead, he reasons, torments them both. The dead, after all, lose that portion of being that anchors the living; And Mary as she is now, caught between stages, must be as haunted by her situation as Joseph is haunted by her.

Her arms are folded, and Joseph ponders the way she always seems to favour the light of a room as once more she is standing by the window, watching. He wonders if she can feel the heat through the glass.

"Wrong number," he says out loud, and then he laughs, an unnatural, forced snigger. Nathan, lying upstairs in the bed, makes him brave.

"Go away," he says to the image, but he is the one who leaves the room.

The phone call is an unpleasant reminder that his own patients are waiting for him to return to work. Colleagues still phone to enquire how he is doing, but their concern is wavering, tarnished by the selfish need to have him back to help with the ever-increasing workload. On this issue he must decide sooner rather than later what he will do.

Still working hard to feel sorry for Nathan and his situation, Joseph knows he cannot have him staying in the house and be a witness to his own mental melt down. He thinks of himself as a human grenade with the pin pulled out, and the explosion, when it comes, will not be shared. Mary should be gone, but it is Joseph that feels trapped between worlds. No longer part of the past and too damaged to move forward into the future, he is haunted, the one who feels like half a person, spiritless and displaced.

"Go away," he says again, this time to the ceiling because he means the young man lying upstairs in his bed, and he wonders if yet another obvious lie will placate Mary. Coffee does not help the headache or his mood.

Nathan has bled onto the sheets. A brown stain, framed now by a lighter wet patch of dribble, marks the silvery grey pattern of the linen. The sheets are well past needing changing, this is Joseph's least favourite task and he has let the weeks drift.

Nathan is awake and needing to use the bathroom when Joseph checks on him. His face is swollen into a permanent scowl which matches Joseph's mood.

"Where's my bike?"

"In the garage."

"Ah'm nae sick."

"Really?"

He sways as he walks, and Joseph keeps his hands ready on either side of him should he fall. The declaration he is not sick goads Joseph, and when Nathan withers back into the bedsheets, Joseph shows a rare turn of speed and leaves the room. He is looking for his doctor's bag, and he searches first where it should be, in the office, but it is not there. He goes out to the garage and checks his car, then returns to re-check the office. He finally finds it buried beneath numerous pairs of Mary's shoes in the cloakroom.

Nathan will surely be asleep again by now, and so all his hurrying and searching will be for nothing, he thinks. But when Joseph gets to the bedroom, Nathan is still awake, his one good eye fixed on the ceiling. He does not respond when Joseph returns to the room carrying his bag. Well worn and old it has a distinctive smell and feel, with the tatty and well-handled leather, softened by use and time, has the imprint of Joseph's working life etched into every scuff, stitch, and stain. His fingers caress the objects as he rummages in the bag, these tools are old lovers, faithful friends, and sometimes antagonists.

Nathan is intent on ignoring him, but Joseph does not need his participation. He is a performer making amends for his earlier indiscretions. Without giving an explanation, he picks up Nathan's wrist and feels his pulse. It bounces and skips beneath his fingers. He chooses the old fashioned thermometer over its newer model, and after wiping it clean, places it under Nathan's tongue. He is efficient as he takes the blood pressure cuff and wraps it around the lad's scrawny arm. As Nathan feels it tighten on his muscle, he makes an insignificant whine. Joseph ignores him and concentrates on listening for the familiar bounce of pressure through the stethoscope. The task fits nicely with taking his temperature, and he can remove both the cuff and the thermometer at the same time. He studies the readings.

"Sit forward for me," he says, but he does not explain why. Still unable to admit his failings and the callous way he has treated Nathan, Joseph knows he is now falling back into this safe and more comfortable role of doctor. Nathan intensifies his scowl. Joseph studied his face while he was sleeping, and it is clear now that most of the damage is to his nose, which is the cause of the black eyes. There is an ominous bump at the bridge, and the perfectness of the nasal bone, something Joseph admired, is compromised. There are grip marks on his right arm and bruising down his right leg. But Joseph has yet to see how bad his torso is. Nathan is reluctant to sit forward and even more reluctant to let Joseph lift his t-shirt.

"Ah'm cold," he says.

"It will only take a minute." Joseph has perfected a no-nonsense voice over the years. Calm, quiet and factual, it is tried and tested and has served him well. He uses that voice now, but it sounds somehow wrong to his own ears. With Nathan he wants to soften his tone, temper the words. There is the desire to offer comfort, but still he is unable to translate that feeling into any meaningful action. Nathan complies but he is not happy, and Joseph smiles to himself as he lifts his clothing. Nathan appears neither distraught nor amenable now, merely inconvenienced by the attention.

Joseph's smile fades. Nathan looks like he has been rolled in soot. His back is blackish purple. Joseph is careful where he places the stethoscope, careful even when he asks him to breathe in and out so he can auscultate his lung sounds, checking for wheezes, crepitations, crackles. He then has Nathan lie back against the pillows and is even more careful when he traces his fingers over his scraped-raw ribs.

Nathan's body gives up part of the story, and in Joseph's mind's eye he sees him as he was earlier, curled into a ball. Only now he also sees his attacker standing over him, kicking him. Perhaps a good enough aim could not be had, and that is why there are grab marks on his arm. Perhaps Nathan, in protecting his ribs, exposed his face, and that was how his nose was damaged.

"Your bed is big," Nathan says. It is, Joseph knows, a move to distract him. They are both reminded of why he was subjected to the beating and how Joseph's words made him cry all the more.

"No one should have this happen to them. Not because they say they love someone, no matter how misplaced the assertion," Joseph says.

"My bed is small."

"I'm sorry for the way I acted. I was embarrassed, but that's not an excuse. It was unforgivable, and I'm sorry." He is, he realises, getting used to apologising.

"Dae you get scared?"

I miss my wife.

"Being scared is different fur us," Nathan says, teasing out the words in his soft breathy voice, testing Joseph's understanding of what such an assertion might mean.

"There's a lot to be scared about."

"Aye."

Chapter 13

Joseph lies down in the darkness beside Nathan and listens to his rhythmic breathing. He feels the warmth of his body. The distance is measured so as to be appropriate, but still this is the first time he has lain in a bed with anyone other than his wife. Perhaps as a child, he thinks, he might have crawled into bed with his parents or his older brother when nightmares had got the better of him, but if that had happened, he does not have those memories now. All he knows is Mary, her back pressed against his hip and her scent permeating the linens. All he has ever known is their bed, their dreams, and for a time, their lovemaking; But now here is Nathan in the same bed: bruised, battered and abused.

Joseph's dreams are filled with images of him, and when he wakes, before any alarm rouses him, Nathan's face is resting against his chest and his breath fans across his skin. There is no distance at all between them now.

It is mid-morning of the third day Nathan has been in the bed. He has stopped protesting about not being sick, and Joseph knows that Nathan is feeling betrayed by his own body. He feels it has failed him because it refuses to work, because it will not move or respond as he wants it to. His appetite for conversation or food has deserted him as well. Since his talk of being scared and Joseph's apology, he has been silent on all matters. So far his presence is not intruding into Joseph's morosity or madness, and oddly, Joseph finds Nathan less an inconvenience than his wife. Mary remains silent as well, but she is also ever present, voyeuristic in her monitoring of them, he thinks. As long as there is light, she is standing in it. Joseph takes food up, trying to get Nathan to eat, but a combination of doing nothing and the split on his bottom lip keep the boy's enthusiasm in check.

A blurred haze through the window in the lounge has washed the colours of the landscape; The heat is uncomfortable through the glass. Joseph opens windows and doors throughout the house to move air about and bring some relief. As he passes the stairs, Nathan is coming down. He is still wearing the t-shirt and underpants, but one sock is lost. He gets as far as the middle stair and sits down.

"Ah am nae sick," he says, and Joseph smiles.

"Are you telling me you are feeling better?"

Nathan thinks about this before he answers. "Ah'm nae feeling any worse," he says.

"Are you going to eat something?"

Another pause and then, "Mebbe."

Joseph proposes a shower, but having come this far down the stairs, Nathan is committed to being up, and with the same swaying gait that concerned Joseph days ago, he comes all the way down the stairs to stand, undecided, in the hallway.

"Come into the lounge," Joseph suggests, placing his hands in an attentive hold either side of Nathan's skinny hips.

"Ah'm cauld."

Reluctant to leave the still unsteady boy, Joseph hurries to retrieve the blanket from the kitchen where it was left. Upon returning, he drapes it around Nathan's shoulders. The heat in the house is energy-zapping and so he cannot believe Nathan feels cold.

"Whoa. What happened tae the wall?" Nathan asks, now standing in the lounge and noticing for the first time the missing portion of the house.

"Sit here," Joseph tells him. He is concerned that Nathan is becoming increasingly unsteady the longer he stands. Although he looks slight, Nathan is a considerable weight, and Joseph has no desire to support him again.

"Did you dae that tae the windae oan purpose?" he asks, now more interested in the missing wall than anything else.

"Yes." Joseph's answer is terse. With everything else that hangs between them, the wall is irrelevant and should not factor into Nathan's thinking.

"Why?"

"To appreciate the view."

"What? You couldnea jist gang outwith?"

Nathan's words make Joseph chuckle, and then the unexpected lapse in pent up emotions escapes in the form of a sudden burst of laughter that surprises both of them. Joseph can't help but grin afterward.

Mary is in the room, and her faded frown and tightly drawn lips give Joseph the impression that she is interested but also irritated by his interaction with Nathan. He lets his own smile die and fusses over Nathan. He realises that he wants, in fact needs, to talk about death. Her being in the room with them perpetrates the need to bring her presence into the conversation between them, he thinks.

But he also wonders why she is here. Is it a result of her failure, of her not wanting to leave this life, or a result of his failure, of him not letting her go that has her trapped this way? Or is she now just hanging around because of Nathan? Losing someone close is something they share, and Joseph is certain that Nathan will want to talk about it.

"I'm sorry about your ma," he says.

"What about her?"

He is surprised at Nathan being so taciturn, more interested in looking out of the window than having any further contact with Joseph. His enthusiasm for being up is wearing off, and his head rests against the back of the sofa. Joseph knows it will not be long and he will give in and sleep.

"Your uncle said she passed."

"Ah'm nae sick. Ah'm cauld," he says, and he cries.

"I'm sorry I mentioned it," Joseph says, and he moves to sit in the seat opposite him. He considers reaching out to touch Nathan, hesitates, perhaps reading too much into an imagined response to any physical contact, and so restrains his hands, folding them into his lap. This is not Joseph's normal seat, and he studies the room from this altered angle. Nathan has the blanket around his shoulders, so his bruised and skinny legs are bare. It is difficult, but Joseph ignores Nathan's tears and hands him the TV remote control.

"Watch something," he says, and he leaves to find a second blanket, deliberately avoiding any further conversation in preference to sorting Nathan's more pressing physical problems.

A song that Joseph does not recognise is mixing with the heat of the room when he returns. The steady back beat hums in time with a pain he has behind his eyes.

"Not so loud," he says, but despite his request, Nathan keeps the music high enough to prevent a comfortable conversation from taking place. Eager now to leave Nathan slouched on the sofa, Joseph, a coward, realises he's not ready to sort out what has happened and so he retreats upstairs.

The bedroom is bogging; Nathan has been festering in the sheets for days, and Joseph for long enough before him. While stripping the bed, he finds the missing sock, and as he bundles everything up he busies himself working on a plan to rid himself of this unexpected guest. A return home to his father, who has made his feelings clear, seems out of the question, but Joseph is holding on to the slim hope that Uncle Tony might be a little more forgiving. He came looking for Nathan after all.

Changing one lot of sheets is bad enough, but Joseph tackles the spare room as well. The room has a sense of the foreboding about it because this is where Mary spent her last remaining days before she chose hospice care over his care. Closed off since her parting, there is dust on the dresser and windowsill. Medical supplies that still have to be returned impregnate the air, even over the mustiness, with the smell of antiseptic, but the forgotten items do nothing to displace the stark emptiness of the room or the memories of Mary's last night there. The room feels and smells like a morgue. The duvet has a lump in it that can't be smoothed away, and Joseph uses a pillowcase to wipe at the dust. It will have to do, he thinks, and he is sweating and miserable by the time he finishes.

Nathan, sprawled out on the sofa, looks for the first time comfortable. One leg pokes from under the blanket, a sure sign that he is not cold at all. Joseph has brought food in on and off while he has been sorting the rooms, leaving it on the table beside the boy. He gave up asking or trying to coax Nathan to eat, but the plates are empty.

"I've made up the spare room for you," he tells him.

He believes he can move Nathan out of his life by first moving him out of his bed and into the spare room. Once that has been achieved, he will contact the uncle. Joseph is certain that the uncle will take Nathan back or find him some place else to stay.

"Clean sheets means clean you. So you're showering at some point today."

"Awerite."

Mary has not followed him into the spare room. Aware now that she has remained with Nathan, standing watch over him; Joseph feels once again replaced. He is surprised and sickened at the realisation that her fixation on someone else, on Nathan, can upset him. Grasping the absurdity of the situation, Joseph realises that, instead of being thankful that she has found someone else to obsess about, he is jealous. He can miss this weird version of her. Her obsession with him and her mimicking of his every move has become meaningful, needed, wanted even.

Chapter 14

Nathan is indifferent about the room, but Joseph in trying to sell the move, shows him the TV on the wall. Again he makes the requests that the music not be played so loud, and again he is ignored. He perseveres as long as he can, but he is in full parental mode when he enters the spare room after an hour to confront his guest about the noise. Nathan is still awake, the light and the TV on, and he is lying across the wrecked bed, naked except for a clean pair of socks. The starkness of the room focuses Joseph's eye on the only thing of interest. Tempted by the impulse to stare, Joseph instead concentrates on the socks, the one thing Nathan has taken from the pile of clean clothes laid out earlier for him. Nathan's nakedness complicates Joseph's plan of attack, and finding he can no longer be the mature voice of reason, he feels the heated stain of colour settle on his cheeks. Forcing himself to stay calm, in the silence is an unspoken truth. Nathan, in exposing himself, has also exposed the very lie that has been Joseph's life. Joseph knows that if he remains in the room, he will react.

Irritated by the heat, the music and Nathan's nudity. Joseph's response to it all is terse. Nathan's indifferent. "Enough. I'm tired, so light out, music off, and go to sleep", he say. He does not wait for a response from Nathan, or for him to follow his instructions. Instead, he takes the TV control and silences the unknown artist himself, and then he turns off the light. He does not say goodnight, just closes the door and goes back to his own room. Images of Nathan naked and the words of the song fixed in his head.

The room is too warm, but Joseph wants to be hidden under the sheets. He has turned one way and then another, and he is considering getting up, giving up on trying to sleep at all. Turning for what feels like the hundredth time, he opens his eyes and yelps. Nathan is standing beside the bed.

"Thaur's something in the room. Come see."

"What?"

"Thaur is something weird in the room. There's a noise. Something's making a noise. Come see." Not giving Joseph time to respond, Nathan pulls at the covers and fumbles for Joseph in the grey light of not quite darkness. Joseph protests, and many of the words are expletives. It does not faze Nathan. He has found Joseph's wrist in amongst the bedclothes and pulls him, first so he is sitting upright and then so he is out of the bed and standing.

"Come see," Nathan says again, and he is neither scared nor perturbed, just insistent that Joseph complies.

It is not the dead Joseph fears, it is what the living will make of his insanity. Frightened that Nathan is about to discover for himself what he has worked so hard to keep hidden, an acidic burn sears the back of his throat. If he could, he would stop their advance towards the spare room but beaten down by everything that has led to this moment, he surrenders to Nathan's request and blindly follows him.

There are no lights on, but Nathan makes his way from one room to another in the semi-darkness. The patches of grey and blackish light that hide and disguise normality are not obstacles to him, it is the bright sunlight that he struggles with. Joseph cracks his toe on the base of the bed and finds a few more colourful words to fill the darkness.

"Be careful," Nathan tells him, he does not let go of Joseph's hand.

The spare room is an alien landscape for Joseph; Nothing is familiar. He says, "Turn the light on."

"No, it willnea work then," Nathan says, pushing Joseph towards the bed and insisting that he sit down. In the dark Joesph misses the smile on the lads face.

"Watch this," he says, his voice now at a distance. Joseph can just about make out the smudged shape of his outline by the door. He thinks he will leave the room, but Nathan shuts the door, sealing them both in.

"Weird, huh?"

Joseph subscribes to the medical model for all things, the process that all doctors are trained to adhere to and the one thing that can still offer him some sense of stability. A heart is a heart whether healthy or broken, for example, and always works in the same way. The result is that blood moves around the body, fulfilling a purpose. The concepts are not dissimilar to the mechanics of a car, boiler, or clock: everything that happens can be explained. Everything that happens can be reasoned out. But Joseph has no explanation for what is happening in the room.

Unaware that Nathan has set this scene, Joseph, recalling the recent history of the room can't keep his fear contained. Nathan, pushes Joseph to the very edge of insanity demanding he explain what is going on in the empty dark and silent room.

Joseph's heart slams against its framework, the beat so strong that it scatters and reaches the very tips of his fingers, resulting in a zap of energy that is both wonderful and painful. With the door closed the room should disappear into blackness.

Instead, shadows in various hues of grey smudge into the corners and make the room seem smaller, tight. The temperature settles to an uncomfortable level, and the air stagnates, the result is a feeling of nothingness that settles like dust and irritates Joseph's bare skin. Now he can only think in terms of what this experience is not. It is not footsteps nor the scurrying sounds of misplaced rodents that he hears. It is not, Joseph thinks, noise or movement at all. The room "feels" of something unlike anything he has felt before. He thinks the feeling comes from the dreich darkness being agitated against its will. Everything has coalesced: the sounds, the grey dusty air, the dirty half-light, and himself. This, Joseph thinks, is the feel of madness, uniting all his senses and in the process becoming something in its own right—a last barrier being broken before insanities embrace.

"Put the light on." His voice is raised the command clumsy and displaced in the soupiness. Unable to hide his fear any longer, as the light routs the gloom, he uses the flat of his hand to guard against its brightness. With the light a memory splinters his brain: a lad sitting at the bottom of the garden on a bucket, the sunlight bouncing off the pail blinding him. That memory quickly replaced with a second: Mary turning away from him, and as she does the light catching her wedding ring as she raises her hand to tuck a stray strand of hair behind her ear.

"Mary." The word is as angry as any expletive he can muster, but she is the one thing that is missing from the room. Pushing past Nathan still standing in the doorway, Joseph turns on lights in the hall as he makes his way from one bedroom to the other. She has in her time commandeered both, he thinks, and if Mary is not now in one, she will be in the other—but both bedrooms are empty. Not done with his outburst, Joseph continues to wash the house with light as he hurries downstairs.

"Mary," he screams again into each empty room as it is lit up, certain that she is the cause of everything that has occurred upstairs. "Where is she?" he asks, as he turns to see Nathan making his way slowly down the stairs.

"Deid."

"Dead," he repeats, sampling the meaning in his and Nathan's frank enunciation.

"Aye."

In their haste to escape the room, save for Nathan's socks, they are both naked. Although, Nathan still wears his bruises, they shine in the sham light of the hallway. Joseph is between rooms, moved by the light, the hour, and his mental fragility. Spittle has dripped onto his chin and chest.

"Should we put this oan the list ay stuff we dinnae talk about?" Nathan asks.

There is a stark and proven insufficiency in his words. "Dead." Joseph tastes the word again and then adds, "Let's put this at the top of the list of things we don't talk about." The dead he thinks need to learn to keep their own counsel.

"We're all haunted." Nathan says, and again Joesph misses the smile.

Chapter 15

Something strong, alcoholic, and expensive is needed. Joseph pours two large doses of whisky, the good stuff, Mary put aside for visitors, who are never expected or invited, and special occasions that have yet to materialise. These occasions also partner table linens that have never been used and tea sets assessed as being too delicate to be put out for everyday use, possessions in better nick now than she is. Had she known her days were numbered, would she have used and abused these treasures; Or with no future, would they have been as obsolete as he had become? Mary had, after all, not made the most of even *me*, Joseph thinks.

Wearing just the garish socks, Nathan slides up and down the hallway. He is dancing, and as he dances he occasionally runs parallel to the image of Mary. Oblivious to her presence, every so often he collides straight into her. Only when Joseph flooded the downstairs' rooms with light did she put in an appearance. Her visual form now offers a sick respite from the disturbing happenings of the spare room. All three of them, beaten by the night's events, share in a silent apathy that fuses misery with ambivalence. Joseph is sure that Nathan's collisions and his own failings, his current ones and also those of the past, will soon anger her. The whisky bites and burns in the most delightful way as it fuses with his most vital parts.

"I have a song stuck right inside my heed that Ah'm dancing tae," Nathan says.

The tune Nathan hums is familiar but still it eludes Joseph, and careful to avoid contact with either of them as he nudges his way past Nathan and Mary to go into the living room, he tries to recall the song. The whisky is so good that it demands to be partnered with soft furnishings and temperate lighting.

"That's not dancing," he tells Nathan, who skids past, now doing a lot of elbow flapping and hip thrusting in amongst the sock sliding.

"Come dance wit me."

"That's not dancing," he reiterates. Then he adds as an afterthought, "Mind yourself. I thought you were sore?"

Joseph makes himself comfortable in his preferred seat, the left side of the two-seater couch nearest the coffee table with a good view of the garden and at a slight angle to the TV. He thinks Nathan is winding up to a massive come-down, and so he tries to encourage him to settle.

"Don't you want this drink?"

Nathan dances his way further into the living room, swaying his hips and giving a very poor rendition of the song that is stuck in his head. He takes the drink and downs it like juice. Joseph watches as his eyes bulge from their sockets and water. The very end of Nathan's nose turns red and he makes a low growling sound deep in his stomach.

"That was silly. Sit down and calm down."

It has been a difficult day, and he has no desire for more drama.

From where he sits, Joseph can ignore Mary and her patrolling of the hallway. Thinking about her but not looking at her makes him concentrate more on what she is wearing rather than the fact that she is a presence still in the house. It is not her best look. Her shapeless dress fades into the mottled late-night shadows, making her appear dusty and drab when in life she had always had style and flair. She was flawless then, but now there is a dishevelled, lost look about her. And given the earlier reminder of how many shoes she owned when he was searching the cloakroom for his doctor's bag, he thinks it odd that she has no feet upon which to wear shoes now. His timid unfunny effort at laughter does not disturb Nathan from his humming. The absurdity of the situation unravels Joseph's wellbeing further. The cavorting, naked, young man in his living room is not someone he should show any attention to. The situation is all wrong, and yet Joseph finds himself able to relate to him, to like him. To need him.

A doctor should be able to explain away what has occurred tonight. Joseph tries to invent an account of what has occurred that will make sense of it all. Nathan, however, content to dance about the living room, is not giving any sign he needs an explanation. There is a lot not being said, an infestation of silence.

"Till death do us part," Joseph says.

Nathan tucking himself into the corner of the room sways from side to side, humming the tune that must sound good inside his own head, Joseph thinks. His movements, however, are uncoordinated, a combination of a lack of talent and skill but also his injuries, which Joseph worries he is making worse.

"Joseph," he says, "did ye ken that wee baby Jesus was born the king ay angels."

Downing what's left in the glass, Joseph stands. He knows he cannot hold his own in a religious discussion. He also now realises that it is not a pop song but a hymn Nathan has been humming. Then, in the overbearing heat of a summer's eve, Nathan sings, "Hark the Herald Angels Sing," a song Joseph has never heard outside of December before. Nathan is at full volume, off-key, and solemn—the moment is surreal.

"I'm going to bed," Joseph says, causing Nathan to stumble from the room and race to the stairs ahead of him.

The heat of yesterday has passed and a fine rain is hitting the window which is still open and letting in a fresh breeze along with clotted early morning light. They have returned to sharing a bed. Joseph's insistence that the spare room is now off limits was met by laughter and Nathan's bragging that he wasn't scared, which caused a half-hearted standoff in the hallway. Only when Joseph returned to his bed, did Nathan follow.

"I'll nae let anything git tae you," he'd said, still finding the situation amusing, and his attempt at wrapping himself around Joseph in a show of protection had been met with a warning elbow to the chest. The blow was not hard enough to hurt the still injured boy but firm enough that the message was clear. Even so, at some point in the night, whilst asleep, they have found each other. In the darkness, the distance between them closed and Joseph has Nathan tucked beneath his torso. Nathan's face is squashed into the mattress, and when Joseph moves, the body beneath him protests. Not ready to face him, he reburies the boy with blankets wanting him to sleep on.

Showered and dressed, he hesitates at the top of the stairs. The door to the spare room is open, left this way in their haste to depart. Daylight makes Joseph brave and he goes into the room, closing the door behind him. Nothing happens, and the non-event is a weighty disappointment. From this vantage point he can see the road and a car making its way up and along the track. The last thing he needs is a visitor. The car pulls into the driveway in a wide arc, swings round, and is already facing back out. The driver, without exiting, drops two bags by the gate and drives off. Joseph, knowing that this is too inconvenient a place to fly tip, is intrigued. The drop must be intended.

The rain is hard enough to dampen his shirt. At first he thinks he might be wrong about the fly tipping. There is one black refuse sack and a smaller white plastic bag. The plastic bag has paperwork in it and what looks like a medium size book. The refuse sack rips at the handles as Joseph tries to untie it. Inside are Nathan's clothes, tattooed by the same stench he used to wear. Joseph reties the sack, puts it in the bin, and jogs back to the house. Not wet enough to warrant a change of shirt, he heads straight to the kitchen. Nathan makes him yelp again. He is sitting at the kitchen table; the chair turned out. Mary is standing behind him.

There was a moment during the histrionics of last night when Joseph hoped he'd lost her for a second time. He feels violated now by her presence but also the boy's.

"I didn't hear you," he says. "Something has been left, and I'm guessing it's yours." He shows Nathan the bag.

"Ah need tae learn tae fly," Nathan says, ignoring the bag.

"Really! Light aircraft or jumbos?" Joseph humours him, which is, he thinks, preferable to discussing anything about the previous night or the meaning of this bag showing up on his doorstep. The bag is a clear statement, of course: Nathan has been soundly evicted from his family. But Nathan giggles, and then he says, "No, fly," and flaps his elbows at his side.

"Oh, " Joseph says, as if he understands. Nathan points at the plastic bag.

"Like a baby bird, Ah hae tae leave the nest. But Ah need tae fly an nae gang splat."

"You look like you went splat."

"Ah've got it aw' figured out," he tells him, and Joseph is envious. If in fact he has it all figured out, then Nathan is doing better than him.

Chapter 16

The white plastic bag now represents all that Nathan has in the world. The dirty clothes in the refuse sack should be part of this, he knows, but Joseph will not have the foul smelling rags in the house. He does not tell Nathan about the clothes.

"Ah'm gonnae mend an' feel better. Then Ah'm gonnae get a job and then Ah'm going tae buy a house."

"You make it sound simple."

"Ah need yer help."

"I thought you might. Do you want breakfast?"

"Give up the ghost."

Joseph has his back to Nathan so he can ignore Mary. "What did you say?" he asks as he turns slowly back to face his antagonists, both of them.

"Can Ah hae toast?" Nathan says, and he pronounces each word slowly and carefully. Then he adds, "An' cornflakes. Always cornflakes, but toast as well."

"I'm going into town. Do you need anything?"

"Ah hae nae money."

"That doesn't matter. Do you need anything?"

"Can Ah come?"

"No. Your face will scare babies and old people."

"Keep a tab of everything Ah owe you, dig money, food, everything. Ah'm going tae pay it aw' back."

"Of course you are. What's in the bag?"

Nathan empties the plastic bag out onto the table: what looks like an assortment of old letters, papers and certificates, a book, and a collection of pencils, one pen, and a black felt-tip.

"Ah hae everything Ah need as long as Ah hae this," Nathan says, and he hugs the book to his chest. Joseph stays silent. Thinking the statement too stupid to warrant a response.

"Maw's bible and my bible pencils."

Joseph has no idea what bible pencils are, and he has no interest in finding out. "While I'm out, don't answer the phone or the door. Don't have the music too loud and don't make a mess."

In his mind he has organised a myriad of tasks for himself that will take him a while to complete. The chores comprise of housekeeping errands that, prior to Mary's passing, would have ended up on the to-do list only after lots of nagging. Some tasks required outright avoidance. He would clean the microwave, for example, if it meant not having time to fill out a tax return. He would undergo root canal treatment if it meant not having to take part in any part of Christmas shopping or entering a shopping centre of any description at any time of the year.

He will leave Nathan on his own and do a skip run of garden waste, finally take more of Mary's cherished possessions to the charity shop, and go to the hospice to pick up the rest of her stuff. Joseph has decided that he would rather do all this than remain in the house with Mary and Nathan.

He has been outside the hospice for half an hour trying to convince his legs that they still function and are not just painted on. He has told himself that the rain-stained building is not to blame. Regardless, the grey Victorian granite pile represents all that has ended, all that is lost and cannot be restored. The smell of the reception area when he finally enters throws Joseph back into the dark age of counting down days, and as he waits for an auxiliary to find the possessions he is there to collect, and that he will then dispose of, he tries to stifle the memories of his previous visits.

The walls, the colours selected for their suppressed formality, are what Mary wanted to stare at during her last days. She chose this, he thinks, in preference to their beautiful home and him—a home that does not smell like death and pine disinfectant. The smell is just in the reception area, Joseph remembers, and further inside the building the odour is more of old lady talc and winter stew.

He finds something comforting in being able to blame bricks and mortar for all that is wrong with his life. The bricks, after all, cannot whine that it isn't fair, and the mortar cannot deliver a scathing attack on his fragile emotions and mental state. The furnishings will not list his failings or criticise his inaction. The staff can, however, still offer their ostensive sympathies in that practised, tolerant, and insipid way. This visit is a suitable punishment to put himself through, he thinks, payback for his ineptness when dealing with Mary and her illness.

Items now in hand, Joseph leaves the building and the memories it has dredged up. It is, he thinks, too soon to return home. There is still too much of the day left to bear, and the house is no longer a safe haven, somewhere to hide. He feels an injustice now in his own situation: Nathan is the one who is homeless, but he is the one displaced.

There is an even more terrifying task he has been putting off, and fooled by the trifling success he has had so far, he decides he will tackle it. Then he will return home triumphant, and neither Nathan nor Mary will take this achievement from him and crap all over it.

Joseph heads to the hospital, Mary's place of work. Parking is a nightmare when he gets there, and he has to leave the car a good distance from the main building. He is angry at having to park so far away that it is as if he is no longer even on the premises. He recalls the many times he has had this conversation with Mary: How are friends and family supposed to visit? It was a rhetorical question because he knew Mary would never criticise her place of work no matter how in-your-face the issue. Perhaps the parking did not bother her because she was lucky enough to have her own space only a hundred yards from the building where she spent the most meaningful part of her life. Somebody else's car is already in what had until recently been her parking spot, and Joseph feels the first parasitic bubble of fear grow inside him.

Mary chose the more dynamic field of anaesthesiology over his own more sedate general practice. She felt the rush of adrenalin when summoned to perform because of some emergency or another, her job a happy mixture of routine and the unknown. She'd told Joseph his strengths were his organised mind and methodical approach to problem solving, his skills best suited to being a GP, thereby securing a separation in their working lives. And he must have agreed because that was what he was. Reflecting on what she told him now, it sounds a subtle way of saying safe, boring.

The hierarchy is in evidence throughout the building, the power struggle of a uniformed and non-uniformed work force segregated into imagined importance by roles, titles, and prospects. In the time that Mary has been gone, Joseph imagines that everything and nothing has changed. The fabric of the place is static, the people, as always, ever changing strangers.

The receptionist wears the uniform of a nurse, he assumes, without having earned the right. Joseph is wise to her for he has a heartless bitch just like her on his own staff team, employed for those very qualities, the ability to protect him from front line attack. The attackers are the sick, who languish at the very bottom of the hierarchy, those unfortunates in need of care and attention who are terrified that their prodigious symptoms are as dangerous as they imagine.

"I'm Doctor Joseph Murphy. I'm here to…." He gets no further. The vanguard receptionist holds up one fat, veined, and lentigos hand to silence him while she answers the phone.

"Yes?" she says, having finished her call. She does not look up from her paperwork.

"I'm Doctor Joseph Murphy and I'm here to collect some items…"

"What items?"

Joseph lets the interruption go. "Items belonging to Doctor Mary Murphy."

"What items?"

"Her personal things."

"What things?"

"Things… items… that she left here when… I'm just here to collect her things."

"Do you have written authorisation?"

"What? No, I was contacted and asked to come in and collect her… things."

"Who by?"

"Who by? I don't know. Look, they told me that her things would be left here and I was to come in and collect them."

The receptionist studies a clipboard. "I have no note of this. What department does the doctor work in?"

"She works… She worked in this department. Here. That's why her things are here."

"I have no Doctor Mary Murphy on my list. I don't know a Doctor Murphy."

A red mist descends upon Joseph and the reception area. A few months, he thinks, and already she is unknown, forgotten.

"You have phoned, and you have texted, and you have emailed asking me to come in and collect her things. My wife worked here; She gave eighteen years of her short life to this place. So find her fucking things or find somebody who knows what the hell they are doing…. now." He shouts the last word. Joseph knows that he is breaking all the rules by shouting at the reception staff, any staff. He knows that they suffer the most unnecessary abuse in the line of duty. He has attended courses about safeguarding against the abuse of staff. Asked to speak at focus groups and prepare guidelines on how to deal with this level of hostility, now he is a perpetrator, but this realisation does not stop his actions. The receptionist stares him down.

"I suggest you calm down or leave," she advises. Joseph knows he should leave. The irony is that he doesn't even want the items he is there to collect. He could go home and write a strongly worded email of complaint. In his head he has reasoned that this is what he must do, but what he actually does is slam the flat of his hand down onto the reception desk.

"I'm not leaving and I will not calm down."

"Then you leave me no choice," the receptionist says, and picking up the phone, she requests security. The situation has the potential to get worse before it improves, but then the standoff is interrupted.

"Joseph!"

"Fraser?"

Doctor Fraser Levitt is ancient, an antique of medical mastery. He was walking the halls of the hospital when Joseph's father was a practising physician, and in all those years Fraser has not changed. He is taupe in appearance, both skin and attire, with wispy hair that crowns a wrinkled face and a chin-grin that never wavers. Joseph looks at the ground rather than any of the participants now in the reception area. Fraser says, "It's good to see you," a clear indication that he has no idea what he has walked into.

"Can you help…?" Joseph asks, thinking the receptionist will once again interrupt and therefore he will not have to explain the situation any further, but he is now angered more because she is refusing to speak than he was by her previous rudeness.

"This inept excuse for a receptionist is being…. well… just fucking impossible," he says, and then under his breath he mumbles, "Troll."

Turning back to Fraser, he adds, "They have hounded me… harassed me, this… this place with demands I pick up Mary's things. I'm here to do just that. I want her things and to leave. Can you sort this?"

Joseph knows his coping strategies have failed him, and so has his ability to hold a civil tongue; his language is unnecessarily indecent. He also knows he has lost the moral high ground before the receptionist has had a chance to utter a word to Fraser. So he turns his attention, and his hostility, on the security guard now instead, the guard joined the group just in time to hear the final part of his rant. Joseph can see that this is no finely tuned athlete as they look each other up and down, and although the security guard is a good ten years younger, he is also three stone heavier. One good push, Joseph thinks, and the guard will go down like a sack of shit.

The guard, already out of breath, makes it clear he is unimpressed at being called to arms. "Ah'm pure done in," he says.

"You out of sorts because you had to pass on the cakes and coffee on the way up?" Joseph asks, determined now to alienate everyone. Annoyed further by the uncalled-for verbal attack, the security guard pulls himself up to his full height. Even so, he is a full head shorter than Joseph. Both middle-aged and, Joseph speculates, both equally unhappy with their lot, they stand facing each other and puff chests. Joseph is thinking the spectacle is worthy of a silent movie as Fraser puts the flat of his hand against Joseph's shirt, pushing himself between the two combatants.

"Now, let's see if we can't sort this matter," he says, and his words, spoken like lines of poetry, are beautifully calm. Turning to the receptionist, he asks her to, "Please find Helen," and whilst she clearly wants to protest the point, making the claim that she is not to leave her post, such is Fraser's importance that her objection is half-hearted.

"Helen," Joseph says, irritated now at his own stupidity. If he had asked to see Helen, everything would have been simple, and it is. Helen, beautiful, and as always, immaculate in her dress, is a vision of calm and poise in her business suit and "taxing" high heels. She greets Joseph with the warmest of smiles and a kiss on each cheek. Helen, who was a colleague of Mary's for more than ten years, placates each warring faction in turn.

"I'm sorry," Joseph says. "I should have asked for you…or better still called to say I was coming. It was just a last minute decision, really…" He lets his words trail away. Helen graciously blames herself for any misunderstanding and sends the security guard to find Mary's things that are, as she explains, on top of the filing cabinet in her office. Once the guard has produced the items, there is a moment of awkward silence. The security guard, then checking his attendance is no longer required, takes his leave, and the receptionist, busy once more at her station, refuses to participate further in any discussion, leaving Joseph to mumble a few more apologies. He wants to run, but fighting his urge to take flight, he hugs Helen once more and carefully says his goodbyes before slowly, purposefully, walking towards the door.

Chapter 17

"You called her a troll," Fraser says. He has insisted on walking Joseph out, in part, Joseph knows, so that the security guard did not have to.

"You heard that? Well, I stand by my assessment," Joseph says, laughing.

"This is funny?" Fraser asks.

Joseph quickens his pace, hoping to leave his escort behind, but for his age Fraser can generate a fair turn of speed and they are still side-by-side.

"She was rude."

"And you were all restrained charm and politeness."

"At first, yes."

"How are you?" That question is what Joseph is running from.

"Fine," he says, and that shitty little word seems perfect.

"Fine is good. I can see being grief stricken and distraught has not affected your appetite."

"Fuck you," Joseph says, and stopping, he sucks in his breath, looks at the ground and then the ceiling. "Sorry," he says. "Do you think this is easy?"

"Coffee?"

"I don't want coffee."

"No, but you need coffee."

Fraser is used to being listened to, when one has been around as long as he has, a certain level of respect is inevitable. Joseph knows he has offended the old man's sensibilities. He accepts the offer of coffee only because he thinks it will afford him the opportunity to make amends.

They sit in the corner of the coffee shop, an enterprising franchise has commandeered several square feet of floor space. A mismatch of plastic tables and chairs are scattered about, adrift from their assigned places. In the corner is a box full of broken and, Joseph assumes, disease-riddled toys for children, sick and healthy alike, to munch on. The coffee is good, hot and strong; Joseph wants it to be terrible to match his mood.

"Helen will explain the situation to the receptionist and it will all be smoothed over."

"I really don't care," Joseph says. Then he adds, "I would hate to work here."

"I don't think you need to worry about an offer any time soon."

"Mary made out she was indispensable, but she's already forgotten."

"Not by everyone… just some."

"I hate this place."

"It's not supposed to be easy."

"Don't," Joseph says. "Don't analyse this or me. Shit happens. Everyone dies. Right?"

"Right. You miss her."

"Not yet," Joseph replies. Then more forcefully, he says, "No." Shrugging, he adds, "I haven't had the chance. Everything is a reminder it's like… Well, it's like she's still here." Then, laughing, he realises he has stepped too close to the truth. "She is… was a pain in the arse, a nag. Now I can… Well, I can masturbate in peace, right there in the living room, any time and as much as I want. I can do what I want, eat what I want… So, it's fine. Like I said. It's all fine."

"Glass half full and all that," Fraser says. "My sister would never allow that sort of thing, lucky boy."

Joseph and Mary were fascinated that Fraser lived with his sister, neither ever marrying, a strange and much-discussed relationship amongst his colleagues. It was said they were more like a married couple than most couples. Trying to shock him, to take the smile from Fraser's face, Joseph hopes will end the meeting quicker. Then he will make good his escape and go back into hiding, with no reason now to ever return.

"I always thought of you two as the ideal couple," Fraser says. Joseph studies his coffee with the same intensity a corduroy-clad biologist somewhere in the building might study gloop under a microscope. He wonders what Mary told Fraser about their marriage.

"Well, you never can tell what goes on behind closed doors, right?" Joseph says, challenging Fraser to reveal all he knows.

"True," Fraser says, and the single word gives Joseph nothing.

Frustrated, and talking more to himself, he mumbles, "I will never have peace or the chance to miss her."

"Do you find you masturbate a lot? I mean, it's good you're keeping busy, got your hands full doing something worthwhile. Not beating about the…"

"You finished?" Joseph says, cutting into Fraser's teasing. He looks about, studies the table top. "I meant to ask you…"

"Yes?"

"Never mind. I have to go."

"Joseph, she loved you."

"I wonder sometimes."

"I hate having to care for doctors because you can't bullshit them as easily."

"I have to go."

"I'm here… anytime."

The seating area is busying up, and an assortment of casualties file past the table, ignoring its occupants. Being amongst the crowd makes Joseph feel more alone than when he is actually alone. Fraser's smile, his kind words, his gentle teasing, and calm manner remind Joseph that at the tattered edges of his life are friends who still infuriatingly persist in offering their support, no matter how objectionable his conduct. The smell of food being cooked is jarring amidst the ever-present smell of disinfectant. Some people don't know when to quit, he thinks.

He must still get rid of Mary's clothes and replace Nathan's, such as they were. Again, Joseph thinks, things could have been simpler if Nathan were a girl. Everything would be simpler. Having just made a fool of himself over retrieving items that he will now have to dispose of, it's easy to think of Nathan in the same way. Allowing him into his home has resulted in Nathan making himself at home, and the situation needs sorting before it becomes public knowledge.

Whilst he has no desire to tackle serious clothes shopping, he can, he thinks, kit Nathan out with practical stuff from the supermarket and restock the kitchen cupboards at the same time. The clothes are reasonable in both price and quality, but not what Joseph would purchase for himself. Given the standard of Nathan's previous attire, Joseph decides that, cheap as they are, they will do. Nathan may be earnest in his desire to pay him back, and he knows he must take this into consideration. Now, with perishables loaded into the car, he has no choice but to return home.

The handles of the plastic shopping bags plait and pull into tourniquets around his wrist, and he juggles car keys into one hand whilst trying to bring some feeling back into the other. Whilst Nathan has obeyed the request not to open the door, as helpful as this would have been, he has ignored everything else. The music is oppressive in its volume, a half empty glass sits on the stairs, and the blanket, which Nathan has claimed as his, is on the floor in the hallway. There is plenty of mess but no obvious sign of the cause. There is also no sign of Mary.

Joseph finds Nathan in the garden, seated at the edge of one of the flowerbeds. He has taken two of the cushions from the lounge with him out onto the lawn. One he is sitting on, and the other has the bible resting on it. As Joseph leans on the railing of the veranda, Mary appears and stands next to him. On countless previous occasions she was very vocal on the symmetry of the cushions in the lounge. Joseph can recall many a heated discussion, sulks, and sighs on this topic. He puts a little distance between them while he watches Nathan; She may be mute but he remains sure at some point she will demonstrate her displeasure. Joseph is certain that, between Nathan being in their home, his mess, and Joseph's own snubbing of house rules, it will not be long before she works out how to punish them both for their transgressions. He imagines he can feel her anger brewing.

Nathan is holding a conversation with himself, Joseph assumes, as there is nobody else about. He is animated, waving his arms around, gesturing the point he is trying to make. Now and then he turns a page in the book, and every so often he bends his head to kiss the open page. Uncomfortable with his voyeurism watching these private undertakings, Joseph makes his presence known.

"Do you like red wine?" he shouts from the veranda, over the music that once more he is reminded is loud and upsetting.

"Huh?"

Nathan leaves the cushions on the lawn but brings the bible with him, putting it down on the table outside where Joseph has said they will be eating.

"Help me with the shopping."

"Dae what?" Nathan asks, now standing in the kitchen, his hands stuffed into the pockets of his borrowed jeans.

"Unpack the bags and start putting the items away. Freezer stuff first."

Nathan is unenthusiastic about the task, but Joseph reminds him he will need to look after himself now. "Nobody will be doing this for you anymore," he tells him.

"Anymore?" Nathan questions, but Joseph is not interested in the details of the boy's past domestic arrangements. He's happy to assume that any lack of skill equates to being waited on. He is reminded that he has often done things for Nathan rather than watch him struggle, and Nathan has so far been a more than willing recipient of Joseph's labours on his behalf.

Together they make chicken curry. The rice is from a packet and the sauce from a jar, and so there is little that can go wrong. Nathan thinks this is cooking, and he is philosophical about the process, realising this is also a skill he will need to work on. They consume the first bottle of red wine before the meal is ready; The second is open and on the table when they sit down. Nathan declares that he likes the wine.

"Ah've never had it before," he says,

"Does your dad let you drink?"

"No, but fur my nineteenth, Uncle Tony took me tae the pub. Ah had beer. Ah like that too."

Sitting in their self-allocated seats, Joseph, himself not a happy drunk, ponders his responsibility in providing Nathan with alcohol. It has been another difficult day. From the moment the sun appeared to announce that another day was here to be survived, Joseph has battled real and imagined demons, all uninvited. However you slice it, he is a man on the edge. Nathan seems happy and content; somehow fitted to his misfortune and rejection. Deciding that he does not want to carry the liability of unhappiness alone, Joseph picks the scab.

"So do you find that helps?" He nods at the bible on the table between them.

"Helps?"

"Reading that," Joseph wants to say "crap" or "shite" because he is angry that Nathan does not immediately get what he is saying. He now has no qualms about abusing Nathan in the same manner that he earlier abused the receptionist, the security guard, and Fraser. No one, he thinks, is off limits. And the memory of making an idiot of himself earlier in the day aggravates his already surly mood further. The voice inside his head is loud, warning that trashing Nathan's beliefs is a step too far, even for him. More wine helps assuage that voice a little. Nathan shrugs, which is irritating.

"Does it offer comfort to you in your hour of need? I mean literally in your hour of need."

"Sure," he says, and Joseph scoffs. He stares at the book and not the boy; It represents a division between them now. Nathan's beliefs are more socially acceptable than Joseph's visions. Those who believe in the unseen hand of God being active in their lives are sanctioned in believing so, their notions validated by those around them. But tell someone you see ghosts and see what happens, he thinks. It's not fair. He waits. Nathan, who was looking away across the garden, now looks back at him. His colourless eyes hold a warning, but lost in his own misery, Joseph is too far into self-destruction to heed it, and the alcohol incites him. Abhorrent as it is to acknowledge, he understands that he wants and needs Nathan to feel as bad as he does.

They both grab for the book but Joseph is quicker, Nathan is injured, after all. Snatching it up, he holds the bible out of reach, and immediately Nathan slumps back into the chair and starts to rock and cry.

"I'm just looking at it," Joseph says, but it is a lie and they both know it. His intentions are clear. He wants to see how Nathan will react to the fear of losing something precious. Joseph, having spent a lot of time reflecting on his own losses— his wife, his vivacity, his career, friends and family, his sanity, the list goes on—now wants to see someone else experience a little of what he is struggling with. Knowing that it makes him a horrible person does nothing to help him reason his way out of what he is engaged in doing to the boy. Nathan, even though he has already suffered so much, is an easy target. There is only loss in life, and the sooner Nathan realises this, Joseph rationalises, the better.

"And that... Does that help? Seriously, I want to know if that helps, because if so, what the hell, I'll give it a go."

Joseph rocks in his chair trying to mimic Nathan but he cannot reach the just-so-fucking-annoying pitch the boy can achieve with his whining.

"Gizze the book an' Ah'll go," Nathan says, and Joseph, achieving the upset he wanted, is now done with the book and so throws it straight back at him. Catching it carefully in both hands, Nathan stands to leave.

"Ah want my bike."

"You don't need to go."

"Ah want tae. Ah dinnae like you. This you is nae nice. Git my bike."

"I know this me is not nice, and that's the point. Sit down." Joseph does not give any sign he will get the bike. He pictures Nathan, still handicapped by his injuries leaving and having nowhere to go, no one to take him in. The thought hits him hard, and the full weight of guilt only expands the distance between them. More than anyone Joseph knows how it feels to be ill equipped for the world's trials. Nathan remains standing.

"Finish your wine."

"Ah want my bike," Nathan says again, and this time he laces attitude and anger into his words. It takes Joseph by surprise. He'd believed Nathan would be an easy and willing victim, but his reactions are an indication he is not so willing.

"I'm sorry."

"So fucking whit. Git my bike."

Nathan's words are pure bravado, however. Joseph can see fear mixed with anger now in his eyes. His intention was never to scare the boy, only have Nathan join him in his misery. But it is all too late.

"Sit down," he says again, forcing calmness into his words and making the tone friendlier. But Nathan, with the bible clutched tight to his chest and breathing hard, paces the veranda. Joseph fancies Nathan is trying to work out whether to go or not. Here, Joseph thinks, is someone rightly alone. Nathan's recovery was only ever fragile. Now wanting badly to find the skills to fix everything, but with no reserves of kindness or empathy to tap into, all Joseph can do is watch as Nathan throws his head back, stretches his neck so the blue veins are prominent against the white of his skin, and screams.

"Ah've bin fecking robbed!"

Chapter 18

He has broken the boy, and an abhorrent razor-sharp pain scratches at the back of Joseph's throat as, rooted to his chair, he watches Nathan. One hand still holds the bible flat against his chest, and the other is splayed, his elegant fingers waggling with a life all their own.

"Why dae bad things keep happening? Nobody takes your stuff… your house. You have all this, and a job… if you want it. EVERYTHIN!" he screams. "Everything of mine has been took'en," and without warning he hoists the rattan chair he was sitting on by the arm and in a fluid arc of movement and anger launches it at Joseph's head. It misses, but not by much. There are six chairs in total on the veranda, and two are now out of commission, the one that Joseph still occupies and the one Nathan has thrown. This still leaves four pieces of possibly weaponised furniture, and whilst Joseph is sure he deserves it, self-preservation kicks in as a second chair, already in the air, crashes down into the centre of the table, obliterating the wine bottle and glasses. He leaves his seat as Nathan moves to grab a third chair. His aim is poor because he is hampered by bruised ribs and using only one hand, and this time the chair arcs wildly to the left and scuttles across the decking.

Joseph has reached an age where very little necessitates him moving fast, but Nathan's actions are now making him move with speed. He throws himself onto Nathan before the fourth chair becomes airborne. They both go down as if they are trying for a penalty. Nathan hits the decking hard and first, Joseph lands most of his weight on top of him, nicely breaking his own fall. The bible skids away and is open, face down on the deck just out of reach of them both. Nathan, now all arms and legs, screams at Joseph whilst at the same time trying to kick, bite, and head-butt him.

"Listen," Joseph says to him, and then says it again. Just that one word over and over.

"Listen."

He has Nathan clutched to his chest. A tangle of limbs, they are both exhausted but neither will give up. Every so often Nathan screams, "Git the fuck aff me."

And Joseph says, "Listen."

Bizarrely, he thinks, if in the past he'd been shown this as a snapshot, himself lying on the decking with a blond boy in his arms, to his future self, he would not be able to piece together the circumstances. Nathan has gone limp, but Joseph is not convinced it is not a ruse.

"You with me?" he asks.

"It's me," Nathan says.

"Listen," he says again, and he rests his lips against the damp hair at the side of Nathan's head. It's as good as a kiss.

"What?"

"Uncle Tony was right. I'm a miserable bastard, and I do and say miserable bastard stuff."

"Why?"

"Because my life is shit and I want everyone, you included, to be as miserable as I am. I want you to hate me."

"Why?"

"Because I'm frightened of the alternative, and… it helps… makes things easier. Only it doesn't. I'm sorry."

"He said ye were a crabbit AULD bastard," Nathan corrects him.

"Yes."

Releasing his grip a little, Nathan doesn't move, just slumps against his chest.

"How come we end up lying on the ground a lot?" Joseph asks.

"Because yer' a crabbit auld bastard."

"Let's drink to that." Joseph untangles himself and stands, offering then to help Nathan up. Refusing the offer, Nathan rolls away and gets to his feet unaided. Joseph is reminded then that he is no better than the uncle, and is perhaps a little worse than the father. His shirt is splattered with red wine, and the table is spoilt with shards of glass, a chair like some crazy centrepiece still dominating its surface.

"You wrecked the place," he says, and he pulls Nathan back in towards his chest, one arm around his shoulder taking him slightly off balance, and this time he kisses his temple.

"Whilst I don't condone this sort of carry-on, and I will insist you help clean it up, nice one."

Nathan, subdued now does not respond.

The wine and glasses are easily replaced, and Nathan rights the chairs whilst Joseph sweeps the broken glass into a cardboard box. Within minutes there is nothing left to show an altercation has taken place other than the dark red wine stains which will forever scar the bare wood of the table. Joseph repours the wine and hands a glass to Nathan.

"A toast," he says, but Nathan is reluctant to take the glass, and so Joseph puts it into his hand and curls his figures around the stem.

"To miserable bastards," he says, and he clinks the glasses together. "Now you."

"Shit head," Nathan says.

"Nice!"

Joseph retrieves the bible and brushes the black cover clean while Nathan makes a pitiful whining noise in the back of his throat as he watches Joseph with distrustful eyes. When Joseph passes the book over, he snatches at it, obviously only wanting to have it safely back in his possession.

"Forgive me," Joseph says, but is ignored. "Doesn't it say in that book of yours that you have to forgive me?" He pushes Nathan down by the shoulders forcing him to sit back in the chair, and he takes the seat next to him. The rain of earlier in the day has left the evening muggy. Joseph drinks the best part of the glass of wine and fills it back up.

"Read me something from the good book, something to make me feel better. There must be something in there about... hope."

The book remains closed and held tight against Nathan's chest. His eyes colourless puddles of disgust, "*Those who hope in the Lord will renew thaur strength. They will soar oan wings like eagles; they will run an' nae grow weary, they will walk an' nae be faint.*"

"Nice. I like that." Silence and then, "I think I'm losing it. This may be the start of a complete mental breakdown you're witnessing here."

"Ah don't think ye're a bampot. Jist a wee bit...excitable," Nathan says. He sips at the wine as Joseph empties and refills his glass. The wine loosens his tongue.

"Madness, let it be swift and permanent," he says, raising his glass again.

"Whit's the problem?" Nathan asks, and the question, an edict straight to the point, tears into Joseph's inebriated rambling.

"Her... She's my fucking problem," he says, pointing to where Mary had been hovering moments before. She's moved however and now stands at the other end of the veranda and so Joseph must realign his sight and point again. Some days nothing goes right, he thinks. A witness only to the unpleasantness, Mary has done nothing to cause or distil events. Her indifference, her lack of involvement, and her placidity stirs Joseph's animosity further. Why is she not angry with any of this, he asks himself? Does she no longer care if he makes a spectacle of himself?

"Who?" Nathan asks, turning in his chair to look to where he is being directed. Joseph rolls his eyes.

"You can't see her? No, of course you can't. Madness must keep its own counsel, right? Right?"

Nathan is silent and Joseph drunk. Somewhere high above them a small aircraft can be heard following the expanses of water that is Loch Ness as it heads towards the airport. Monsters lurk all around them.

"Is it… a ghost? Is the ghost still here?" Nathan asks, his voice no more than a whisper. Joseph ignores him. "Is it looking at me? Is it mad or something?"

"Not it. Her," Joseph says, correcting him. "Yes, she's mad. She's fucking furious," he says, lying, needing to put right this wrong version of Mary.

"Why?"

"Because you're in her house, taking her place—and you messed up her cushions. That's why she's mad at you. I think she's mad at me because… well… you're in her house, in her place, her side of the bed… Lord, this makes no sense," Joseph says, having given an answer he knows only fits with how he thinks Mary should act and not how she is acting.

"Amen."

"I swear to God, shut the fuck up."

"Amen… again."

Nathan, looking like he's received a few jolts of electricity, his hair standing straight up on end, an energetic blond mass atop a fatigued, pale face with bruised and sunken eyes, is obviously spent. Despite his past harsh words, Joseph smiles at him.

"It's a ghost, right? Ah know you said you dinnae want tae talk about it, but you brought it up, so…"

Joseph's smile withers. "SHE," he says, over emphasising the word, not afraid to show the hurt now that he feels each time Nathan refers to his wife as an inanimate 'it'. "And SHE is not a ghost."

"Then what is SHE?" Nathan asks.

"Madness."

Joseph takes another mouthful of wine and refills the glass while he thinks on his answer. There must be, he thinks, a better answer.

"*When Jesus therefore had received the vinegar, he said, It is finished: and he bowed his head, and gave up the ghost.* That's in The Bible," Nathan tells him. "If Jesus gave up the ghost, then so should you. And mebbe the vinegar."

"There's no ghost," Joseph tells him. And for his own sanity, he adds, "There is just madness, the result of grief, of not being able to handle the loss. It's grief and… and now… too much wine."

There is a lot more that Joseph wants to say, would like to put into words, but the wine and the events of earlier spiral his thoughts into nothingness. He lets his arm fall casually from the chair, displaced from his body. He watches, as with a life all its own, it sways in a metronomic rhythm.

"There was a time just after Mary died when I thought I wouldn't survive the loss of her, and now I'm afraid I will."

"Ah dinnae hate you. Ah cannae and Ah willnae."

There's no scaffolding to hold Joseph's thoughts together. Forgetting that earlier he'd told Nathan he wanted to be hated, he is puzzled now at the statement.

"I'm drunk," he announces, pulling himself upright in the chair and taking back control of his limbs.

"Aye," Nathan says, stretching his mouth out in a sad contortion, not a smile but an expression, Joseph thinks, of how things will look tomorrow. For now, they will sleep it all off, but tomorrow the demons will no doubt return for both of them.

"Help me up to bed. It's only fair. After all, I have been lugging your sorry arse around for days."

"*And when ye stand praying, if you hauld anything against anyone, forgive heem, so that your Father in heaven may furgive you yer sins.*"

"Yeah, that's what I'm talking about. Forgive me and help me up to bed."

Chapter 19

Nathan rarely smiles. In recent days he has had little to smile about, but even way back at the beginning, Joseph cannot recall him smiling often. He giggles, and sometimes laughs, but he doesn't smile. Joseph smiles. As angry, frustrated, and unhappy as he is, still he smiles.

Nathan is curled up cat-like, his head on a cushion scrunched into Joseph's thigh. He is taking up more than his fair share of the sofa. Joseph left the bedroom in search of fluids and cool air, he came downstairs to sit in the lounge and nurse the worst hangover he has ever experienced. It is that part of the day when a person is undecided whether it's really late or really early, and so Nathan confused by the hour has been told both it's too early to get up and it's late and to go back to sleep. Even so, he has followed Joseph downstairs and curled up beside him on the sofa. One knee pokes from under the blanket, and because of the trauma to his nose, his breathing is still congested.

Joseph is hot, thirsty and tired, but he cannot sleep. He cannot consume enough fluids to abate his thirst, and he cannot control the inner furnace that indulging in too much red wine has created within his core. It is a wretched start to another wretched day, he thinks.

There are no unwanted images in the semi-darkness, just the sound of Nathan's breathing and the various noises the house makes at this strange hour.

Seeing Fraser yesterday at the hospital has unsettled his already precarious emotional well being. Unjust as it is, Joseph now wants to blame Fraser for everything. He thinks it is easier to blame Fraser for how he treated Nathan earlier than attribute any wrongdoing to himself. Heaping further transgressions onto a kindly old man who has only ever meant well, he also makes it all Fraser's fault that to rid himself of the painful memories the hospital dredged up, he indulged in too much red wine. And while he's at it, he thinks it is also Fraser's fault that the crap he went to the hospital to collect is still in the car and not, as it was intended, a donation in some charity shop by now. Joseph knows there is no logic to his thought process, knows it is a small step from blaming Fraser for the present state of his psyche to making him responsible for everything that is wrong in the past. After all, they can't both be right, and Fraser's retrospective account of the marriage has done nothing to exonerate Joseph from his belief that either Mary didn't love him, and therefore didn't need him, or she loved him and he let her down.

One sentence keeps repeating in his head now: The wrong treatment might be worse than no treatment. Fraser did not and would not have uttered these words, but now immersed fully in his funk, Joseph attributes them to him.

The sentence is a reminder that shoves him back into his past, back to when there was no madness, anger or morosity, when routine and work and Mary were the fundamental elements to Joseph's life. Back to a time before Nathan, to a time when Joseph could still suppress and manage the lies and deceit. Inevitably, his thoughts reach the moment when normality abruptly ended—the instant everything changed.

Joseph recalls Mary giving him a list of items she wants collected from the supermarket. That was the start of it all. In answer to his sulky question why he must do the shopping, she'd explained that she would be home late. Casually she mentioned a doctor's appointment. It was a Thursday afternoon. Joseph assumed that her appointment was at the Well Woman Clinic and was routine, and she had not said otherwise. And he remembers now that he had been too focused on fitting grocery shopping into his already busy day to ask further questions.

He recalls being irked upon returning home because her car was already in the driveway, meaning she would have had time to do the shopping. He was further annoyed because she did not help him bring in the shopping and it took two trips. It was raining and he was wet, cold, and tired. The house, he remembers, was chilly, the fire not made up and the heating not on. Mary was in the lounge, seated by the window, a bottle of water loosely held in one hand. She was so lost in thought she'd not noticed he was home. He'd been sarcastic, saying, "Thanks for all your help."

When she'd turned then to look at him, she was crying. There is no need to embellish on the crappiness of that moment. Now, as then, there had been the sense that they would never be happy again.

He recalls Mary factual in her account talking in an odd, disjointed and aloof way, as if it is all happening to someone else. She tells him she'd felt unwell, nauseous, dizzy, and unsteady when walking for the past six weeks. She said she'd had an fMRI that day. The fMRI had shown up metastatic brain tumours and she now needs a total-body CT exam. She has been sent home to wait. Waiting makes no sense to Joseph, and the need to do something, the need to have some involvement in his wife's treatment, consumed him. He'd had a thousand questions vying for position in his head, but he settled on the most insipid.

"Why didn't you tell me?" That was the start of being shut out of his wife's illness and all her subsequent care.

In the days that followed, the CT scan showed tumours in her lungs, liver, and adrenal glands. Mary was then referred to the local oncologist, who arranged for a biopsy. Waiting on the results delayed her treatment further. It took less than a week for Mary to succumbed, she looked, sounded, and acted unwell. During it all Joseph was assigned the benign task of chauffer, his doctorate—obsolete among the many that perform tests, procedures, scans and biopsies. From that cold Thursday evening when fear and resentment replaced normalcy and contentment Mary endured just thirty-one days and then she was gone.

Joseph wonders: did knowing the facts of her fate encouraged Mary to give up, or was her condition at the point of diagnosis already beyond hope? The question joins a list of things he is troubled by. Foremost amongst them, as a doctor, as her husband, could he have done more.

Dull shades of sunlight are just starting to filter in past the drapes. Intrigued by the specks of dust that still dance in the blackness, keeping time with his thumping heart. Joseph feels the beat sometimes as an intense thump in his chest but also as a back beat behind his eyelids. He thinks the dust looks trapped forever caught in this sham of a night sky. The wretchedness of the day and the inconvenience of his symptoms take their toll. Despite the hangover, he believes how he is feeling has nothing to do with drinking too much and everything to do with grief - it has him trapped just like the dust.

Nathan is clingy, and as unpleasant as Joseph has been towards him, there is now an intimacy between them that was not experienced in all his years of marriage. The boy, who rarely smiles, sighs in his sleep and stretches his scrawny white legs out over the sides of the sofa. In sleep, the deep lines at the corners of his mouth turn up into a sedate grin.

Chapter 20

Mid-morning brings a break in the clouds and the sun washes the veranda. Nathan has Joseph's ancient CD collection laid out on the decking, and despite being told twice to hold the discs at the edges, he is still leaving incriminating and perfect fingerprints gifted onto each delicate surface.

"I give up," Joseph says, more to himself than the boy. "I need to be out of the sun."

The passing hours have amassed to toy with him, and instead of easing his discomfort, as the day unfolds his symptoms real and imagined are worsening. Still suffering an internal liquor-fuelled heat, it pushes him to find relief back indoors where the sun cannot abuse him, where he hopes Mary will be unable to find enough light to manifest. Nathan has recovered, showered, and dressed, now full of toast and cornflakes, he appears to suffer no ill effects from the night before. Joseph, however, is fighting a feeling something akin to a surge of vomit. It forces him to hold his thumping head in his hands and reflect on how the day has been upended in this way.

Nathan, still outside, busy with his newfound interest, soaking up the sunshine, satiated with vivacity, is the day to Joseph's night, the laughter to his tears...

"Joseph... Joseph," he says, "Dae ye want tae choose?"

"No." Forced to answer, knowing that if he doesn't Nathan will come inside to find him, Joseph thinks letting him choose the music might mollify him for a bit. He does not want to be found.

"Awrite, Ah'm gang tae put this one oan then, cos Ah ken ye like this one," Nathan says, muttering under his breath, more to himself now than to Joseph.

It is on catching the beginning of the song Nathan has chosen that the heave comes, not as projectile vomit, but grief. Now instead of being redundant alcohol or spoiled food, it is heartache and sorrow, mixed in with a whole load of self-loathing. Carrying with it as much force and the same intentions that any expulsion of unwanted food would deliver. He allows the sobbing to ruin him.

He hears Nathan: singing along to a song; it is clear he is unsure of the words; he is four or five beats adrift. Dressed in baggy shorts and no t-shirt, he has a sock on one foot with no shoe and a shoe on the other with no sock; he is dancing up and down the decking. The heat of mid-morning has made his hair damp, the top still a blond halo, but the sides are darker and glisten. He favours being in a state of semi undress.

The tears come hot and sting Joseph's eyes; they will not stop no matter how hard he wills it. Crying is not helping his pounding head; watching Nathan is not helping his mood; the boy is everything Joseph is not: young, happy, healthy, and carefree. Closing his eyes, Joseph slumps forward in the chair, letting his head hang.

Knowing he must put himself back together and get a grip, he tries to kill his demons. He holds a private conversation with himself - an internal dialogue, sounding out the issues? But the problems fold back on themselves. He cannot now stand the daylight. It is the shadows; the dark corners of the house - his home - where he seeks out sanctuary. He listens as Nathan comes inside and stands to attention just in front of him. He reaches out to hold the waistband of Nathan's shorts. He rests his aching forehead against the boy's hard flat stomach. There is no give, no softness, just the faint odour of clean sweaty young male. Joseph has thought about reaching out for him before - thought about it but never done it.

"Why are you here? Why am I letting you stay?" Joseph finds his voice is barely recognisable, throaty from crying, and angry from shame. "I don't think I even like you... much," he says.

Nathan laughs. With Joseph's head bent against his stomach, he runs his fingers into his hair.

"Mebbe God sent me," he says.

"Why?"

"Fur you tae take care aff."

"No, that's wrong. God wouldn't have sent a blond...." Joseph says, trying to be funny. "I didn't take care of Mary; and she didn't want me." He feels he must say the words; must hear them said out loud, like a confession to his priest, Joseph is bearing his troubled soul. "I'm such a failure... and you mean nothing to me, and my wife is...was everything. Why do I let you stay?"

"It' s jist different."

"No."

"Yes."

"I hate you."

"No...."

Silence. Nathan continues to run his fingers into Joseph's hair; it eases the headache but not the tears or guilt.

"God sent me," he says again.

"Why?"

"Providence," Nathan whispers, sounding out each syllable of a word that holds a lot of meaning to him.

Joseph looks up. Nathan is blocking out most of the sun. Now there is just a dim hazy, blurred halo of light behind him. The tears and the half-light make the boy's silhouette look odd, faded and displaced; Joseph blinks, all the talk of God getting to him.

"Why wouldn't she let me take care of her, Nathan?"

"Mebbe you did yer best."

"Not even close."

"Then she didnae need ye."

"Her eyes say different." Joseph says, looking then towards Mary who is standing in the far corner of the room having found the only patch of light - still she owns the place. Wordlessly she stares him down – judging him. Even though her image is shredded by Nathan's obstructing of the sunlight, she looks more alive to him now than she did in the final days before she passed. She confuses, torments and goads him

"Fuck you, get out of my house." It is Mary's presence he is angry with not Nathan's, but still Joseph pushes him away in place of her. It's all he can do; the thought of having any inter-action with her sickens him.

"Joseph, how far dae ye want me tae gang?" Nathan asks, and immediately Joseph regrets the loss of him. Not answering is easier than answering, and he puts his head back in his hands.

"You cannae dae the dying fur her," Nathan says, as he goes back outside and from the veranda shouts, "Ah'm going tae put that song back oan again, cos Ah ken you like it so much. Come and dance wit me, it'll make you feel much better."

"Leave me alone. Let me be miserable. I want to sit here and feel sorry for myself."

Nathan, still all smiles and laughter, says, "An' Ah want ye tae come outwith, intae the sunshine and dance wit me."

Joseph missing Nathan's fingers running into his hairline, pulls and digs his own hands into his scalp yanking at the roots and saying over and over "Why, why, why… why is she here?"

"Ask her," Nathan says, standing again in the doorway, half in and half out of the light.

"You're crazy."

"Ah am nae the one seeing stuff."

Escaping Mary and going back out into the daylight, Joseph studies the boy before him; eyes with no discernible colour, hair a blond halo of innocence. His, Joseph thinks, is the supple body of an angel that has fallen to earth in error, wings a little crumpled, brain a little shot, perhaps. The shorts have slipped and are precarious - low on his hips, his external obliques, the swimmer's V very visible.

The music has changed and a song that is all frantic guitar and banjo music now plays; there are not a lot of vocals.

"Ah love this song, come dance wit me," the boy says, and he grabs at Joseph's hand as he whirls past. Gravity, the veranda steps and his persistence drag Joseph down onto the lawn. He clenches his fists, pulling his arms up into crooks before bending his knees and jerking them up and down, sort-of in time with the music. Nathan watches and tries to copy. Joseph thinks they must look quite a sight, spinning round and bumping into each other, sometimes by accident, sometimes not. The song winds into a frenzy and then ends and they both fall onto the grass breathing heavily. Hangover be dammed, Joseph thinks as he manages a smile despite the throbbing pain in his head.

"Ah love dancing." Nathan says,

This is no way for a grief stricken grownup to act, Joseph thinks.

Sitting in the dying embers of a late afternoon sun and having both sworn off wine, they drink beer, back on the veranda where they re-kindle their interest in music. For Joseph, it has lain dormant; for Nathan, not easily available. Joseph's musical offerings are as deficient as the technology he uses to play the discs on. Nothing very modern, all very mainstream,

"What music do you like?" he asks, hoping to turn the spotlight. He sees himself as victim and perpetrator, baffled by Mary's rejection of him when alive and her obsession with him in death. Thrown by Nathan's acceptance of this spectacle that is their life he sips beer straight from the bottle and picks at the label. Nathan sitting with one foot pulled up, so it rests flat against the seat with his chin balanced against his knee, gives the question some serious thought. If Joseph tried to sit as the boy is, his thigh muscles would protest by now, and he knows that he would have lost all the feeling in his foot. Nathan is a patchwork of colour, blood black bruises contrast with ghost white skin.

"Ah like hymns."

"Of course you do."

"Ah like Be still my soul and Thine be the glory, but my favourite is I vow to thee my country."

"Isn't it everyone's?"

"Feeling better?" Nathan asks,

"No. A little... maybe," Joseph says his answer as muddled as his head. His stomach has settled and the headache of earlier abated a little but his apprehension over what tomorrow will bring fills him with self-loathing and dread.

"Maw says whit's done is gone, move on," the boy offers.

"Sometimes that's easier said than done".

Still concentrating more on rolling the damp beer label into brightly coloured strips than on Nathan's prophesising he says more to himself than his guest, "Why would someone that's dead still feel the need to be the centre of attention?"

Chapter 21

The day is dreich. The house is shut up; the temperature settling now at a cooler, more acceptable level. Inside is constricted, but outside looks damp and uninviting. Nathan has asked twice for his bike, insisting he has been out in worse weather. He is done with being confined to the house, done with convalescing. Joseph would love some time alone, but he is trying to be a better person, trying to do right by the boy and so he says, "Find something in the house to do."

Over the last view days, Nathan has been picking and choosing which instructions he will adhere to. He has played the "you're not my dad" card, and in turn Joseph has played the "if you want to stay in my house then you'll do as I say" card. The rain has caused an uneasy standoff.

Joseph thinks he can hide in his office where there is mail unopened on the desk and emails unread on the laptop that need his attention. The office door being shut does not deter the boy, however, and he invades Joseph's last sanctum.

"Can you give me some space?" Joseph asks.

"Aye, nae bother," Nathan says, but then he sits at the table in front of the window with his back to Joseph, who is already tucked in behind his desk. He has brought with him the white plastic bag, which he empties onto the tabletop.

Sorting through the items, he takes just the pencils from the contents.

"Can Ah have some paper?" he asks, and Joseph inhales and clenches his jaw before he answers.

"Yes. Take it from the printer," he says, careful to give Nathan nothing from his tone. "I need to do some work, so be quiet."

"Ah am being quiet," Nathan says, standing and leaning in close against Joseph to get to the paper. "You smell nice," he says. "But yer mood stinks."

Joseph assumes Nathan means his aftershave, but then he remembers he isn't wearing any and now he can't think of a response. Outwardly, he ignores him, whilst inwardly he analyses everything not said and in the heavy silence of the room ponders what is left.

For an hour, nobody speaks, it is only when Joseph's back sends painful messages to his brain, saying "enough, move, stretch," does he get up and leave the room to make coffee. Standing in the kitchen rubbing the base of his spine and waiting for the kettle to boil, he shouts back to Nathan, "Do you want a drink?"

When there is no answer, he walks back to the office and leans in against the doorframe. "Don't ignore me," he tells him. Nathan is hunched over the desk; he holds several pencils in his left hand that stick straight up in the air, reminiscent of how he holds his knife.

"Huh?" he says,

"I asked if you want a drink."

"Aye please, cold… juice. Is there juice?"

"Yes, what are you doing there?"

"Drawing. It's a picture of you. Ah'm nearly finished."

Nathan has never shown any inclination for art, not before he became a permanent fixture in Joseph's life and not recently.

Walking back to the kitchen, Joseph appreciates the dullness of the interior of his home. There is insufficient light for Mary to manifest and the gloom offers him a certain respite. He knows his next exchange with Nathan will be awkward, and that he should ooh and ah over this piece of crap Nathan has produced. These are the games people play, he thinks. He hears Nathan's footsteps padding up the hallway behind him, surprised that he has left what only moments earlier he was engrossed in. He takes a sip of coffee. Side on now to the doorway, he watches as Nathan hangs back, reserved. He appears to be waiting.

"She's not here." Joseph says. Then he adds, "There's not enough light."

Nathan nods, comes further into the room, and places a white sheet of paper face down on the table.

"Ah need out of here. If not, Ah'm feared Ah'm gonnae end up as mental as you."

"Tomorrow," Joseph tells him, "if the weather is better."

"Ah'm nae bothered if it's cosy or perished wi' the cold. It can be sweltry or rainin' a pure stoaner. Ma heid is minced with being indoors aw this time. Ah am nae staying in tae-morrow."

"Really."

"Aye, really. And Ah need to gae tae church anyway, cos Ah huvnae bin fur a while now."

In the ensuing silence, Joseph keeps a steady gaze on Nathan, who is playing with the glass of juice left out on the table for him, running his finger around the rim as if he might get it to pitch the perfect tune.

"Gonnae come wi me?"

"I might burst into flames."

Nathan laughs. "Have you sinned?"

"Not exactly."

"Mebbe just had sinful thoughts, then."

Joseph thinks Nathan is spoiling for a fight, goading him with his religious talk and direct references to his questionable mental state. "I've changed my mind about your bike. You have my blessing. Go visit with your loving deity if you think it will help."

"My what?"

Turning his gaze away from Nathan, Joseph studies the kitchen; it needs a good cleaning. He will, he thinks, tidy up the place if Nathan goes out.

"The omniscient, omnipotent, omnibenevolent being, the one you like to lecture me about so much—God."

"That was a lot aff unnecessary words."

"Well, I'm struggling to understand how you can believe in a god who supposedly cares deeply about the fate of each of us when your own mother died before her time, and Mary as well. Please, no quotes from The Bible, not today."

"God gave me a way tae remember my maw."

"That's nice. I have insanity and hallucinations as a way of remembering Mary. And storms, damage to my property, and oh yes—best of all I've got you. All God's work, I'm assuming?"

Joseph watches Nathan as he stretches out his face, pushing his eyebrows into his hairline and dragging the corners of his mouth down into an exaggerated pout, a sure sign he is deep in thought. Ignoring Joseph's litany, he says, "It will be a way tae remember you as well."

Nathan's words are a reminder that at some point soon he will be gone, leaving Joseph alone. At the very edge of the kitchen a slither of sunlight casts a faint image against the back wall. Mary is there, he thinks, trying to find enough light to manifest. And unlike the boy, she will never go, never leave him alone. Wanting a change of subject, he places his free hand flat against Nathan's skinny neck and gently pushes him towards the table where the piece of white paper is.

"Show me your picture then," he says.

Forgetting coaster etiquette and the permanent consequences of ring marks, Joseph places his drink straight down onto the table, and with a not too steady hand, he takes the now offered picture from Nathan.

He has always been saddened by his own likeness. He finds photographs of himself to be disappointing and flawed, as is the image in the mirror—substandard, aged, and imprecise. There are very few pictures of him, and the ones that have survived are mostly of him as a child. Yet here, on what was a very ordinary piece of white printer paper, Nathan has drawn Joseph how he might wish to be.

Leaving a small portion of the paper white for parts of his shirt and collar, the rest of the paper has been coloured in. Joseph stares at himself staring back. The portrait's eyes follow him, and he looks away to Nathan and asks, "How did you do this?"

"Ah jist colour in the paper," Nathan says, which tells Joseph nothing that he hasn't already worked out for himself. Nathan then laughs and beats out a rhythm with his fingers on the tabletop.

"Is nay tay bad fur a nae rite," he says.

There is something predictable about Nathan dripping with talent, hidden or otherwise. Joseph has long suspected that the weirdness of his eyes and the steady and certain way he views the world hides the capacity for something wonderful. He knows he now holds in his hands that something, and it is very special. The portrait is better than any photograph or any image reflected out from a mirror. For Joseph, it captures a sense of hope. Done in a smudged palette limited in scope of greys melted into black, the lack of colour gives the picture a history, a timelessness authenticity. It also fades and softens the laughter lines tempering the uneasiness he normally sees behind his eyes so that, instead, he thinks he sees a hint of amusement. Even the colour and style of his hair are more vibrant somehow, more in style, and not what he sees when he looks at himself each morning in the mirror. It is, Joseph hopes, a true reflection of how Nathan sees him and how he might come to see himself. But unable to let Nathan have this achievement, Joseph says, "What else have you drawn?"

The question seems to present a problem, and Nathan looks out of the window across the miserable, rain-sodden garden whilst he works out an answer.

"Ah might show you," he says. "Ah might show you my memories. Ah might but… Ah dinnae ken."

Joseph gives Nathan his best smile, but he thinks it is still a long way from being the smile from the portrait. He stays silent, worried that saying the wrong thing will make him rescind his offer. But suddenly filled with purpose, Nathan leaves the kitchen and returns moments later with his bible pressed between his praying hands. Joseph has mishandled, moved, and retrieved the book at various times, but he has never yet opened it. This is not a book he would read.

"Look inside," Nathan says, but then he pauses, and sitting down at the kitchen table like an old man taking the weight from tired arthritic limbs, he rests before handing over the book.

The pages of the Bible are, like any book of an age and quality, fine. Like tissue paper, they crinkle when touched. The only part of the book that has any substance is its black cover. To redress his past mistreatments, Joseph is careful.

And there she is: he recognises her straightaway, even though he has never seen or met her. Nathan is the living likeness of her. His beloved maw's portrait stares out at them from the title page. Nathan has sketched her likeness into the text, incorporating the words so they are now his mother's eyebrow, cheek, and tumbling curls of hair. Nathan does not draw by the normal rules, Joseph thinks, but has merged the text with her image or coloured straight over it to produce her likeness. The Bible has seven hundred and sixty-five pages, and all but a handful have been drawn on. Every picture is of Nathan's mother.

"She's lovely," Joseph tells him, as he continues to turn pages.

"It's maw."

"I can see that. You are so alike, it's amazing. She's very beautiful...like you."

"Yes," Nathan says, in his soft whispery voice, and just for a moment there is nothing else that needs said.

Then Joseph asks, "Nathan, why did you draw your mother in the bible?"

"When maw died Ah was greeting an' Uncle Tony said, 'Boy why are you crying?' Ah tauld him that maw was gain and Ah didn't have a single picture and Ah was frightened Ah would forgit her. Uncle Tony tauld me tae use the pictures in my heid. But things slip out ay my heed, you ken. They're safe in here, cos he won't touch the bible. Everything else of maw's is gain but he won't touch her bible. These are my memories."

Joseph has watched Nathan turn the pages while talking to himself. He has seen him bend and kiss what he assumed were the scriptures, but now he understands that he was doing far more than that.

"You mebbe want tae find a better way aff remembering ye're wife than what ye're daeing now," Nathan says.

And smiling, Joseph replies, "I can't draw."

"Shame."

Chapter 22

In the cold clear light of a day that is trying to shrug off its damp and dreariness, Joseph stands with his back to the room. Framed by the window, he ignores the world and its bid to get going, more concerned with the events that have occurred inside his home and how they fit with his view of the future.

He isn't interested in the odds or in hedging his bets. The doors of opportunity are swinging open and slamming closed at the same time. Solutions present themselves, but in turn have offered up further problems. He wonders: How will *we* get from here to there? The "*we*" settles as comfortably within his vocabulary as Nathan does within Joseph's life.

Nathan needs a job, a way of earning money so he can be more independent. He has shown a good work ethic, but they both know his willingness to work hard will not be enough. Art, Joseph is sure, is the solution. But in trying to solve the issue, Joseph has yet to work out how Nathan can turn such talent as his into a meaningful career.

Joseph has connections in the community, and he knows someone who can help someone who can probably advise them both on how to pursue this. But he classes this someone as a close friend, and to introduce Nathan would cause two separate parts of his life to come together, something he'd planned never to let happen. There is also the niggling thought that solutions are never that easy. Still, he resolves to take the risk.

Able now to shrug off the corrosive self-loathing of yesterday and wrap himself instead in a protective, manic cheeriness, Joseph sees Nathan's way out of this current situation taking them both down an interesting, if daunting, path. He believes that, if salvation can be achieved for Nathan, then he too will be redeemed.

"Just how good are you?" he asks, goading Nathan to brag about his talents.

"*Let another praise ye, and nae your own mouth; a stranger, and nae your own lips.*"

"Right," Joseph says, and raising his hand he dismisses Nathan's preaching. Taking it to mean he is free to go, Nathan drags himself up from the table, more exhausted by the efforts of sitting still than he has ever shown when doing manual labour.

"Such a talent is God-given for sure," Joseph says, causing Nathan to then pause in passing. "Can you draw anything else?"

"Aye. You."

"Yes, I know that, but can you draw anything else?" Joseph asks. In amongst the pleasing pictures of the boy's mother, he has found other drawings of himself. They are scrawled on the backs of used envelopes and scraps of paper, then folded with great care and tucked into the delicate pages of the bible.

"Like what?" the boy asks.

"I don't know. Trees, boats, cars, animals."

Nathan laughs. "Why?"

"Because that's what people like. This could be your thing. No. Fuck it, Nathan. This *is* your thing."

In trying to get the boy excited about his talent, Joseph paces the kitchen. It is not dissimilar to how Mary paces, and he finds the thought amusing.

"Draw something else."

"What?"

"The garden."

The boy turns to look out the window, then shakes his head.

"No."

"Why not?"

"Why?"

"Because it's beautiful. You love my garden. Draw it for me."

It is still raining and dull, and the garden is not at its best, far from beautiful. It has a depressing fatigue to it. Joseph sees the landscape bleed sadness; Today, it is nothing more than a scrambled and murky haven of dreariness. He knows Nathan cannot understand why a picture is wanted of something that can be seen every day, no matter what its current state. There is a pause while together they look out the window, both lamenting the loss of the good weather and the freedom of outside.

"Let's go for a drive," Joseph suggests, wanting to appeal to Nathan's longing to be out of the house. "I'll bet we can find better weather, and I'll bet we can find something you'll be inspired to draw."

"Ah bet we cannae, and Ah bet you willnae."

Reeling Glen, a steep-sided gorge scored by the hastening waters of the Moniack, is far enough from home to leave the rain-soaked scenery behind and create the potential for dry, if not sunny, weather. Relaxed enough in each other's company to let silence inhabit the confined space between them, the journey passes in a hushed and contented quiet that suits the stillness of the passing scenery beyond the windshield.

As Joseph had hoped, the weather outlook ahead looks a lot more promising. The circular walk leads them through conifers, Douglas fir, and broad-leaved woodlands. Trees that stretch 170 feet upwards crowd the skyline, displaying their maturity and longevity to passersby.

"Ah came here once oan a school trip," Nathan says. They walk side by side, close enough that their knuckles brush as they fall into step. Nothing in his words or expression shows he enjoyed the childhood trip. The light beneath the canopy is mottled, causing shadows to dance on the carpet of mud, leaves, and pine straw. The earthy aroma stirred by their steps mixes with the now familiar scent of the boy. Joseph inhales, and ignoring the obvious track, he makes his own path. Nathan, always compliant, follows. He stops at the base of an impressive tree, places his hand flat against the bark for balance, and looks up along the trunk skyward. A break between the branches shows a china-blue sky.

"Amazing, isn't it?"

Nathan mirrors his actions, placing his hand against the tree as he looks up.

"Amazing," he says, and Joseph thinks he is trying to be funny. Half-heartedly, he throws out a hand as if to skelp him around the head, misses by a fraction, and lets his arm rest across Nathan's shoulder. Refusing to let Nathan's apathy dampen his own forced joviality, Joseph says, "How can you not be inspired?"

"It's a tree," Nathan says.

"A really impressive tree."

"Mebbe Ah could work fur the forestry commission."

"I think you need a driving licence."

"Shit."

"But you know what? You don't need a driving licence to draw a tree."

Letting go and pushing Nathan away from him, Joseph eases himself to the ground and sits with his back pressed against the trunk. The rejection is intentional. Sitting in the debris of leaf litter in amongst an orchestra of other trees, the forest floor reminds Joseph of a fine oriental rug, like the one that once covered his parent's hallway. For a moment, he thinks only of the rug and what was once his family home. He can feel the ridges, humps and bumps of bark beneath his shirt. Here nature is at work hiding and camouflaging and protecting all that need it. Settled amongst the foliage, Joseph feels safe in the same way. There are no ghosts in the dappled light of outdoors. Pulling his legs up, he lets his arms rest against his knees, hands dangling down and fingers laced together.

"I just feel really good about this. I think art is something that will save you."

"Ah need saving?"

"Yes. From a life of doing something that's a drudge."

"Aye, and dae you need saving tae?"

The question is beyond Joseph, the answer swaying between the past and the future. He'd thought that he was happy with his lot. Being a doctor validated him, but in the end, it was easy for him to walk away from it, a relief even, and now he cannot imagine returning to such a demanding lifestyle. Occasionally he wonders about the fate of certain patients, wonders how the practice is coping without him, but over time it is becoming easier to quash the thoughts and forget that the place even exists. Nathan makes it easy.

"This isn't about me," he says.

Once more indifferent towards Nathan, he hangs his head. "Do what you want," he says, and then looking up, he forces a smile.

"The ground's damp and my arse is wet. Help me up."

Chapter 23

Walking through each of the rooms of his home, Joseph remembers Mary agonising over the pieces of art on the pristine walls, choosing each with great care and consideration. Now they blend, merge, and camouflage themselves from Joseph's eye. Long past considering them, he neither likes nor dislikes the paintings, and that is, he thinks, the shame of it. Now with fresh eyes and Nathan's talents to use as a comparison, he sees the pictures differently. His conclusion: they are all the same: landscapes busy with movement, bright with colour, and stubbornly obvious. A tree is a tree; water looks like water; clouds look like clouds. As Nathan says: boring.

He makes his instructions to Nathan clear and simple, or so he thinks. Gathering his jacket and car keys together, he tells Nathan as he heads towards the door that he must spend his time thinking about what he will do with himself.

"You are healing," Joseph says. "Before you leave here, you must have a plan. Life's not all dancing and sitting about in the sunshine."

Nathan's answer is a beautiful blank expression. He hiccups, then stretches his face out in a very impressive grin and says, "Is this about the tree again?"

"It's about you taking responsibility for yourself and no longer relying on me. If art isn't your thing, then fine. Find something else. But do it quick."

The conversation is dry, Joseph the inarticulate one, childish in his manner, unable to tolerate not getting his way. He is frustrated by Nathan's lack of worry. The boy, he thinks, should panic about the future. He hopes leaving Nathan alone in the house will give him time to reflect on what has been said and perhaps to act. Joseph wants him to see sense and pursue art. Nathan, in defiance of Joseph's harrying, remains indifferent to the uncertainty he faces.

Inside the car the air is heavy, and Joseph fiddles with the settings until the temperature drops and becomes unnaturally frigid. He has tasks to do that will take him away from the house for a while, and he needs the distance from Nathan for an unhealthy closeness, an attachment even, has been building between them that will make the inevitable separation all the harder.

Staying out of the house, wasting time and avoiding the issues, diminishes Joseph's fragile mood, however. Now he is weighted with the feeling of wasting the day and it irritates him more than Nathan's clinginess. Even though they'd had no plans, there is still the sense that Nathan has prevented him from achieving all he'd hoped. As Joseph circles the house, entering the property from the garden into the kitchen, he hopes to catch Nathan unawares, busy wasting time. It will serve as ammunition in the argument, proof, Joseph thinks, that the situation and his instructions are not being taken seriously. The now familiar *thump* of music fills the gloom and it takes a moment for Joseph's eyes to adjust.

He finds Nathan sitting on the floor in the hallway, looking up and along the curve of the wall as it follows the path of the stairwell. Scattered beneath his legs are the bible pencils. Joseph follows the boy's gaze, unsure at first what holds his attention. Then he sees it. Incorporated into the pristine teal paint is a drawing. Now, instead of unblemished paintwork, there is a life-size representation of Joseph sitting beneath a tree, the branches of which curl in a tangle of braids that follow the line of the stairs. Nathan, aware now of Joseph's presence, turns his tired face towards him, sighs, and then stretches himself out flat on the floor. Looking like Leonardo's Vitruvian man, he closes his eyes, giving Joseph the impression that he is affirming by his finished handiwork that he is now permitted to rest.

"What the fuck? What have you done?" Joseph's words whisper out, strangled by his barely contained anger.

"You wanted the tree. Ah drew the tree."

"Not on my fucking wall!"

"Ah cannae find paper big enough, and so Ah had tae use the wall."

"Run. Run far and fast, wee man, because I am gonnae kill you." In his haste to get the words out, Joseph's cleaned-up speech slips, slides, and sludges into a more natural dialect. "You're deid."

The boy, prone on the floor with his arms and legs splayed, his eyes closed, looks like he is making an offering of himself. Submissive, spent, satisfied, he says, "Have a word wit yourself, Joseph. Dae you want the tree or dae ye nae want the tree?"

"Not on my fucking wall," Joseph says again, "this isn't art. This is… graffiti. This is criminal damage."

"Ah guess it's all tae do whit how you want tae look at things."

"It's all to do with damaging property that isn't yours." Pulling his hands up through his hair; Joseph paces the hallway. Stepping over the boy, he looks in the office and then the living room.

"She will be so fucking mad. You think I'm mad, you wait… until she sees this."

"Nae this again," Nathan says. "You ken she's deid, reit?"

"You're fucking dead, you wee shite."

"Ah'm nae feart aff ghosts or feart aff her; its nae me she's haunting."

Motionless, eyes closed in his languorous pose, Nathan's no-never-mind attitude unhinges Joseph. Kicking out at the boy's foot, he screams, "I told you she's not a fucking ghost, and she's not haunting me." The kick connecting with the sole of Nathan's shoe has not hurt him, but it, and the screaming, suffices to get his attention. Sitting up, he balances himself on flat hands and open arms.

"Then what?"

Joseph, although steadfast in his assertions that Mary is not a ghost, having claimed as much many times now, both to himself and out loud, is still uncertain in his own mind what in fact she is. True, he sees her as something ethereal needing sufficient light to manifest, but his objective thinking, the still rational part of his brain tells him it, she is nothing more than a delusion. But there is no peace to be found in the answer. If he is seeing the ghost of his dead wife, then he is mad. If his dead wife is a ghost, then they are both mad; and if he is seeing things that really aren't there then he is still mad. Nathan's questioning only piles on the torment until it physically hurts him. He feels it as a burn in the pit of his stomach. Not being able to explain this intolerable situation has plagued him night and day. It hijacks his thoughts. Distressed at having drunkenly admitted seeing her, whatever "her" is, now Joseph is further enraged that Nathan would use such a stupid confession against him, seeing it now as a clear betrayal. At every turn, he feels hounded, first persecuted by his wife and now grilled by Nathan. There is no let up, no respite from his misery. He sees a murky future shadowed in madness and coloured by the incitement of anger and hurt, and it scares him.

"I'm not doing this again…not with you. No, not again. I keep going back to this, doing this. You're both making me crazy. Go…leave." Joseph screams the words at the top of his lungs, unclear now if he means Mary, who is nowhere to be seen, Nathan, or both of them.

Nathan slides around on his bum, the Caithness stone floor making the move seamless. Facing the picture, he ignores Joseph's shouting and says, "If you look at the tree from this angle, it's much better."

"It's not *better*. Nothing about this is *better*, and it's not a fucking tree. Once again, all you have drawn is me, life-size and grinning like an idiot."

The boy, with an exaggeratedly sad face, pouts at the picture and not at Joseph, "Ah am sad that you dinnae like it."

"Leave," Joseph tells the boy again, but it is in fact he who removes himself from the quarrel. Going into the office, he slams the door closed, hoping it will send a clear message and deter Nathan from following. Now alone, he sits in the window seat and once more scrabbles for an explanation. He feels forced by the escalating events and his own unravelling to make sense of what is going on. "She's a hallucination," he thinks, "perhaps created by an over-excited and unstable visual cortex, which has mixed incoming data with existing information?"

So many memories. Her possessions everywhere are reminders of the life they had. A desperate need simmers inside him, a longing for his old safe, boring life… and Mary. Everything has amassed, he reasons, to over-stimulate his visual processing, and so information tumbles and twists and fragments with the light. "It's the bloody light," he says. Harmless mental images, memories tricked, altered somehow so they are projected out instead of staying safely within. Like long suppressed feelings they are suddenly free to escape and become experiences of their own. His medical mind is comforted but not convinced by the assessment.

"Shadows," he tells himself. "Nothing more. Just an image of what was and what might have been caused by the wired light and unstable memories, that and mental fragility produced because of all the crap I'm having to deal with." Joseph knows his explanation does not consider what Nathan has or hasn't experienced—that is beyond any accounting he can muster. The memory of the incident in the guest bedroom scuttles his thoughts further: the dreich and dreary darkness agitated against its will, everything coalescing—the sounds, the grey dusty air, the dirty half-light. The very real feel of madness. How much of that did Nathan see and feel?

Memory of the incident and the jumble of past memories assaulting his senses causes his heart to pound in his chest, and the acidic taste of heartburn settles at the back of his throat. For a moment, he thinks his suffering will all end here with a heart attack, and that would be fine, he thinks, and he scoffs then at his choice of word.

"Fine! Everything is just fine!" he tells himself sarcastically. "I will drop dead and Mary and Nathan can prowl about the place free to annoy each other. Then there will be no need for me to worry about explaining all this."

Nathan—who finds the walls of the house magnetic to judge by how he slams into them, who trips up the stairs and falls down them, who drops, bangs into, and dislodges various possessions of Joseph's as he goes about his business, who if he cannot be seen then his whereabouts can still be judged by the audio clues he gives—is now silent. And still Joseph does not believe that he has left. The directive was a bluff, the boy will go nowhere without his bike and he has not asked for it. The bike remains locked in the garage. The silence of the house is bothersome; it tells Joseph his future. His plan cannot change: a retreat inwards and the suppression of all feelings. He must subdue every emotion before his plan can take hold. Sort the boy, he thinks, get him gone and then… Mary.

Both Nathan and Mary are in the garden. Nathan stretched out on a sun lounger, his face relaxed in sleep, looks younger than his years. The sfumato image of Mary grips the wooden railing with cobweb-sketched fingers and turns her face to feel the last of the sun's rays. The now sleeping boy could easily have drawn her. The sky has turned a rose pink in the dying light of a mid-summer evening. Can she, Joseph thinks, feel anything, or are her actions his, merely transposed? There is a connection not felt before. He and Mary have both, in their own way, died. Both have been removed from every vestige of their past life and are now just shadowy images of who and what they once were. Joseph by choice and Mary forced into this nightmare. Her sullied looks and the ringing of her hands choreograph perfectly Joseph's anxious pacing and loss of self-control. Then there is their shared obsession now with Nathan, his whereabouts and antics. Mary has yet to react to the drawing that now adorns their staircase, and Joseph, working hard to manage his anger, has not quietened enough to appreciate what Nathan has made possible in pencil. The real tragedy is that he knows now there is a great work of art on his wall; but his indifference to the picture and to Nathan is unjust, self-preservation having a tight hold of him, prevents any appreciation.

The chair scratches the decking as he pulls it away from the table. The sound wakes the boy which was Joseph's intention. Mary, however, keeps her back to both of them, and Joseph is fine with that. He has two bottles of beer in his left hand, a peace offering. The lingering light of evening brings out the sickly yellow bruising around Nathan's eyes.

"You owe me," Joseph says as he eases into the chair, stretching out his legs. Sprawled, he feels the familiar ache of damaged muscles protesting in his lower back, forcing him to adjust his position to a more upright posture.

"So this is what will happen. Tomorrow we are both going into town. We will meet a friend of mine who knows something about art. You will act appropriately and not argue about any of this with me. And you are not to draw on anything but paper. Understand?"

"Fine."

"And then, if you do all that without your normal fuss and bother, when we are finished you can choose where we go to eat."

"Whit about the tree?"

"It's not a tree, and tomorrow, along with everything else, you will paint the wall... all of it."

"Shame. Ah think that's some of my best work."

Nathan has made himself at home to such a degree that, when the phone rings as he passes from the living room to the kitchen, he shouts, "I'll get it." The first time this happened Joseph was mortified, easily imagining a colleague or friend on the other line asking difficult questions, wanting to know who and why he was in Joseph's home and answering his phone. Instead, Nathan had intercepted several unwanted and unwelcome calls, cold callers and acquaintances of Mary's who had just heard the news and wanted to pass on their condolences. And not familiar enough with the family set up to question Nathan's place within it, the arrangement had worked out well so far.

Joseph, busy battling a roast chicken, still feels the need to monitor the conversation, however, and so, abandoning the bird to stand at the doorway, he eavesdrops.

"It's Nate... Nathan. Who's this? Hang on. It's for you. It's Kenneth. That's your brother."

"I know."

Joseph would have screened the call and probably not taken it, time and distance has damaged what was an already fragile relationship. He has not seen his brother since he moved to Australia twenty-four years ago, taking their parents with him. Neither phones the other often and so Joseph is never expecting a call.

His brother says, "Hi." Then, "Who was that?" Joseph mentally kicks himself for ever letting Nathan near the phone.

"Nathan."

"And who's Nathan?"

"Did you call for a reason?"

"He sounds as thick as shit."

"So do you with that accent. You've forgotten where you're from."

"So you're not going to answer the question?"

"How's the wife? How's the kids? How's the parents? How's the weather? How's work?"

"Good, good, okay... Bloody hot and good. How are you?"

"Fine. It's all fine, even the weather."

"Now I know you're shitting me. I'll bet it's raining. It's always fucking raining. I don't miss that. Sometimes I miss the snow, but not the rain. So, who did you say Nathan is?"

Joseph registers that his brother does not say he misses him. "I didn't. What do you want?"

"Fraser spoke to Dad the other day. He said you're still not working. He said... Well, everyone's worried about you."

"Is this why you rang?"

"Yeah, we're worried about you, of course we are."

They, Joseph thinks, are all *so* worried, but not worried enough to put themselves out and visit him. Even back at the beginning, when he and Mary were still lying to themselves and pretending she would be fine, his family had not offered to come. Instead, his father had suggested that they should be the ones to make the trip to see them. And when Joseph phoned to tell them she had passed and to give them details of when her funeral would be, cruelly they'd sent their apologies. Kenneth had said it wasn't a good time to take his kids out of school and his own work was full on. It was a bad time to ask for leave. Kenneth is in electricity. Joseph never understood what this meant, being in electricity, or why Kenneth needed to go to Australia to do it. After all, they had electrical needs here too. His father, now retired and comfortably well off, could have made the trip with his mother, but he didn't. Now Fraser is gossiping about him, and that alone is the reason his brother has bothered to phone.

"Joseph, why don't you come visit? Meet the kids and Meg. Maw and Dad would love to see you. If money's a problem…"

"It's not."

"I'm just saying that I'm happy to pay the fare. Perhaps you can get your friend there to house-sit for you. Who is he again?"

"No."

"No… to which part?"

"All of it."

The distance now between Joseph and his family suddenly feels like a godsend. The last thing he needs, he thinks, is them thrown into the mix.

"Fuck, Joseph, why do you have to be such an arsehole?"

"I hadn't realised I was."

"Mum and Dad worry about you."

On the verge of saying too much, venting and then regretting, instead he says politely, "I have to go. I have a chicken in the oven that needs my attention." He puts the phone down.

"Did I do wrong?" Nathan asks,

"No, but if he phones again and you answer, just say I'm out."

"Lie?"

"Yeah. As we both know, you're good at that."

The phone rings again, and they both ignore it, then, competing with the sound of the chicken roasting in its tin, Kenneth can be heard recording his own inimitable voice mail: "Joseph you're a dick. I'm telling Dad."

It doesn't matter how old we are, Joseph thinks, we are always somebody's child and can be made to revert.

"You're in trouble," Nathan sings out as if he is the one telling tales, and Joseph feels the childhood thrill and fear of a parent finding out that he has done wrong.

Chapter 24

Nathan looks out of place at the kitchen table, a flawed but beautiful character from some long forgotten time in history Clothes that were once Joseph's have somehow migrated into the boy's rotation. Borrowed black Oxfords are teamed with tan trousers from one of Joseph's better suits, partnered now with an off-white dress shirt and dark wool blazer. Nathan is the only person, Joseph thinks, who would wear smart shoes and no socks. His hair is a blonde madness of mess and energy, his face insipid, bruised and sulky.

"Wear these," Joseph says, finishing the look with sunglasses. He will not quibble about the clothes, if this is how Nathan sees himself—as an artist—then so be it. The focus is on the meeting, and on getting Nathan to the meeting. There are not a lot of movable parts to Joseph's plan. He needs Nathan to be independent of him. Joseph might not want to be alone, but neither does he want any more of his slow but inevitable mental breakdown witnessed. Which means Nathan needs to be gone from the house, and sooner rather than later.

Joseph's psychological situation feels frantic, the madness escalating. Mary is a constant presence now. When she is not walking aimlessly about the rooms in the house folding and unfolding her hands and fidgeting with the sleeve of her dress or a stray wisp of hair, she is there in his dreams. She messes with his progress when he reaches out for Nathan or she prevents them from leaving the house by getting in the way. Asleep or awake, Joseph's anxieties are barely manageable. Knowing he has the shakiest grip on sanity incites his need to resolve the situation the only way he knows how. Nathan must go because Mary never will.

He has not phoned in advance to arrange this meeting, imagining too many awkward questions being asked. But in his head Joseph has played out how it will transpire, squashing any bubbles of doubt as they rise. The drive is done in silence, Nathan staring out the side window with his body turned away from Joseph. Twice he has tried to leave the bible and pictures in the house, and twice Joseph had to remind him not to. Now the white plastic bag hangs from Nathan's fingers and dangles down between his legs.

The plain red-brick building was once used by the council, and as a child, Joseph remembers an odd assortment of people would gather outside its glass doors at different times of the day, obstructing the pavement, oblivious, it seemed, to the problems they were causing. The new sign does not fit in the space left by the old one, and the faded logo for the council butts against the brighter colours of the sign that says Art Workshop. If first impressions matter, then this is not a good start.

When it first opened, Joseph had shown his support by purchasing a green ceramic bowl, giving it to Mary as an unexpected gift. For a while it sat on a table by the front door and they used it to keep keys in. Neither the bowl nor the table remain, and Joseph can't recall the story behind why that would be.

There is an acrylic smell to the place that irritates his throat and causes him to cough before he speaks. If there is such a thing, then the middle-aged woman working the till looks arty. She is a mash-up of styles but blended to her environment. She looks well placed. She is keen to make a sale, as no sooner are they in than she is asking if there is anything she can help them with, anything she can show them, something perhaps that they are looking for. Nathan, in trying to occupy the same space as Joseph, has walked on his heel twice; it is clear they are together. Joseph pushes the boy away from him and asks, "Is Talia here?"

"She might be out back," the woman says, but she makes no move to find out.

"Could you go ask her if she has a minute to see us? Tell her Doctor Murphy would like a word."

"Sure, sure, nae bother," she says, and she slides from her chair.

Joseph has told himself that Talia, will not be interested in Nathan. Even with Nathan's connection to Joseph, she will not be interested in him. There is nothing other than hopefully his artistic talents that will interest her. Nathan is slightly younger and at their age this difference is significant. Intellectually, Nathan will frustrate her, growing up fast with an alcoholic mother and a feckless father, she does not suffer fools. She will judge Nathan an idiot as soon as he opens his mouth. Even so, hopefully she will offer some advice point them in the right direction and that will be it—and that he believes is his safety net.

Talia is the definition of beautiful, On seeing her again now he can't help but recall the fragile thirteen-year-old, back when she was all long pale limbs, and wild auburn hair. The crazy dash of freckles across her cheeks is still there but now at twenty-two she has grown into her body and her beauty, and she is confident without the arrogance that might have gone hand in hand with such a gift. Dressed to appeal to the tourist trade, she is wearing the smallest of lilac kilts and a white bodice top the laced front strains to keep her perfect breasts contained. She squeals, giggles, and tucks her arms in around Joseph's waist. Her head fits nicely under his chin. She does not normally greet him this way, and it temporarily side tracks him from his plan.

She makes a deep growling noise when she hugs him and says, "Doc, it is so good to see you. How are you doing? You okay?"

Nathan, instead of moving back to give Talia the space she needs for such an intermit embrace, moves forward once more. Joseph sandwiched between them, is now very aware of limbs and scents mixing, bodies touching. It is unravelling his crumbly composure. He manages a laugh, ignores her questions, and steps back into Nathan.

"I'm wanting some advice… We're wanting some advice," he corrects himself, bringing Nathan into the conversation.

"Can we talk somewhere private?"

Noticing Nathan for the first time, Talia folds her arms across her chest and furrows her brow. She takes longer to study him than Joseph is happy with before questioning, "You want advice… from me?"

"On art… drawing. I want to… we want to show you something, but not here."

"Ah dinnae," Nathan says.

"Don't start." The warning is whispered, Joseph turning his head slightly so Nathan minds that his words are directed at him in case there is any doubt.

"Please," he adds, and looking neither at the boy nor Talia this time, his request is up for grabs.

Perhaps sensing that any further public dealings could be bad for business, Talia suggests they go into the back of the workshop. They walk in single file, Talia leading the way and Nathan now pushed in front of Joseph so he can be sure he will follow.

The room is empty but for a large artist's table and chair angled to get the natural light from the bare bay window. Nathan holds the white plastic bag tight to his chest.

"Nathan, Talia; Talia, Nathan," Joseph says by way of introduction. "Show Talia the pictures, Nathan."

The boy seems detached because of his sunglasses, and Joseph considers asking him to remove them. But Nathan is already ignoring them both; Joseph watches as he moves away to stand by the window, resting his head against the pane. He is himself a work of art, Joseph thinks.

"Ah'm nae happy about this," he says, the words directed inwards and not at either of the other two people in the room.

Talia is confused; Joseph can see it sparkling in her eyes and in the half smile that comes and goes with each new event. He grins at her, and trying to make light of the situation, says, "You get used to him." Then to Nathan, "You promised, and you owe me, remember?" Not confident that Nathan will obey him, Joseph walks to the window, puts an arm around his shoulders. Taking advantage of the closeness, he whispers, "Don't fuck with me, not here, not now," and he guides Nathan firmly to the chair, pushing him down into the seat behind the drawing table and taking the plastic bag from him.

"Look," he says and, taking the loose pictures out, he places them on the table in front of Talia. The images of himself line up soldier-like. A parade of smiling facsimiles looks out: happy, handsome, satisfied with life—a lie of wordless composition.

"Wow," Talia says. "Seriously, wow. He did this?" The question is directed at Joseph, but Tail is looking at Nathan as she asks it, then back at the pictures, unable to correlate the two. The moment is marked then in Joseph's mind as a terrible mistake. He was wrong to bring the boy here, he thinks. Talia is in fact very interested in Nathan.

Chapter 25

All beauty and brains, Talia leans in over Nathan so she can study the portraits better. She stands like this for a long time in silence, and then says, "This is good, very good. What else have you got?" As she asks the question, Nathan groans and drops his head onto the desk with a loud thwack.

"Is he okay?"

"Nothing about him is okay." Joseph holds the bible in his hands, and he pauses before giving it over to her. "This is what he's getting all worked up about," he says, needing her to understand. Taking the bible to the window, she leans one hip against the sill and turns the pages.

"Who is she?"

"His dead mother."

"I see."

"What do you think?" Joseph asks, wanting to get to the point, needing the meeting to produce something that is worth the effort, something to enable them to leave with a clear plan.

"Pictures of you, of his mother… What else?"

"Ah drew a tree," Nathan says, his head still low on the desk, shoulders hunched.

"He didn't," Joseph corrects him. "He drew part of a tree, but it's not exactly portable and it's not even a tree. Forget it."

Nathan then thwacks his head on the table again. "Gie us maw's bible back."

"How'd you meet?" Talia asks. The question coming out of the blue and having nothing to do with art annoys Joseph.

"The storm blew him into my garden, and nothing has blown him back out again—yet." He needs to get Talia back on track. "So what do you think?" he asks again.

"It's clear that you're very good," Talia says, looking at Nathan, but then she stops short of committing herself further. "Do you prefer just doing portraits then?"

"Aye."

Turning to Nathan and wanting to once more be part of the conversation, Joseph says, "See, I told you. This is why I was trying to get you to draw the damn tree."

"Ah did," Nathan says as he moves his head so he can look at his own feet under the table.

"I'm sensing that Nate here isn't as keen on pursing this as you are, doc."

"Nathan likes to listen to music, dance about the place, and eat me out of house and home. I'm trying to get him to focus and start thinking about his future."

The gleaned knowledge that Nathan is living with Joseph registers on Talia's face. Joseph knows his confession is an invitation for her to ask more probing questions about the arrangement.

"He's staying with you?"

Joseph, having no intention of parting with any more information, holds out his hand for the bible. He has all but made up his mind to leave. Perhaps sensing this, Talia says, "There's no development."

"Huh?"

"With the pictures. They start off perfect, but Nate here hasn't improved his skills. I guess when you're this good, there's no need. But can we try something?" Again, Talia's attention is only on Nathan, but it is Joseph who she hands the bible to before she leaves the room. Joseph pushes his fingers deep into the roots of the boy's hair and pulls him upright.

"Maybe we should just go," he says. "I'm thinking this is a mistake and you're not interested." Perhaps it is the fact that Joseph is giving up, or seeing the bible back in safe hands, whatever the reason Joseph's assertion has the opposite effect from what he was expecting. Sitting up, Nathan puffs out his chest and moves the muscles in his shoulders around as if he is preparing himself for some heavy work.

"Na, we're here now," he says. "So we might as well stay and see what the lassie has tae say for herself." They wait in silence until Talia returns with art materials in her arms.

"Take the sunglasses off," she says. "We're about to get busy." Talia manages them both with a degree of confidence that suggests there will be no discussion. She stops once in her task to take a closer look at the boy's eyes as he removes the glasses.

"Ouch," she says, then, "Nice." This Joseph thinks, is an observation about the bruising and also about the beauty of Nathan's eyes.

"Doc, stand here and put your hands together like your praying. Like this," she demonstrates with her own hands, and Joseph obliges.

"Now, Nate, draw just this." She makes a circle with her fingers around Joseph's hands. "Just this," she says.

"Ah dinnae have my bible pencils whit me."

"You can use my pencils."

Mumbling something to himself about hands not being attached to anything and floating about, Nathan settles to the task. It's painstaking. He sorts the pencils into his left hand, in an order that makes sense only to him, and drops his head, hunching over the paper.

"Do you need me to stay like this?" Joseph asks, his back already aching from standing, and holding his hands in such a way is an added aggravation.

"Nope," Nathan says. He does not look up, and Joseph smiles at the boy's curt response.

"He likes me really," Joseph says, trying to make light of the situation.

Nathan is unhappy with the picture when finished. He sighs and pushes it away. Finished, flawless and perfect, the praying hands swim up and out from the paper.

"It's shite," he says and spins slowly round on the chair so he is facing away from everything, from everyone. Talia beats Joseph to a response.

"What don't you like about it?"

"Hands dinnae float about like that, nae attached tae naething."

Talia shows amazing tolerance, Joseph thinks. Leaning over the table, she pulls Nathan by the shoulder back around so he is facing her; the boy's eyes are level with her breasts and while she's speaking he does not raise them.

"A picture of your mother or the doc here, whilst good, has no real value. It's interesting to a few people. But a picture like this one can be copied, and we have the equipment here to do that. Then from this one picture you have many possibilities. As an artist, you must find the balance between creating pieces of work that have meaning for you on a personal level and work that will sell. Often art that sells isn't necessarily what you enjoy doing, but we all have to survive, make a living somehow, and so we must find that compromise." Talia's words resonat with

Nathan. Dragging his gaze momentarily away from her chest, he now looks at the picture differently.

"We can put this image on t-shirts, mugs, greeting cards. Here we can reprint it over and over, and we can add colour or a slogan. Several guys who work here do that with their artwork, and then they sell it in the shop."

This is the gem Joseph has been looking for, and briefly a thread of hope weaves its way into his vision of the future. But something is transpiring between girl and boy, coy smiles flash between them, and Nathan listens intently to what she is saying.

"And Ah could dae that? Draw stuff and copy it and then sell it here in the shop?"

"Well, I could speak to the others to see what they think. It's not just up to me, you understand, but the more artists we have the better it is for business. Let me see if Dougie's about—he's kind of in charge. Do you have time to wait while I go find him?"

"Aye nay bother," Nathan says without hesitation. And Joseph is left with the realisation that he has not thought things through at all well. He waits for Talia to leave before he squares up to Nathan.

"You're not to discuss me. You understand? If you end up spending time here, you are not to discuss me at all—or any part of my life.'

"Ah'm nae the one that tauld the lassie we're living tae-gether." Joseph is taken aback by the brutality and criticism in Nathan's words.

"We're not living together. Don't say that. Christ, people will get the wrong idea if you say things like that. If anyone asks you're just staying with me until you get sorted. Understand?"

"Aye right," Nathan says, and he swivels on the chair as he speaks. Joseph is about to say more to reinforce his request for Nathan's silence, but Talia returns.

Chapter 26

Talia goes straight into introductions, calling Nathan Nate, which annoys Joseph. He is feeling that there is no longer a place for him in the meeting, but too concerned about what Nathan might do or say, he is rooted in place. Her companion, whom she introduced as Dougie, studies the pictures still laid out on the table.

"You're a very handsome man," he says, turning to look at Joseph and compare the real version of him to the portraits.

Joseph feels his cheeks stain red and he mutters, "He should draw something else. Perhaps you can get him to listen."

"Why did you draw this? Tell me the story behind it," Dougie says, turning back to look at Nathan and not responding to Joseph's request.

"Showing aff."

"To who?"

"Joseph."

"Why?"

"Ah dinnae ken."

Dougie laughs and then says, "Lies, outrageous lies! Tell me the story behind the picture."

"Ah tauld you, Ah was showing aff."

"Tell me more."

"Joseph was all busy with his work. Ah had neathing tae do so Ah so ah drew the picture."

"You knew it would impress him."

"Ah suppose."

"No. Not suppose. You knew. Showing off implies as much, a confidence, a belief in one's own abilities."

"So?"

More laughter, and turning to bring Talia into the conversation, Dougie says, "What a miserable boy you have found us." Turning back to Nathan, he asks, "Why are you here?"

"Ah dinnae ken. Joseph thinks Ah can make money aff a this. And the lassie here made me draw this shite."

"Why is it shite?"

"Hands don't float about, nae like that."

"Draw this." Dougie holds his middle finger up close in front of Nathan's face, and without a word of protest, Nathan obliges. Turning, he sorts the pencils once more in his left hand.

"Where did you find this genius?" Dougie asks, filling the silence whilst Nathan is busy drawing.

"The wind blew him into the doc's garden and hasn't blown him out again yet," Talia says, copying Joseph from earlier.

"Ah love him," Dougie says, and Joseph feels the first prickles of excited hatred for the man begin to manifest. Talia laughs; Joseph does not. With the drawing finished, Nathan turns it around to show his admirer.

On seeing the picture, Dougie says, "Art is remembering and replicating. The artist chooses each moment, each mood, and preserves the experience first for himself and then for others. Are you understanding this?" he asks Nathan.

"No." It is an honest answer, but Joseph winces on Nathan's behalf because of what it gives away.

"If the message is in the detail, it need not be fixed. The message in this picture of my middle finger held like this is clear. It says 'fuck you' the world over understands this…" After pulling the picture of Joseph's praying hands out from under Nathan's arm, Dougie holds it up. "Here is another message without written words or speech. We can infer from this: prayer, devoutness, a belief perhaps in something greater than ourselves. So there is no need to draw the whole person."

Nathan, in trying to understand, looks from one picture to the other. Taking one of the many pictures of Joseph, Dougie holds it up in front of Nathan. "Here. This picture is a moment in time that *you* selected. The beauty, the movement, the emotion captured within this portrait has its own message to tell. This person has their own identity, and you have preserved them in that single moment that might otherwise have been missed. Art can be selfish; you did this picture because it pleased you, and only you. And these pictures…" He holds up the finger and the praying hands. "These you did because you were told to. You love this…" He holds up the portraits. "And you say this is shite." He holds up the praying hands.

"Yes."

"Unfortunately, although all of this is art, 'shite' like this sells."

Silence and then Dougie says, "You get me?"

"No."

Dougie laughs and turning around on his chair, he looks Joseph up and down.

"I love him," he says. "I really do." And placing his arm around Nathan's shoulders, he kisses his cheek. "We can keep him, right?" The question, directed at Joseph, throws him off guard, and at a loss for words, he nods.

In wanting to free himself of Nathan, Joseph realises he has inadvertently allowed this tamely handsome, effeminate-looking, verbose individual to usurp his place as Nathan's champion. Dougie's claiming of Nathan as his own private student and the kiss, offered with an ease and honesty that Joseph can only envy makes him unhappy.

They leave the workshop, and standing outside on the pavement, Joseph surveys the high street. The day pitching between events has unsettled his understanding of what the desired outcome was supposed to be. He'd fantasised about being rid of Nathan, but now he realises Nathan might well be rid of him. There are also the pictures they have left behind at Dougie's request, pictures of Joseph that he does not want shared. He thinks Dougie is someone who enjoys his own utterings and is full of guff; but he also had to admit that he showed perceptiveness when he referenced the portraits, one picture in amongst many that all tell a story. "Art," he'd said, "is insight and understanding."

"What now?" Joseph says, more to himself than Nathan.

"Chippy. You promised."

Giving Nathan a sideways glance, he says, "I did?"

"Aye, you said if Ah gei a job out of this tae-day, doing art stuff, then Ah could choose what we eat. And Ah choose chippy."

"Fine."

"Fine," Nathan mimics. "Ye're nae as happy as Ah thought you would be."

"It's complicated, Nathan. Talia knows a lot of my close friends, spends a lot of time in their company, and if you're working with her... Well, like I said, I don't want you discussing me."

Nathan sighs before he answers. "Joseph, two things," he says. "One, ye're nae that interesting, and two, Ah'm nae a leaky boat."

The Fish and Chip shop is almost empty, just a mother with two children. Unable to stand still they circle her legs in a weird game of hide and seek. There is also a man who stands side on to the doorway, leaning against the countertop. Preoccupied with ordering, it takes a moment before Joseph realises Nathan's excited chatter has stopped. Being tuned into his habits, his quirky mannerisms, and the behaviours that are so uniquely Nathan, Joseph registers something's wrong. He searches back over their conversation, trying to recall what he has said or done that would have upset him. The nasty florescent lighting takes the last traces of colour from Nathan's skin but emphasises the bruising that lingers around his eyes. He has tucked himself into the corner of the shop, his head down. He is using Joseph's frame to block himself from view. It is then that Joseph realises it is from the man who has now straightened himself out and is glaring at them. Everything about Nathan now reminds Joseph of the boy at the bottom of his garden on a bucket, obediently waiting his work orders. The man has done nothing other than glare, but with a minimal amount of effort he has undone the boy. Using his own body to block Nathan now from the man's view, Joseph stares back. The deadlock is broken only when the man's order is placed on the countertop and he must turn his attention to paying for the goods. Just to ram home his displeasure, after paying the man returns to scowling at them, he refuses to break eye contact as he leaves. In a rare show of nerve, Joseph returns the non-verbal insult by glaring back until the man steps outside and disappears.

They walk in silence along Huntly Street, Joseph mulling over the order in which he will ask Nathan all the questions that are zipping around inside his head. Nathan, head down and shoulders hunched, is thinking over his own matters. Home is too far away and so their supper will spoil before they get there, and Joseph will not allow food to be eaten in his car. They head to the banks of the river Ness in the centre of the city, find an empty bench, and sit down. Nathan has the white plastic carrier bag close against his chest. Joseph has the food.

"So, that was your father," Joseph says matter-of-factly.

"Yep."

"Are you all right?"

The silence stretches. There is a refreshing breeze coming from the East, and Joseph watches a solitary duck trying to paddle upriver only to be caught by the current and held for a moment in place before being swept further away from its destination. Scrabbling from the bank, the duck then casually labours along the path. Joseph can empathise with the duck's struggle. Still Nathan has not answered him. As Joseph hands him his supper, he realises Nathan is crying.

"Don't," he says, immediately putting the supper to one side, and using the cuff of his own shirt, he tries to dry his tears. "He's not worth it." He knows his words are banalities. Joseph knows what it is to be rejected by family. There can be no recovery. It is a pain that lasts no matter how much time passes.

"It's nae him."

"Then what? Did you think it would be different? That he would be sorry?"

"No, never. Ah ken he would nae dae that."

"Then what?"

"It's me."

Silence, then Nathan, using the pad of his hand, smacks himself repeatedly on the side of the head.

"No. Don't do that." Taking hold of Nathan's hand, Joseph places it carefully on the bench. Leaving his hand on top of the boy's, he shields their hand holding with his body.

"Ah am a fake. Ah gae on about God and The Bible and all that, but Ah cannae in my heart find any forgiveness for him. Ah'm feart of the hatred Ah still feel."

"Some things are unforgivable."

"What he did, yes, but nae him. Ah should find it in me tae forgive him."

"Why?"

"Tae be a good person, tae be the best kind of person Ah can be. Also, my maw was pure insistent about it."

"Nathan, I aspire to be more like you…"

"What's that mean?"

"That I'm trying to be more like you."

"And you couldnae just say that."

Supper is getting cold, and they both remember the food at the same time.

"I mean that I wish," Joseph says, "that I could be as good as you when faced with difficult situations, when things aren't going the way I want them to. You've seen me losing it…"

"Aye."

"Well, this is what I see. I see in you someone that might not feel forgiveness, but in your actions and in your inactions, you show forgiveness."

"Huh?"

"You've never once said anything bad about him, threatened him, wished bad things would happen to him. The things you haven't done say a lot more than you think. They show what a good person you are."

Joseph throws cold chips onto the grass in front of the bench, a gesture to a duck that is having a hard time of it. But the seagulls that have been on look out from nearby rooftops swoop in and harass the poor bird further. Some days nothing goes right, Joseph thinks.

Chapter 27

Dropping Nathan at the Art Workshop feels like Joseph has just left his only child at the school gates for the first time. Stopping by at his old practice skips into his head and is quickly dismissed. Instead, he finds a coffee shop off the main street and sits at a window seat. Mothers with prams and shopping bags clog the aisle, making the waitresses' job an exercise in agility and restraint. He imagines how he is feeling is akin to how the mothers will feel in time. Nathan is spending his first full day away, and Joseph has been cast adrift. The memory of a different coffee shop, of wasting time waiting, slips into his thoughts. He searches the traffic of people with blurred faces outside the window, imagining the familiar figure of Mary negotiating her way through the crowds to find him. But it is only within the safety of their home that her image manifests; elsewhere he has trouble even picturing her in his mind. The idea that he can survive the loss of her, even welcome it, becomes a conscious thought. The only thing missing from the picture is what will replace her. Even in an unsatisfactory, wasteful marriage, he realises, the other participant can be missed.

He spends too long food shopping and purchases junk specifically for Nathan. Joseph is not losing weight and Nathan not gaining any, the boy is still without arse or stomach. Nothing has been arranged regarding picking him up, but while he is waiting in line to pay, Talia sends a text message saying they will be in the pub between five and six. There is time to go home and return later, but Joseph chooses instead to stay out. He heads for a park in the centre of town and sits on a bench watching children play on the apparatus. He feels lost as the children run from place to place in a boundless search for something new and exciting. It is sad, he thinks, that certain activities look sinister when done alone. If he had a partner, dog, a child of his own, then his presence in the park would be acceptable. As it is, he feels uncomfortable and heads into the shopping centre, where the only place of interest is the bookshop. He scans the shelves for a book on art that might appeal to Nathan. He is forcing himself to think of anything other than that he is now without goals or direction. It is only thinking of Nathan that gives anything significance—everything is for or about him. Which Joseph finds odd. Nathan was only ever meant to be a minor distraction, but now he is the vital part of Joseph's happiness. His sanity even. The novelty of having nothing pressing to do, no work to make demands of him, he thinks, might finally have worn off.

He is hoping to intercept Nathan before he goes into the pub. The friends Joseph has neglected frequent this establishment, and he has no desire to see them just yet. Timing his arrival for half-past five, and with no sign of Talia's car, he remains in his own car and thumbs through the book he has brought. After ten minutes, the thought occurs to him that perhaps Talia doesn't have her car here. Perhaps it is off the road or she has traded it in and will drive something else. The thought persist and convincing himself that Nathan is already inside Joseph unkinking his back muscles gets out of the car, he starts the short walk towards the side entrance. His hand is flat against the wood of the door when he turns to see Talia's car pull in and park, and even though he would like to turn and leave, having come this far he continues into the bar where not so long ago he was a regular.

The three James's, Mackintosh, Macleod and Macpherson, are playing pool. Ian Myers, Ian Wilson, Duncan McPhee, and Grant Paterson are at the bar, a mixture of friends he has known since school and patients he has known even more intimately.

"Doc, dae you owe me money?"

"Never," Joseph says, and he forces a smile for George, an old friend who is trying to make light of the time that has lapsed.

"Then Ah cannae mind why you have been avoiding my establishment."

"It's nothing personal, George. I've just been busy." They both know that nothing could be further from the truth. He thinks it will be assume that he has been sitting alone at home consumed by grief, and he's happy with the deceit. George, too dear a friend, and too good a landlord, does not push the issue. Instead, he turns his attention to Talia when she enters, and taking a deep breath, he sings out loudly, "*Gentleman it is my duty. To inform you of one beauty. Though I'd ask of you one favour. Not to seek her for a while. Though I own she is a creature of great character and feature. No words can paint a picture. Of the Queen of all Argyll.*"

Talia is used to such a carry-on, George is landlord, substitute father figure, and antagonist.

"*On the evening that I mention. I passed with good intention. Through a part of our dear country known for beauty and for style. In a place of noble thinkers. Of scholars and great drinkers. But above them all for splendour is the Queen of all Argyll.*" He holds the tune well, and what he lacks in talent he makes up for in enthusiasm.

"You done?" she asks, smiling.

"Ah have another verse but… who's this?"

Standing at six foot six, George has the corned beef skin of the Highlands that has been slapped pink by the rawness of the weather. His hair is thick and coarse like the bristles of a broom and with as much style. His eyes, small and watery blue, flirt and skip about, refusing to commit or settle on anyone.

"Nate, George; George, Nate."

"And what's Nate's story?"

Nathan does not answer, and it is left to Talia to bring George up to speed.

"He's staying with the doc. He's an artist, and the doc brought him down to the workshop to see how he'd get on. Dougie says he's a genius."

"Nae another one."

Joseph buys the round. Standing leaning against the bar, surprised at how he can ease back into the natural rhythm of the place, with Nathan standing close beside him, it is the boy that appears on edge. He does not know how to take George, and the affable, teasing and careful questioning causes his normally hesitant speech to dry up completely. It is only when the pub busies up and George is occupied elsewhere that Joseph can speak to him in private.

"So, how did you get on today?"

"Guid."

"That's it? Just good?"

"Ah'm gonnae gae back tae-morrow."

"Okay. Did you learn anything? I mean, was it fun? Interesting? Did you meet some of the others who work there? Did you get on alright with everyone?"

"It was guid," Nathan says again. Even now when they are alone, the boy is anxious.

Joseph, keen to pursue their conversation, turns face on to him, but he is interrupted before he can say anything more.

"Joseph, how are you?"

The voice hits his stomach and causes it to lurch. He'd not seen Lachlan come in, had not considered that he would be there this early in the day. Turning away now from Nathan, he says, "I'm good. Yourself?"

They grew up falling in and out of each other's lives and homes, they have a shared history of which they can be ashamed, indifferent and proud of in equal measures, but presently they are strangers. Lachlan, short and thin, wears the disappointment of his life like a suit. Joseph intentionally blocks Nathan from view with his body.

"It's been a while., Lachlan says, and he stretches over the bar to get George's attention. "Is this you back now in the land of the living?"

Joseph winces at the choice of words; if Lachlan notices, he does not react.

"Just catching up... getting Talia's help..."

Lachlan interrupts, a familiar trait of his. With Lachlan, there is always more talking than listening. "You back working?"

"Uh...no, not..."

"Cannae be good staying up that hill on your own all the time."

"He's not on his own," George interrupts as he places a drink in front of Lachlan. "He's got the boy, Nate here, staying with him," he says, and having thrown the information into the conversation like a grenade, he then stands back smiling.

"Oh."

The "oh" hangs in the air and Lachlan studies the drink now in his hand. He neither looks towards Nathan nor asks after him. Joseph registers the snub.

"What about you? How's it going with you?" Joseph asks, desperate now to fill the silence.

"Same old, same old. Working hard. Nothing changes except the hair, which is greyer."

"Give him long enough and he'll find something to complain about," George adds and walks away. Talia stays.

Lachlan talks and Joseph is happy to let him. He tells Joseph how his son's second year at St. Andrews University is going, the cost both financial and emotional that it is having on him, how difficult work has been. There is no shortage of subject matter, nor an opportunity to participate. This is not a conversation but an exercise in attentive listening.

Joseph is thinking time is getting on and that he and Nathan need to be making a move towards home. Joseph is thinking it, but Nathan is the one that says it. Interrupting Lachlan's banal talk, he says, "Joseph, gonnae gae hamen now?" Nathan can be blunt and sometimes harsh with his words, but he is not rude.

"Is the bairn tired? Is he wanting his jammies and a bedtime story?" The tone is mocking, even for Lachlan, and Joseph thinks it inexcusable behaviour. Nathan's interruption had not warranted it. Joseph, bracing himself to go into peacekeeping mode, is not given the chance. Nathan has other ideas.

"Ah dinnae wear *jammies,*" he says. "And my business isnae any ay yours anyhow."

Joseph is standing between them and wishing he wasn't. He blinks at the sudden turn of events. As Nathan says his piece, he moves, passing Joseph so he can stand in close to Lachlan.

"Wheesht," Lachlan says, silencing and dismissing the boy with his words and a wave of his hand. Nathan retaliates straight away.

"Gonnae nae dae that?" And he crowds in on Lachlan some more, forcing Joseph to put his hand flat against the boy's chest.

"Let's go," Joseph says, pushing gently and trying to get Nathan to take a step back, aware that the boy is purposefully invading Lachlan's space.

"Is there a problem?" George asks from behind the bar, keen to make sure there will not be any trouble. But Lachlan, not about to let the matter go, adds more fuel to an already incendiary situation.

"Wee bairns tired and crabbit and needs a bath and bed." He turns his back on Nathan as he speaks, which Joseph thinks is probably not a good idea. Nathan's response is to rap loudly on the bar directly in front of Lachlan with his knuckles. The noise is loud enough to get Lachlan's attention—and everyone else's. A furnace of embarrassment spreads throughout Joseph's body. Everyone knows the boy is with him.

Uncurling his fist, Nathan stretches out one long pale finger and points it straight at Lachlan's chest. "Ah dinnae like you."

"And Ah dinnae give two fucks," Lachlan says back.

"Is that so?"

"Aye."

"Mebbe you should."

Pushing himself in so he is now standing directly in front of Nathan, Joseph says. "Enough." Then he mutters, "Sorry." The apology meant for George because *they* have caused a scene in his pub.

"Dinnae bring him back," Lachlan says, wrongly assuming that Joseph is apologising to him.

"Hey," George interrupts. "This is my place and Ah say who is welcome and who isnae."

Sidestepping Joseph once more, Nathan holds out his hand to George. "Ah am sorry if a caused any bother sir," he says.

"Nae bother," George says, and they shake hands. Then to Joseph's utter disbelief, Nathan slides his arm around Talia's waist. Leaving his hand flat against her tummy, he plants a delicate little kiss on her cheek.

"Thanks for all your help tae-day," he says. "Ah am excited fae tae-morrow."

Having witnessed the carry-on between Lachlan and Nathan, Talia is momentarily stunned. "Yes tomorrow," she says, recovering her wherewithal and kissing him back. The look on her face says she is both intrigued and confused by what has transpired.

Chapter 28

The temperature has dropped. Low-lying clouds have tucked the night sky up in a blanket of darkness. It makes walking across the car park tricky. The only light they have comes from the garage forecourt across the road. Nathan's face is mostly in shadow.

"Nae wonder you're looking for new friends." he says.

Joseph's reply is curt. "I'm not… I wasn't."

"Ah remember you chasing about after me and making all those fancy lunches and all that. Ah dinnae get lunches like that now. And waving tae me and wanting me tae visit you at weekends."

"That's not how I remember it."

"That's cos yer old and a little bonkers."

"Do you want to live on the streets, Nathan, because I swear to God…"

"Amen." Silence, and then as Joseph pushes him none too gently towards the passenger side of the car. Nathan asks, "Are you mad or something?"

"Whatever gave you that idea?"

"Yer shitty words and the shitty look oan yer face."

Joseph knows that Nathan cannot see his face clearly enough to make this assessment.

"Explain this to me, if you can," he says, leaning on the roof of his car and looking across at the vague outline of Nathan. "The other day you were sat on a park bench crying because you couldn't find it in your heart to forgive your father, a man who kicked you black and bloody. Lachlan makes one silly comment about jammies and bedtime, and you get all up in his face wanting to pick a fight."

"What bit dae you need explained?"

"Where's your forgiveness now?"

"For that prick?"

"You don't get to pick and choose. The Bible doesn't say *if you feel like forgiving this person but not that person, fine, no problem.*"

"How dae you ken what the Bible says?"

"Don't get fucking smart with me."

"Ah dinnae get smart with nae one."

"Get in the car."

"You want Ah should gae back in there and tell that prick Ah forgive him?"

"Jesus Christ, no. Get in the car."

"Amen."

In the dull light of the interior of the car Joseph laughs. He imagines Nathan going back in to tell Lachlan that he forgives him and the outrage that would follow. In the safety of the car he finds it amusing.

"You only get one father, Joseph, but pricks like that, they're aw ower the place."

Alone with Joseph, sitting in the front seat with the book balanced on his knees, Nathan is back to being pleasant and chatty. He starts each sentence with "Dougie said" or "Dougie did," and Joseph wonders if this is how it was when Nathan first met him. Had he gone home and spoken to his father about what Doctor Joseph Murphy said and did? Nathan's words cut into his thinking.

"Thanks fur the book. Dougie has loads of books. We were looking at them tae-day. Dougie said Ah should get some books, so thanks fur this oan."

"You're welcome."

"Dougie says tae-morrow he's going tae show me… Well, nae him but someone else that does it, is gonnae show me how they can copy my pictures on tae stuff."

"That's great."

When they arrive, the house is in darkness. Normally, Joseph would leave a light on, but his intention when he left this morning had not been to stay out all day. Having stopped to get pizza, the smell of the boxed food has tormented their senses on the drive home. As they sit at the table, Nathan's stomach growls. Impatiently he pulls at the food with his fingers, scalding himself on melted cheese. They are eating a lot of take-away food, and Joseph knows before long he will pay the painful price of indigestion.

"Ah am starving."

"Did you get lunch with the money I gave you?"

"Aye, but that was ages ago."

They sit at the kitchen table in semi darkness the only light coming from the hallway. They drink beer straight from the bottle. Nathan, having already downed a pint at the pub while Joseph settle for a poor non-alcoholic substitute, is noticeably more relaxed.

"So today was good? You enjoyed yourself?"

"At the workshop, yeah, but not so much at the pub."

Collectively, they disregard the ringing telephone and carry on their conversation, both indifferent to the disturbance.

"So what time do you have to be there tomorrow?"

"Any time after ten. That's what Dougie said. He said he could spend time with me after ten."

"Did he say if you could work there? Did he say whether he thinks this could be a job for you?"

"He said he loved me."

The reminder of Dougie's softly delivered endearment frays further the torn and tattered edges of Joseph's heart. "Yeah, I heard that," he says, and his words are sludgy, thick with unhappiness.

"And he said Ah am a genius."

"Yeah, Ah heard that too." Joseph's minimal response does nothing to deter Nathan's immodesty.

"And he said to be there after ten. Shall Ah gae oan my bike?"

"No, Ah'll take you. Ah have things tae do in town."

"What?"

"Things."

The telephone cuts off and then instantly starts ringing again. Nathan flicks his eyes quickly towards the sound and then back at Joseph, the glance meant to elicit a reaction.

"Nae wonder you love me so much."

"Nathan, I'm serious. You have to stop saying these things. I don't love you and we are most definitely not living together."

"Right."

"I care about what happens to you, that's all."

"Then why'd you fuss ower me so much?"

The question, teasing and testing as it is, refocuses Joseph's thinking. He side steps the subject. Like one of Nathan's dance moves, it's done with ease and grace.

"Because long before Dougie came on the scene, I already knew you were a genius. Now, genius, help me clear up."

Straight from the shower, Nathan stands naked in the bedroom that they still share. Mary is there too. The bedside lamp casts her in a turbid light. The lamp illuminates the darkest corners so that now she looks to be her own shadow. Drops of water sparkle across Nathan's wet back. The book on art lies open on the bed, distracting him. Holding his head at a slight angle, he dries himself half-heartedly as he reads. With his head bent towards the book, Joseph see Nathan's smile reflected in the dressing table mirror. Taking the towel from his idle hand, Joseph looks at Mary as he dries the boy's back. Mary's reflection should be there too, but the space is empty. Putting one arm around Nathan's chest in a loose hold, Joseph pulls him in against his own chest; and all the while he keeps eye contact with Mary, waiting for, wanting, a response from her that never comes.

The day has piled past memories and new possibilities on top of each other. Nathan's actions, at times, remind Joseph of the boy he once was, the one that sat on the bucket, dirty, unkempt, and unsure of himself. But now there is also this other Nathan emerging, one who swaggers and puffs his chest, ready to give his opinion. Joseph thinks back on the last time he took a towel and dried him. He tells himself that an indifferent person would not behave this way. If he were disinterested, he would not bristle each time Dougie's name is mentioned. Dougie's admiration would not burn like the worst heartburn.

"Is the book any good?"

"Yeah."

He holds Nathan for longer than he means too, resting his chin against his back, and then giving a gentle push he moves him away and runs his hands into his hair.

"This needs cutting," he says. "Unless this is how Nathan the artist looks."

Free of the embrace, Nathan closes the book and places it on the floor at the side of the bed before crawling in and hiding himself under the covers.

"Ah'm nae Nathan the artist yet."

"Soon, though," Joseph says, and his words are full of hope for them both.

"Aye and then Ah'm gonnae pay you back fur everything."

"Sure you are," Joseph says as he goes into the bathroom.

When he returns, Mary is gone, and the room has just the beautiful empty darkness of nothing. Joseph leans in and removes the bedclothes from covering Nathan's face. He marvels at how comfortable they have become in each other's company. They have found a routine that satisfies and appeals to both of them. Turning out the light extinguishes the incessant monologue within his own head, and silencing his conscience allows him the freedom to press himself up against Nathan's back, no longer faking the distance between them.

Joseph smiles. The darkness makes him brave and not care. Sleep comes easily now, and the future is undreamed.

"Aye," Nathan says, his voice already thick with sleep. "We dinnae live taegether, you dinnae love me, and we definitely dinnae share a bed every night."

Chapter 29

"Dougie says Ah should make the most ay myself. Ah dinnae understand a lot ay what he says, but Ah think he means tae work hard."

The "Dougie says" litany continues and is unaffected by minor matters like whether or not Nathan fully understands what Dougie says. Nathan has spent at least part of every day at the workshop since his introduction to the place. Today, Joseph has been waiting for him to return. It is a nice afternoon, and he wants to go out; Nathan is dragging his feet and wants to know where they are going before he commits himself. The boy, with his lack of enthusiasm for Joseph's own efforts and his over enthusiasm for Dougie's pontificating, is disappointing Joseph.

"If Dougie's so great, why don't you go live with him?" Joseph says. It is a throwaway comment, but somewhere, hidden within the charged words, he knows is a test. What is Nathan's future intentions? It's clear he is growing away from Joseph. Every day brings a new level of confidence to his vocabulary, and new names are introduced from a social circle that Joseph has not been asked to join. Joseph tells himself this is for the best, but in fact he is hurt to be so easily replaced.

"Talia said Ah could live at the pub wit her. Ah mean not wit her, but at the pub where she lives."

"Very good," Joseph says, and he takes his coat from the back of the chair. Sidestepping Mary on the way out the front door, he leaves his frustrations—Mary and the boy—behind in the house. He doesn't want to be stuck inside any longer, and he doesn't want to be at work. He doesn't want to be on his own either, and Nathan is no longer fulfilling the role of dependable diversion. Jealous of the boy, his talent and the excitement and passion he's showing for his art, Joseph can feel resentment eating into what little time he has left with him. Now to add to the problem, there is the mental image of Nathan ensconced in the pub with *his* friends while Joseph is stuck far away from everyone, up a bloody hill on his own. The worst of it, he realises, is that he knows how to fix this, knows what he *must* do, but the fear of that next step dries his mouth and makes his heart thump so that its beat can be felt in the back of his throat. It takes a week, seven short days to sort the arrangements.

"I'm returning to work," he tells Nathan, but only when it is a done deal, only when everything has been worked out and he has received confirmation that he is welcome back and that there is a place for him.

"What abit me?"

"What about you?"

"Ah wulnae see you."

"You hardly see me now because you're working. But we will still see each other after work. If you want. I am not going back fulltime, not yet anyway. And there are the weekends and days off."

"Is it what you want?"

"I don't know what I want." The answer is honest and Joseph is surprised that he has said it out loud. Then he adds, "I have to do something. You're putting me to shame, going off to work and being a big success and all."

Joseph hopes that putting some distance between them will make them both happier. Their future can then be sorted in a way that will suit them both.

Joseph has stopped by the workshop a couple of times since the initial visit, wanting to see for himself the display of Nathan's work for sale. Now T-shirts, mugs, and greeting cards carry images in Nathan's unique style.

Above the door that leads to the back of the workshop hangs a framed portrait of Talia. She is leaning out of the picture with her arms resting on some unseen support. She smiles out at potential customers. Nathan has illustrated her breasts perfectly. There is a sticker saying, "not for sale."

Joseph thinks perhaps he is not the only one who thinks the breasts in the picture are perfect. The once-empty art room where Joseph first showed Talia Nathan's pictures now has a shabby red sofa whose seat cushions seem unable to remain in place and spill onto the floor. A coffee machine has been rigged to only serve hot chocolate and is pulled up close enough to Nathan's seat that he does not have to get up to use it. Canvases, boards, and paper tubes lean against every wall. A radio that looks very much like the one that should be in Joseph's garage sits on the windowsill, its aerial poking out of a gap in the glass. The room belongs to Nathan. He is making money, and over the weeks he has asked Joseph repeatedly to tell him how much he owes him. The debt remains unsettled.

Joseph is relieved to find Nathan alone. The last time he'd called in, an assortment of youths lolled about, their excited chatter tapering off to a chilled silence at his appearance. He'd looked and acted and felt like the only adult in the room.

Nathan had said afterwards that "his friends" were frightened of him. Joseph had been more interested in criticising Nathan's use of the word friends than making any judgement on his own actions. Now they are alone save the host of faces that look out from the many portraits that represent hours of work.

"You smell like hospital," Nathan says.

"You smell like chemicals."

"We have tae go tae the pub."

"Have to?"

Nathan sighs as if preparing for a tiresome round of negotiating, and he looks up from his current piece of artwork, an outline of a naked female in shades of blue. There's just a shadowy hint of the girl's face, but Joseph knows she is one of Nathan's new friends. The girl was part of the group that had commandeered the sofa during his earlier visit, and her picture is as much of a hindrance now as her being here in person was previously.

"Dougie's giving Talia some paperwork, and we have tae gae there and get it. You have tae read it over and check it's okay."

"Have to! What paperwork? Why am I reading it over and checking for what?"

"Ah dinnea ken."

"Well, if you don't know, how am Ah supposed to?"

"Speak to Talia."

Nathan's collar is twisted, and Joseph runs his finger between the material and skin of the boy's neck to flatten it out. There is a moment when Nathan looks up. Joseph, done with the task, makes eye contact with him. It is just a moment, but to Joseph it feels like the end of something; he believes he is an expert now on endings, and this feels to him like another one.

"Is Talia still here?"

"No. Ah tauld you she's gonnae be at the pub."

It's an ambush, Joseph thinks. Talia has orchestrated several such meetings to take place over recent weeks, all in the vain hope that the lingering unpleasantness between Lachlan and Nathan can be resolved. Joseph believes it is in preparation for Nathan's inevitable move to the pub, a clearing of the decks so there will be no further altercations that might cause George unnecessary agro. Looking back down at the picture, it does not escape Joseph's notice that Nathan has drawn the anatomy of the female form perfectly.

Every time Joseph waits at the pub for Nathan to arrive, Lachlan is civil. Each time Nathan appears however, Lachlan finishes his drink and leaves without a further word being said. Talia is the only one who seems upset by this. Joseph sees in her a puzzling desperation to have harmony within the group, although he has yet to work out why it should matter so much to her. George hasn't noticed a problem, and Joseph sees Lachlan's exit when Nathan is around as a blessing. Nathan, however, seems obnoxiously pleased by it all.

Chapter 30

As they leave the workshop and walk back towards the car at Rose Street, Joseph is aware of three boys sitting on top of the wall bordering the car park, their legs dangling like twigs caught in a breeze. These are hooded youths the kind he avoids at all costs. Lost degenerates, he deems them, alienated in every sense from the world Joseph is most comfortable in.

"McGill, you knob," the smaller skeletal-looking one of the group shouts. Nathan, responding to the taunt, spins around on one foot and looks back at the group.

"Aye?"

"Gie us a fag."

"Ah dinnae have none."

"Gonnae gae us some money then."

Nathan spreads his hands out to show that they are empty. Joseph says, "Come on," giving what he thinks is a clear enough message that he does not want any involvement with these boys.

"Whit abit ya boyfriend there?"

Nathan plants his feet, and Joseph pats his arm lightly, saying again, "Come on," but with a little more force now in his voice.

Ignoring him, Nathan shouts, "Wait, Ah do have something her fur you." He shoves his right hand hard into his pocket.

Pulling it straight back out, he winds his middle finger up into the air and gives it to the trio. The emancipated troublemaker who has so far done all the talking then lets out a torrent of abuse and jumps down from the wall. In height, he would do well to reach Nathan's chest. His two associates who have so far remained silent in the altercation now find the carry-on amusing, and the laughter rumbles like far off thunder around the empty car park.

Joseph puts a still firmer hand on Nathan's arm and repeats his request to "come on." Nathan, pulling away, takes one step towards the younger lad, arms now spread wide, chest pumped. "If you think you can, wee man," he says as his fingers flick in a beckoning motion.

Jumping down from the wall, the three lads stand face on to Nathan, and Joseph has a very bad feeling. His body language says I'm walking away, but he's stays put. He will not leave without Nathan. Preparing to be the mature voice of reason, he turns to face the three troublemakers. But it is the larger of the boys that speaks.

"McGill, chill. It's cool. We're cool," he says, and he smiles, which Joseph thinks is not the best idea, the boy being without a single tooth in the front of his mouth.

"Ah am nay happy," Nathan says.

"I'll sort it. Chill. Be cool," the gangly toothless youth says again, and to prove his point, he slaps the instigator of all the trouble around the head with the back of his hand. The boy howls and holds his injury. For a moment the group is silent, and then, the same boy says, "McGill, it's good—we're all good here." The boy rallies his troops and they disappear into the shadows off a side street.

"Are you wise?" Joseph asks, now taking a firmer grip of Nathan. "Do you ever give any thought to me and how this looks. I can't be seen getting involved in carry on like this."

"Ah wisnae gonnae let um away with saying that."

"Do you enjoy getting beaten up?"

Nathan chuckles. "By them? Are you having a laugh? Those bairns."

It is a minor altercation, but it peeves Joseph because Nathan will not see his side. Lecturing at him as they make their way to the pub, he makes it clear he is still mad about it. Attempting to drive home his point still further, he says, "Nothing good comes from fighting, and you just let yourself down if you have to resort to violence to settle an issue. When you do that, you've already lost the argument."

It's still early and the regulars have not yet piled in, meaning there is a depressing vacuity to the place. Two lads are playing pool at one end of the bar, and an elderly couple seated at the far side drink coffee. George, sitting with an assortment of daily newspapers spread out across the bar, is working himself into a temper. It seems he is annoyed both at the inconsistencies of the reporting and the repetitiveness.

"Is Talia here?" Joseph asks.

"Nope."

"Did she leave some paperwork here for Nathan?"

"Aye."

Joseph thumbs through what appears to be a contract detailing the terms and conditions of renting a space at the workshop, commissions, and the selling of pieces of work. A part of the document has sticky tabs showing a signature is required. He puts the document to one side and orders drinks, asking George at the same time if he thinks Lachlan will be in soon.

"Aye."

George needs to work up to being warm, friendly, and sociable, and the night is still too young. Given that he is not for talking, in the dour space that's left, Joseph attempts to explain to Nathan what the paperwork is for, but he is just as uncommunicative. He's focused instead on asking Joseph about buying art supplies and whether he will drive him to some place Talia knows where he can get everything he needs cheap. Exasperated and still not over the confrontation in the car park, Joseph's tone is abrupt. He's further annoyed at the inconvenience of being forced to come to the pub and the lack of co-operation he's receiving. He finds it a struggle just to contain his frustrations with the day and Nathan, and so he's relived when Nathan says, "Ah'm gonnae play pool," and takes himself off.

George smiles. "You have your hands full," he says, and Joseph puts the cold, wet glass he is holding to his forehead.

He is forcing down his second non-alcoholic beer when Lachlan arrives. Joseph offers straight off to get him a drink. It is important to get on his good side before asking any favours; Joseph knows Lachlan needs careful handling.

"I was hoping… well, can you look at this for us… for Nathan? I know that the two of you got off on the wrong foot and Nathan can be hard to take sometimes, but as a favour to me, can you look at this?"

Lachlan gives only the quickest of glances towards the paperwork before taking the drink.

"It's fine," he says, not even bothering to read the front cover.

Joseph persists. "I think I will have to sign this either with Nathan or on his behalf. I want to make sure it's all in order, that I'm not signing him up to something more than he can manage, tying him into something that's going to take all his money. I know I'm going to be the one who has to deal with everything if it goes wrong, so can you just…"

Lachlan says again, "Its fine," but he still hasn't looked at the document.

"Can't you just read it?"

Lachlan sighs, then glances along the bar and away from Joseph. "Ah said it's fine," he says again, and there is impatience in his voice that Joseph feels is unwarranted.

"Well, you know, that's great. Yes, great, and thanks for that. I'll remember this when you come to me with something embarrassing…medical next time…" Joseph lets his words trail off to nothing. Gathering the papers together, he plans to find Nathan and leave. Lachlan makes a poor attempt at laughing off the situation.

"What? Ah said… Ah've told you it's fine, good enough for your precious boy there."

"You haven't even looked at it."

"Ah don't need tae. Ah wrote it. Ah wrote it for Talia, and if it's good enough fur her, then it's more than good enough fur him. Where is the fucking retard anyway? When you gonnae see sense and rid yersel ower that particularly annoying skin tag?"

Lachlan might have been about to say more, but the opportunity isn't given. Without engaging in any rational thought, thinking only of avenging the cruel, malicious words said about Nathan and acting on autopilot, Joseph forms a fist and makes a defined, direct, and devastating dent in Lachlan's face. His nose gives a very satisfying crack under the strike, the force of the blow taking him off his feet. In slow motion, Lachlan puts out a hand to steady himself as his other hand goes automatically to the injury. One hand is inadequately trying to stem the flow of blood while the other tries unsuccessfully to grab hold of a support, any support. Unwisely he chooses a bar stool, and both the stool and the man end up on the floor.

Then there is nothing, only silence, before Nathan says, "Joseph?"

"We're leaving," Joseph says, but in his haste to get away, he trips over Lachlan, now sprawled in his own blood, and falls into Nathan, who in turn is pushed backwards and collides with Talia, who it seems has just arrived.

George, standing behind the bar, watches as the dominoes fall one by one. Chaos has erupted out of the boring tranquillity of mid-afternoon, and as surprised as anyone by the sudden downturn in events, he's left a stoic spectator.

As chairs and people are righted and gain more solid footings, Lachlan scrabbles from the ground, his suit bunched around his shoulders, ruined with gore and dirt. Blood and bubbles of froth form between his fingers and drip onto the stone floor.

"Oh God," Joseph says on seeing first-hand the damage that he has caused. And then, as surprised as everyone else, he vomits, adding to the carnage.

"Amen," Nathan says, artfully sidestepping the splash back of spew.

Again, Joseph says, "We're leaving," but his legs refuse to cooperate and they wobble as he takes his first full step towards the door.

Chapter 31

Witnesses to the incident would later laugh and say that George cleared the bar like a gymnast, placing one hand flat on the polished wood and skipping over it, his legs perfectly straight so as not to disturb a single drink.

George shouting, "Wait up, wait up." Grabs Nathan from behind, holding him like a hostage, one arm slung around his neck and all the while pulling him backwards, determined to prevent him from following Joseph out the door.

"Let him go. We're leaving," Joseph says, but he is almost incoherent. He is making very slow progress to the door and needs Nathan for support, needs to lean on him. He cannot contemplate leaving without him. The realisation of what he has done sucks the energy from his body.

"Nate, if Ah let Joseph gae, he wullnae come back. And then you willnae come back either. Is that what you want?" George asks, whispering the words close against Nathan's ear. Their faces are side by side, bodies still pressed together because George has no intention of loosening his hold. George knows Joseph will not leave the boy even to save his own embarrassment.

"Please, let Nathan go," Joseph says, his tone imploring George to understand.

"Nate, is this what you want?" George says.

"Ah jist want tae help Joseph."

"Ah want tae help Joseph tae, but we need tae fix this," he says. Then, directing the assertion at Joseph, he says, "Come back and we will sort this."

Nathan, taking advantage of George's attention being focused more on Joseph than him, struggles free from the hold. Gently he reaches out and places his arms around Joseph's waist, an offer of support and a show of unity. The cause is now all but lost and George apparently knows it.

He says, "Well dae what you want," but it is just his way of stalling for time. Pulling a bar stool up close behind Joseph, he makes it easy for him to rest to gather himself together.

Nathan knows that somehow this is about him. He carries the guilt in the way he hangs his head and in the way he manages his body: shoulders slumped, arms folding in on themselves. He watches Lachlan, who is now sitting on a stool with a bar towel against his nose, and he glares at him from under his unruly fringe. The front of Lachlan's shirt, both hands, the towel, and quite a bit of Talia is covered in blood. Later, Joseph knows, there will be a lot of laughter and piss-taking. A doctor who can't cope with the sight of blood is funny, he supposes, but it was not the blood, although there was a great deal of it, that made him vomit. It was the fact that he was responsible for it. The scratchy, unpleasant feeling he has at the back of his throat from having brought food back up against the grain has not abated.

"Wonderful. Just fucking great," George says. "We have blood and we have vomit. Now all we need is whisky." And vaulting back over the bar, he takes down the single malt, the one put aside for special occasions.

Joseph is shattered. All the sensational melodrama that he has devoted to the moment—the physical violence, embarrassment, and emotional investment—has left him drained and discourages him from speaking.

"Taxi home tonight," George offers. The first sip of whisky Joseph takes is ruined by the lingering taste of vomit, but the second and third efficiently erase that.

Joseph might be exhausted, but Nathan is transformed and is now a zap of energy. Directing his anger at no one in particular, he shouts, "Ah'am not that boy anymair. Dirty… nae right in the heed, well you never saw him, but that's nae me now. Ah'am a fucking genius. Ask Dougie. Ah'am nae putting up wi this shite. Nae anymore. Ah'm telling you all you can jist gae tae fuck. And you…"

Joseph's heart is breaking. If it's possible, he feels sadder for Nathan with his history of being persecuted, bullied, and ruined by incidences just like this one than he does for Mary and her death and Lachlan, whose snivelling torment of those he thinks are weaker has earned him a broken nose for his troubles. In Nathan's anguished words there's a miscarriage of justice.

"I have a fucking diagnosis," Nathan screams, now directing his anger and aggression squarely at Lachlan. Astute enough to realise what is about to happen, Joseph blocks Nathan's path, using his tired and still shaky body to hold him pinned against the wall. An odd thought now crosses his mind the skinny boy with no reserves of fat is gone and it will only be a matter of months before Nathan, whose physique, attitude and temperament seem to change daily, will be stronger than him. He watches as Talia, now incited by Nathan's aggression, also puts herself between him and Lachlan. She is protecting him, Joseph thinks, but then his thought process goes no further.

"Ah have autism and obsessive-compulsive tendencies that are worse cos Ah have learning difficulties… and dyspraxia."

There is a pause in Nathan's rambling while he thinks over the information he has revealed. Then as an afterthought he quietly adds, "And asthma." Then riding his own private roller-coaster of emotions, the volume raises again and he shouts, "You wantae try being me fur a fucking day, dealing with all this shite, you fuck." Now utterly exposed, it leaves him a sobbing wreck. This small inconsequential gathering of people shouldn't matter to him, but Joseph realises they do. In time Joseph hopes Nathan will see them for what they are, but fixed as he is in this moment, every little detail and event is overly significant to him.

"Ah am trying tae nae get things wrang and nae fuck up aw'er the time, and jist learn shite and be awerite... and keep care of Joseph. Fuck you," he screams and pushes again at the obstruction that *is* Joseph.

Lachlan is clearly shaken. The squashed and bloodied nose must hurt, but Joseph sees there is also the humiliation of being decked of falling on the floor and now the added concern that Nathan might break free and finish what Joseph started. It is clear to everyone that Nathan's anger is directed just at Lachlan, and within the group the realisation now that he must have heard what Lachlan said.

"Listen," Joseph says. Still using his body to brace Nathan against the wall and hold him in place, he gets one hand onto his scrawny neck bringing it down so that his head rests against Joseph's chest.

"Listen," he says again, and he adds soothing noises to his words, his own heartbeat slowing, the rhythmic beat bringing the boy back to a more stable footing.

"That fuck," Nathan says, and there is more struggling.

"No, listen. I've sorted it. It's okay. Listen."

Nathan cries, the sobs wrack his body and set off a chain reaction—hiccups intrude into his words. For a while he persists, and then the words dry up and there is just crying; eventually the crying stops too.

"Listen," Joseph says again, "I've got this."

Lachlan says, "Sorry." Just the one word grafted into the many that Nathan has screamed, shouted, and sobbed out and so it is easily missed. He does not shame himself further by trying to explain or justify what he has said and done. Joseph's hope is that that will come later, not tonight.

Chapter 32

Talia and Lachlan take the first taxi and head off to A&E after a cursory look by Joseph at his face confirms that Lachlan's nose is most likely broken and needs attention. A substantial amount of whisky later, and Joseph and Nathan too are in a taxi, both seated in the back. Nathan laces his fingers into Joseph's and rests against the seat in the dark.

The temperature has dropped significantly. The sky is bible black and cloudless with an abundance of stars. The noise of the wildlife inhabits the night when the taxi leaves them at the end of the road, the driver making it clear he is not happy with coming as far as he has. Joseph sways and inhales, willing himself to sober up before embarking on the walk towards home. On one side is a deep ditch that ensures the road does not flood and wash away; on the other, nothing but the steep down-slope of the hillside as it falls into blackness. The ditch, Joseph thinks, would surely break your ankles; the nothingness of the hillside would take your life.

"Be careful," he says to Nathan, who is in as bad, if not worse, condition than he is.

"What's the danger?"

"Falling."

Nathan giggles. Joseph can only make out the blurry, vague shape of him standing slightly to the side.

"I'm serious. If you fall down there, you'll never stop."

"Ah thought you meant a wild animal would get me."

"Maybe a hare. That's about as wild as it gets out here."

They are above the midge line, which makes Joseph happy. The torment of being eaten alive as they make the walk would be too much to deal with.

"You want... Ah should leave?"

"What?"

"Dae you want me tae leave... to live someplace else?" Nathan's words coming out of the darkness have taken Joseph by surprise. He did not expect the conversation to turn to anything deep and meaningful.

"Why?"

"Ah embarrass you in front of your friends, like tonight. My fault."

Nathan sighs a lot as he talks, and Joseph knows that he is trying to focus his thoughts, engage his brain, and speak all at the same time.

"Friends, such as they are, embarrass me, not you."

"Talia and George are okay."

"Yes."

"Ah mean, what the fuck is Lachlan's problem? Seriously, what is his problem? Ah never did anything tae him. Never even spoke tae him, nae after that first time."

Sober Joseph would censor his response, be careful with the private information of others, but this drunken version of him is more free with information. "It's his wife," he says.

"What about her?"

"She's rough. I could use a lot of fancy descriptive words, and you know I know some, to describe her, but... Well, in her case there's no point. One word will do: ugly. She's pure ugly. Turns out she's lazy as well, but it's mostly the ugly thing. Lachlan doesn't love her, never has.

"How's that my fault?"

"It's not. It was never about you. You're just an easy target."

"Why'd he marry her?"

"They have a child."

"So?"

"So it's like there was a gun to his head. Don't underestimate the power of social pressure, Nathan."

"Huh?"

"You know, it makes you do and say the right thing. We torture ourselves and others to do what we think is the right thing. There's always this pressure to be something or someone... different, better... normal."

"And who had a gun tae yer heed?"

"No. I love... loved my wife."

"Aye right, so why'd you let yersell be haunted by her?" The words are a sobering reminder of Joseph's ongoing nightmare. "And how am Ah an easy target?" Nathan asks, breaking into Joseph's thoughts and causing him to refocus.

"Because they think you're stupid," he says.

"Who's they?"

"Don't interrupt, and move away from the edge." Joseph pulls then at Nathan's arm, trying to make sure he is safely away from the edge of the road, but he pulls too hard, which causes Nathan to swing widely across the track, arms flailing about, legs working hard to keep balanced.

"Shit," Joseph says.

"Ah'am okay."

"No, shit," Joseph says again, and he scrapes the sole of his shoe along the edge of the road trying to dislodge the muck that he has stepped in.

"Ah am nae stupid."

"You're a little stupid."

"Ah am nae the one wit shite oan my shoe, and Ah'm nae being haunted. And Ah'm also…nae the one wit an ugly wee wifey."

Joseph finds the seriousness of Nathan's tone and his words amusing. Alcohol-infused laughter ensues. It cannot be controlled and the unbalanced pair now clings to each other for support. Only when a deer, startled by the noise, breaks cover, skips past them on the road, and leaps effortlessly up the bank and out of sight do they stop.

"Man, Ah nearly shit myself then," Nathan announces.

"Is that what I stood in?"

The laughter starts again but is more subdued. Nathan, still holding on to Joseph to steady himself, says, "What did you mean, when you said 'she dinnae let me take care of her'?"

"What? I never said that."

"Yeah, you did."

"When?"

"Before."

"I was drunk."

"No, upset."

"Forget it."

"No, tell me."

Nathan's questioning launches Joseph into a drunken ramble, words jumbled together in a confusion of time and place, without context and still no censor. Everything that he has worked hard to squash and keep inside him for so long spills out. Nothing is now off limits.

"The only thing that has ever validated me is being a doctor… and her husband. I'd have gone unnoticed if not for that. I went unnoticed, you know, by my parents. Well, they never… Anyway, they never, and Mary said…"

Joseph is now no longer on the road, no longer with Nathan. His recollection of past events takes him to the very moment where he sees his nightmare rising. Once more he is back with Mary, and they both know she does not have long. The timeline from diagnosis to death has been charted by change. If changes occur monthly, that means the patient has months; if it's weekly, then the patient has weeks. Mary is fading daily. Her demise is rapid, but confusingly, time seems to have slowed to an agonising crawl. She's consulted with her medical support team, excluding Joseph from the discussions. He remembers being involved only when the arrangements have been finalised. She has made her decision.

"Mary said... Well, she told me," Joseph recalls now, "that she wanted to spend her remaining days at the hospice. She said that there her pain treatment would be carefully controlled and monitored." At the time, this had confused him. Mary was short of breath even when at rest and she required oxygen, but she was never in any real pain, just discomfort. "Why would she say that?" Joseph asks himself now. He recalls the moment they left the house they shared for eighteen years. Mary looked back only once and said, "It's sad to think I will never see this place again." Inside Joseph's head, he recalls, an argument had raged. He wanted to make her stay and allow him to do this one thing for her, allow him to take care of her. Out loud he'd failed to utter a single word of objection.

He is aware that Nathan has slipped his hand inside his again.

"Go on," he says.

Joseph is tempted to change the details of the story and make them fit better, but he has relived it too many times to drunkenly deviate from the script.

"Mary is settled at the hospice", he says, "and I hate the place. Visiting is torture. There is nothing for me to do and we are beyond words, and so there is nothing more to say. When I visit her a few days into her stay, she has rallied and is a little brighter. She's pleased to see me, and although it is a struggle, she wants to talk. She tells me how she has made 'the worst mistake ever' and that she wants to come home. I remember her begging, and she repeated the request three or four times, forcing the air into her lungs like sobs."

Joseph pauses then in his recounting, caught up as he is in seeing again the events unfold.

"Go on," Nathan says.

"A needless problem has arisen. Mary insisted I take her winter coat and boots home with me. She said she wouldn't need them again. She was adamant about it, and I was too worn down by then to argue. I remember standing in the room wanting to take her home, but also realising not having the coat and boots would cause a delay. That delay proved... costly." This is the moment more than any other that shuts Joseph's brain off from further thought.

It is only Nathan's gentle, "Go on," and his hand tightly holding Joseph's that enables him to continue.

"So I go back home to get the coat and boots. Only... well... I can't drive in my big winter coat. The weather was bad for three days, snow falling on and off. The back roads had not been gritted. Mary had predicted that A&E would be busy with all sorts of fractures. I throw my coat into the back of the car and with it my mobile. The radio is on and I never hear my phone."

"Go on."

"If I could have one moment back, the opportunity to rewind events and do things over again, I would choose that one. The simple act of not throwing a coat into the back of the car."

"Go on." the gentle nudge of Nathan's words pushes Joseph to finish.

"The moment I walk into the house and hear the phone ringing, I know. I know that she is gone. Dead. The nurse said that they had checked on her shortly after I left. They thought she was sleeping but…"

"Go on."

"That's it. That's the story. There is nothing else. She said she'd made a mistake and wanted to come home, but she never got the chance to. The mistake was mine, letting her go in the first place but then taking the boots and coat home once she was there. That and not having my phone to hand. Who does that?"

"*Whoever conceals his transgressions will not prosper, but he who confesses and forsakes them will obtain mercy.* That's in The Bible," Nathan tells him. "God disnae mind mistakes."

They have reached the driveway and Joseph stops. Once more the house is in darkness. He thinks of a moment when it will be his turn to leave and never return. Nathan turns to stand face on and pushes his body in close.

"Ah would kiss you, but nae efter you've boaked."

Taken aback by the frankness of Nathan's words, Joseph stands in the darkness wondering what it would be like to have someone want to kiss him. He puts both hands on Nathan's shoulders, pushes him gently away, and then turns him around so he faces towards the house.

"Walk," he says, encouragingly. "It's late, I'm tired, and I want my bed."

"Tell me again, Joseph, how naething good comes from fighting and how you just let yersell down if you resort tae violence."

Chapter 33

The phone is ringing. Drunk and pumped now from the walk, Joseph rushes inside to answer it. His father's voice, level, rich and familiar, fills his head.

"Ah've been ringing for ages."

"Hi. How are you? How's everyone?"

"Your brother said you put the phone down on him."

"Well, once a snitch…"

"What's wrong with you?"

Joseph wonders if his father means in general or apart from the obvious things such as confusion grief and loss. He is tempted to ask for clarification, and he imagines himself doing so, but then Nathan distracts him. Ignorant of the fact that it's impolite to listen in on a call, he has sat down on the stairs next to him. Joseph leans against the doorjamb, but a stomach empty of food and full of whisky is taking its toll on his ability to remain upright. He slides down onto the floor, and Nathan laughs. From this angle, he can just make out the drawing of himself that still disfigures the stairwell. Since Nathan started work, there has been no further talk of it being painted over.

"Who's that?" his father asks.

"Who's what?"

"I can hear someone. Who's there with you? Kenneth said a boy answered the phone."

"Nathan's here, and we just got back from the pub. Do you remember Lachlan?"

"The accountant?"

"Lawyer."

"Right."

"I broke his nose."

"You did what?"

"Yeah, get me, that's a first. Never thought it would be Lachlan. Never thought it would be anyone."

"An accident?"

"No, I meant it."

"Joseph, I think you are having a breakdown. I think this er…episode has manifested itself as severe stress, and you are overwhelmed by everything that has occurred, if this is not resolved… Well, you need help. I will speak to Fraser and he will recommend someone…"

"Don't go to any trouble."

"Joseph, we're all worried…"

"So worried that not one of you made the effort to come over here. Not one of you came… to be here with me, and it's not an episode. It's death. It's… Never mind. Forget it, please, and goodnight."

Joseph puts the phone down on his father, something he has never done before. Then just to make sure there will be no further intrusions, he pulls the jack from its point.

"What'd he say?"

Nathan's words are a little slow, his eyes heavy. He's still sighing a lot, after each word.

"He thinks I'm having a breakdown."

"Are you?"

"Fuck knows."

Laughing, Nathan repeats those words, and sliding off the stairs, he pushes himself up close to Joseph on the floor.

"I should chuck you out my house," Joseph tells him.

"Why, because of Lachlan?"

"Tomorrow, when I'm no longer bolstered by bravado and whisky, I will regret EVERYTHING."

"I like whisky… What's bolstered bravado?"

"I'm so tired."

Sitting on the floor at the bottom of the stairs, Joseph watches the vision of his dead wife walk along the hallway. As she passes, she gives them both an apparition's equivalent of a sullied look. Mary is mute, Joseph thinks, but her non-verbals can still pack a punch.

"Her boots and coat are still here," he tells Nathan, picking up the story again as if there had been no interruption.

The fear of forgetting her, his once most constant companion, has abated slightly. Mary being dead is not as dreadful as it once was, and that makes him sad. He thinks this is what "time heals" means and it is not a good thing.

"Keeping her best coat and favourite shoes and her important bag hanging where it's always been, that says it best: Ah remember you," Nathan says. "Why can't her stuff stay here? So it can say 'remember me.' It's better than putting dates on a block of stone."

Somehow not doing something makes sense, leaving some of her possessions where they should be is akin to a bandage wrapping a bloodied gash. Joseph tells himself, "It will do." Nathan is right. Her things hanging where they should be says more than a stone that marks nothing other than a sad ending. Her possessions should stay because they say more and they say it better.

Nathan is not in the bed when Joseph awakes, and this alone is enough to put him wrong. The boy is now so much a part of his life that he minds when he is not there. There's an alcohol-induced amnesia, but last night comes back to him in fragments. Patches and parts of yesterday's events are mixed up, however, no longer linear. He has gone to sleep still in his dress shirt and tie, although at some point he has removed everything else.

Nathan is easily found. He is lying face down on the sofa, and he is fully dressed save for one shoe and sock. On the floor beside him is a bag of peas that were once frozen but now are not. There is the hazy memory of the walk along the road, but of nothing untoward happening.

"You with me?" Joseph asks. It takes some poking and gentle hair pulling before Nathan responds with grunts and a hacking cough that concludes with him dry-heaving. He turns over and says, "Ah dinnae feel great." He then breaks wind.

"You're a delight to live with."

"Aye."

Rolling off his makeshift bed, Nathan ends up on all fours. He remains like this for longer than Joseph feels is necessary, and then using the sofa as support, attempts to stand. He is no sooner upright when like a marionette with its string cut he drops once more to the floor. Joseph shouldn't but he finds it funny when, sitting with his leg bent, Nathan studies his foot.

"Ah'm hurt."

"Did you fall over on the walk home?"

"Nah, Ah fell down the stair going up tae bed."

"So you made it all the way home only to fall down the stairs!"

"Stair," the boy says. "The first one."

This explains the thawed peas and the exposed foot. At some point Joseph must have attempted to attend to the injury before giving up and taking himself to bed. He studies Nathan. His eyes that are normally colourless are bloodshot, cheeks sunken, mouth dry.

"You look bad."

"Ah am nae well," Nathan says again, and pulling himself up and back onto the sofa, he lies down and curls back into a ball.

"Don't go back to sleep. Get up and get showered. It will help," Joseph tells him, and perching on the sofa cushion, he runs his fingers across Nathan's rutted forehead. He is suffering. In the past, Nathan has shown no sympathy for Joseph when worse for wear with drink, so now he can't help but enjoy the turn in fortune.

"Do you want to dance?" he asks him, finally getting him upright. Nathan sits holding his head in his hands.

"Mebbe later," he says, and Joseph thinks it is both the sweetest and saddest thing he could have said.

They debate, over breakfast, how best to get the car back. A taxi would mean walking back along the road and possibly further down the hill, and that's if one would come at all. Nathan favours cycling back to the pub. Showered, he now has more optimism about life, but he still limps badly. Joseph, not wanting to cycle anywhere, plays on Nathan's injury for his own interests. His preferred option is to use Mary's car.

"How will we gie that back?"

"Why bother. I'll take it to a garage and sell it. I don't want it."

The car, another item on the list of Mary's things that needs to be disposed of, is shut away in the garage and has been easily forgotten.

"Ah dinnae want tae go. Ah might stay here."

"Is it your foot?"

"No."

"Drinking too much?"

"Aye, a bit, and the stuff that happened last night."

"If anyone should be ashamed and embarrassed about last night's carry-on, it should be Lachlan… and… possibly me."

"Ah don't think Ah want tae go back there."

"Ever?"

"Mebbe."

"I think that's just the hangover talking. You don't normally let people get to you. Give it a few hours and you'll feel different."

"Ah willnae. Ah tauld um way too much. Sometimes Ah jist cannae help mysell. Ah start spouting aff. It's nae ideal."

Chapter 34

The doorbell interrupts Nathan's raw reflections. "Hide," he says.

Joseph, crafting a grin, says, "I will not."

Nathan still serious and morose, tells Joseph as he goes to answer the door. "It's always bad."

At times Joseph wishes Nathan wasn't so perceptive. He is right about the door. Lachlan and Talia are standing in the driveway admiring the view. Joseph's car is parked in front of the garage doors. It solves one problem he thinks, but another might be sailing right behind. Lachlan holds out the car keys, letting them dangle by the fob from one finger. Stating the obvious nasally he says, "I've brought your car back."

"You drove my car?"

"You're welcome," Lachlan says, choosing to ignore the obvious displeasure in Joseph's voice.

"We tried phoning, but your phone is off the hook."

There is the scuttled memory of a late night phone call. Joseph thinks it may have been with his father, but the details are missing. Without being invited, Lachlan manoeuvres himself into the hallway.

"I always forget how nice your house is."

"Please come in," Joseph says, his voice heavy with distrust and annoyance. Lachlan is not known for his helpfulness, and his tone is flippant as he asks, "Where's Nate?"

"Leave him alone." Joseph's own words are rapid, like repeated gunfire. Beads of sweat appear on his brow. Lachlan, unbalanced by Joseph's defensiveness, avoids eye contact. He looks up the hallway, apparently his intention is to find Nathan on his own if Joseph won't help.

"I only want to apologise to him," he says.

"You already did."

Joseph considers telling him they are both feeling the worse for wear, insisting that he go, but such a confession does not sit well with him, and then there's Talia still standing in the driveway looking awkward and out of place. She gives him an apologetic smile.

"You'd better come in," Joseph tells her, his voice too soft, too quiet to be welcoming. Lachlan might carry on as if nothing has changed, but it is clear Talia has been dragged here against her better judgement. She nods, keeping her head tilted to one side as she passes him. It makes her look years younger than she is and Joseph sees a hint of the little girl he remembers from years past.

"Speak o' the Devil," Lachlan says, spotting Nathan at the end of the hallway. He is loud, obnoxiously, so and Nathan limping further into view, with a hobble that is just pitiful, says, "How am Ah the Devil?"

"It's just a saying. How are you?" Lachlan asks, and Nathan is clearly confused by this attempt at exchanging pleasantries. He looks past Lachlan and down the hallway to Joseph for help. No one comments on either Nathan's limp or the elaborate white dressing that covers Lachlan's squashed and swollen nose.

"No bad. Yer sell?" Nathan says, his mumbled Invernesian response automatic.

The hallway is spacious, but with Mary now opting to join them and, as is her preference, pacing the passageway, Joseph knows he must do something about her, Nathan, his visitors, work, but where does he start. He shudders as Mary passes through Talia, and the shudder does not go unnoticed by the group. Talia frowns and Lachlan raises his eyebrows, silently questioning Joseph's agitation. Nathan smiles.

"You all right Joseph?" Lachlan asks.

"Sure... Sure, let's go into the lounge or the kitchen or outside." He would like them all to leave, Mary included, but knowing that this is not an option, he hopes that by ushering them into another room, Mary will stop inconsiderately walking into anyone else. His guests might be unaware of her, but Mary invading their personal space is bothering the hell out of him.

Lachlan makes it to the bottom of the stairway and is heading into the lounge before he says, "Dear Lord..."

"Amen," Nathan says, and Joseph sucks in his breath, certain now that the day will be long and difficult.

Lachlan is face on to Nathan's graffiti picture, brows pushed close together, a crazed, slick smile on his lips.

"Did you do that? Is this what you do? Holy crap! Right on the wall. Right there... on the wall. It's... big."

"It's beautiful," Talia says. Having moved herself up the hallway, she now stands between Lachlan and Nathan.

"Is this the tree?" she asks.

"Yes," Nathan says.

"No," Joseph says, cutting into the conversation. Attempting to get them to move into the lounge and away from Mary and the picture, he bunches everyone up by standing too close.

"It's not a tree. I mean, if you have to ask."

"It's a tree," Nathan says again, and there is fierce resolve in his voice.

"So this is your thing, huh?" Lachlan turns as he speaks, so he is facing Nathan and away from the picture. Joseph thinks it's a start.

"My thing?"

"Yeah, people like you all have a thing, don't you, like playing the piano or being a whizz with numbers? And this is your thing."

"People like me?"

"Yeah, you know. Special people."

Nathan's bloodshot eyes dance about, refusing to rest anywhere. Joseph watches his fingers flicker, long and elegant and choreographed by an energy all their own. Joseph's mind is now made up, any motivation to be peacekeeper gone. He will not stop him, if Nathan decides to show his displeasure with Lachlan, Joseph will not stand in his way.

"What the fuck?" Nathan says as he takes one step closer to his adversary, necessitating a hop then to get his feet underneath him and be pain free. Joseph notices that he has the toes bent inwards and favours standing on the edge of his injured foot.

"Who are you calling special? Ah'm a fucking genius. Ah'm nae special. You… you're fucking special."

Lachlan looks from Joseph to Talia and then back, and his face suggests he's realised his attempt to be sociable has gone wrong somehow.

"Ah only meant…"

"Ah ken what you meant."

Joseph, thinking it will bring a speedier end to the visit, is content to let Nathan vent. That is until he says, "How's yer wife?"

Now not so content to let Nathan vent, Joseph catches his eye and tries to signal him not to say anything else, dragging one finger across his throat.

Lachlan stares Nathan down. "What?" he says.

"Yer lazy, ugly wife. How is she?"

Joseph screws his eyes up tight, the voice inside his head screaming just one word that echoes with torment: Why?

Talia says, "Dear Lord," and she shakes her head before moving as far back as she can in the restrictive space of the hallway. Opening his eyes, Joseph can see she is wishing that she were anywhere else and not standing between the two combatants.

Nathan says, "Amen." And then, "Is yer lazy, ugly wife special too?"

Joseph shakes his head, unknowingly mimicking Talia. He sighs, hunches his shoulders over, and goes back to avoiding all eye contact. There is nothing that he can say to explain this breach of trust, nothing to excuse such a cruel indiscretion.

"Ah guess it was a mistake coming. Ah just thought returning the car would be helpful and… Well it would give me a chance tae apologise properly tae you, but clearly there's nae point," Lachlan says.

"No, there's nae point. Dinnae try tae apologise tae someone like me. A retard, a skin tag, special like Ah am. There's just nae point." Nathan sings out the words, absurdly proud of the way he is defining himself, and evidently pleased with his competitive antagonism.

"Well, Ah am. Ah am sorry. Every time Ah say something, Ah make it worse and nae better. But Ah'm going tae say it anyway. Ah am sorry for saying those things. Ah realise now how offended you are, and Ah am sorry. Even so, there's nae need tae bring the wife intae this. That's bad shit."

Nathan, tired and sore from standing on his injured foot, slides down the wall and sits in front of Lachlan. He is silent and in the silence Lachlan turns to Joseph.

"Ah have always thought you have every kind of luck, Joseph," he says.

"My wife died."

"Yeah, well, Ah have wished that my wife died."

"Dear Lord," Talia says again.

"Amen," Nathan says.

"Ah went home last night after you knocked some sense intae me, and Ah tauld her Ah didnae love her. Ah tauld her Ah dinnae even like her. Ah said Ah was leaving. Then, well she disnae even turn the telly aff. Disnae even look at me. Just says 'fine'."

Spent from his confession, Lachlan sits on the floor next to Nathan.

Joseph thinks, "There it is, that shitty little word again."

"All those years spent worrying about how she would cope, worrying how she would react, and she can't even be bothered tae turn the telly aff and talk tae me about it. What's that all about?"

"Mebbe," Nathan says, "she's as pissed aff with you as all of us. You're nae a very likeable person."

Lachlan smirks and leans his head back against the wall, facing the picture.

"Wow," he says. "That tree really is magnificent."

"It's not a tree," Joseph says.

"It's a tree," Nathan says. "It's best from this position."

Talia joins them on the floor.

"It's not a tree, and can we sit someplace else?" Joseph asks. "I have chairs." He is very uncomfortable now with the group sitting staring at this life-size grinning version of him.

"We're appreciating Nathan's tree drawing talents, and you'd think you'd want tae join us for this," Lachlan says, and having indicated only moments before that he was leaving, he now appears to have made himself comfortable. Legs outstretched, arms folded into his lap, head still resting against the wall, the slick smirk still fixed in place, he's settled.

"Let's be clear here: it's not a fucking tree. I'll make drinks," Joseph offers.

Mary, having about-turned, marches back up the passageway; this time she misses the occupants. But Joseph, making sure he avoids any contact with her, pushes in against the wall. Lachlan, seeing an opportunity, catches his wrist. "Sit," he says, and he pulls Joseph down. They sit like ducks in a row, backs to the wall, face on to the picture.

"It's a tree," Joseph says.

And Nathan, a delicious kenspeckled smile on his face, says, "Ah tauld you."

Sitting as he is on the floor, Joseph can appreciate what Nathan has created on the wall for the first time. Standing above the picture looking down there is only the portrait of Joseph. The pinstriped shirt with sleeves rolled up to just below the elbow, hair falling in pliant waves across the brow and resting against an open collar. Eyes that follow you complement a smile that never wavers. What little there is of the tree is additional to the portrait of the man. The man is the whole picture. But from the floor looking up any vestiges of the man are gone. The pinstripe shirt, waves of hair, collar and unwavering smile somehow have merged and melted to become bark. Knees drawn up to the chest and fingers that dangle are now roots, branches, twigs, and leaves. The sensation of being hidden and safe, sitting in the pine straw beneath the tree comes back to Joseph. How had Nathan seen and drawn what was at the time just feelings, hopes, daydreams and desires?

They sit outside in the pleasant heat of mid-morning, a sorry quartet of bruised and battered souls, and one seraph, who in death looks in better shape than the living.

Lachlan states that it feels like the first day of the rest of his life. He is, he says, staying with Talia, which Joseph interprets to mean he is lodging at George's. Lachlan's recovery from a marriage that is over is more straightforward than his own, Joseph thinks. Lachlan's wife will not torment him.

"They call my wife ugly, not plain-Jane," Lachlan tells Nathan. But Talia will not let him away with such a blatant lie, forcing him to confess that it was he who started this unfortunate tag.

"Why would you dae that?" Nathan asks.

"Because she made me a joke with my friends. So Ah made the joke about her, made it work for me. Then it didn't hurt so much."

"And that worked?"

"No, it just hurt both of us—and our son. And Ah'm sorry about that. Ah will make sure she's okay. Ah think that this will be best fur both of us. At least that's what Ah'm telling myself."

"*The soul who sins shall die. The son shall not suffer for the iniquity of the father, nor the father suffer for the iniquity of the son. The righteousness of the righteous shall be upon himself, and the wickedness of the wicked shall be upon himself.* That's in The Bible remember that," Nathan tells him. Lachlan, shocked by Nathan's recitation of scripture by heart, is lost for words.

Finally he says, "Aye, you werenae wrang there. You're a genius awerite." Nathan, leaning back in his chair, nods his agreement.

Chapter 35

The blemished light of early evening colours what's left of the day in mottled watery shades. A day that started off with all the markings of war is now an evening of peace and tranquillity. Joseph feels content for the first time in months, giving him time to reflect, perhaps even to make a little sense of the mass of information that has battered his belief system.

Has Nathan seduced him? Until that moment he'd felt it was he who was the principal player in everything that had happened between them so far. But having seen Nathan win over Talia and now, against all the odds Lachlan, perhaps he realises he might be mistaken; perhaps he was never the star, and it is Nathan who stolen the show.

As shadows lengthen, Joseph knows he needs to question the issues that face him now more intently. Can he really live without Nathan? Would he want to? He has tasted solitude and loneliness and found it ugly, bland and dull. Nathan has brought art and music, dancing and differing dietary requirements into his day. Now Joseph no longer has to contend with the meaningless urgency of work or of maintaining a sensible persona. Instead, he manages occasional whining, the constant possibility of tears, and the always unexpected but welcome surprise of unplanned laughter. How could he give that up? Why would he want to?

Lachlan sees his failed marriage as a new beginning. Joseph is trapped by his. Death, it seems, has provided less of an ending somehow.

"I'm in love, and it feels like a first," Lachlan says.

Nathan and Talia have their heads bent close together and are discussing music. It has not escaped Joseph's attention that the two of them have a lot of shared interests, mostly art and music.

"I want to dance," Talia says, and instantly Joseph feels the heated pinpricks of jealousy trapeze across his skin. Mary was a good-looking woman, but she put men off. She was too confident, opinionated, and righteous. The average male trying to flirt does not want or need those odds. So while she had commanded respect, Joseph had never had to deal with competition. Nathan gives off a very different vibe.

Moving from her seat to the grass, Talia sways with the music, letting her hips roll and shimmy in time to the vocals of a solo male artist, his soft soulful, if a little nasal, voice complemented by a lone piano player. Her actions are neat and economical. She is good to watch, but Joseph prefers the boy, his rhythm more constructed, familiar. Putting her hands onto Nathan's skinny midriff, she manoeuvres him so he sways and grinds in time with the rhythm of the song. His face set in concentration, head bent forward, eyes fixed on Talia's best assets.

"Do you think it's madness?" Lachlan asks.

"What?" Joseph says. Engrossed as he is in watching the two dancers, he has lost the gist of the conversation.

"Us," Lachlan says.

Joseph, still more intent on what Nathan is doing than paying heed to Lachlan, at first does not notice that Lachlan is also watching attentively. And like Nathan, Lachlan focused on Talia has a possessive, predatory glint of need in his eyes. Only because he can't follow the conversation does Joseph turn to look at him. Then he understands.

"You and Talia!"

"Don't say it like that."

"It's quick, that's all."

"No, and Ah'm ashamed, but it's been going on a while."

"She's very young."

"She's older than your boy."

Joseph, looking away, misses the meaning in Lachlan's reference to Nathan.

"How does George feel about all this?"

"He's letting me stay, but he's nae happy."

"Understandable, perhaps."

The dancers, with the change of song, put some distance between each other. Nathan turns circles on one foot, still protecting his injury by holding it slightly off the ground.

"It's our song, Joseph," he says, and for a sweet and serene moment, he's all smiles.

Lachlan chuckles, and teasingly he shouts out, "You have a song!"

Straightaway it kills the mood, and embarrassed, Nathan slumps into the chair opposite Joseph.

"It's a good idea to rest your foot. No more dancing," Joseph tells him.

"We should go," Talia says, always perceptive. Joseph thinks she is predicting another fallout.

"I'll get organised," Joseph says, pulling himself slowly out of the chair, believing that he has to drive them both back to the pub.

"Nae need. Talia's car is at the end of the road. She refused tae take it any further, but we can walk tae it. It's a nice evening," Lachlan says, and he is back to being helpful and pleasant.

But keen to keep their momentum towards their exit going, Joseph thanks them both for returning the car and makes convincing inferences about enjoying their company; and wishing them well, he shepherds them out of the house and on to the driveway. He watches as Lachlan takes Talia's hand and they walk away. Seeing her once more as the little girl that they have watched grow up, he cannot reconcile that girl and the woman now with Lachlan. At what point did she become attractive, a sexual being? And at what point did she become interested in someone of his and Lachlan's age? Shaking his head, he steps back inside the house.

Nathan is at one end of the hallway, Mary the other; looking like bookends, they await his return. Walking towards Nathan and intending to summarise the day's events, it surprises him when Nathan drops to the floor and curls into the foetal position.

"Dinnae hit me."

"I never have and I never will."

"Aye, you say that, but look at Lachlan's face."

The words are thick and half lost in the folds of the boy's clothes. Stepping over him, Joseph makes his way into the kitchen. Realising then that he has moved away, Nathan uncurls, rolls over and, facing into the kitchen, watches. Joseph lets his antics go unchallenged, putting away plates and cups and wiping mess from the kitchen surfaces.

Then, minding that Nathan is still lying on the floor, he asks, "Did you say you were asthmatic?"

"Aye. I was. I might not be anymore."

"Best not to roll around in the dust on the floor just in case."

"Are you mad?"

"That depends on who you ask and on your definition of madness." Tired of confrontation and drama, Joseph attempts humour on the boy, hoping for a quick resolution. Stepping over him again, he leaves the kitchen and returns to his seat in the garden. Fresh warm air fills the evening with the scent of vegetation and cooked earth. Leaning back in the chair, he angles his face to catch the last of the sun's heat.

"I love it here," he says, the words are spoken out loud but still a selfish pronouncement.

"Ah am sorry fur what Ah said jist then. Ah was nae minding my words as well as Ah should have been."

"Forget it. They were here parading their relationship. I don't think they are very interested in anyone else right now. Did you know already?"

"Aye."

"Why didn't you say?"

"*Keep your tongue from evil and your lips from speaking deceit.*"

"Right. Bible?"

"Yep."

"Was there a phone call last night?"

"Aye. Yer dad said yer a bampot."

Joseph surveys the garden. Eden he thinks has lost its Eve. Branches of plush green leaves have already spread into the space left by the fallen tree. He plans to cut them back. He wants the gap to remain, to be a reminder of what is lost. Nathan can help, he thinks, and he realises then that Nathan is now and will always be in his future.

"I want you to stay."

"Aye. Nae bother."

Chapter 36

Wiping steam from the mirror, Joseph studies his own reflection. He is disappointed. The image in the mirror is not as good as the picture that will remain on the wall in the stairwell. He smiles at himself and then frowns, smiles again, and childishly pokes out his tongue. Mary is in the bedroom, and he expects Nathan to be under the bedclothes, if not already asleep. Returning, he finds the room busy, crowded. Nathan is not in the bed but standing by the side of it, and he seems uneasy. Like in Joseph's dreams, Mary blocks Joseph's path to him.

"What?" he says, and there is the feeling that dead wife and boy are colluding.

"Ah still want tae kiss you."

"It's late." Lachlan's statement that Talia is "older than your boy" bobs into his memory, and he blushes now with the realisation of what Lachlan was implying, and of missing something so obvious.

"Perhaps," he says to Nathan, "they were here to be nosy after all."

"Ah never thought otherwise."

Joseph bends his head slightly to the left to look around Mary. Nathan, who rarely smiles, lets his lips part slowly in a shy, skilful grin. His steps are tentative, possibly because of the painful foot. But two small strides and they merge.

"She is using him to get to me," Joseph thinks.

A lack of food, staring too hard at her faint image, or madness, has made him feel lightheaded. There's a need to put out a hand and steady himself against the very solid furniture. The amalgamation of the two, Nathan and Mary, gives him a look that says, "Aren't we clever."

If this is madness, that defining moment when you become aware of the very instance of losing it, then Joseph believes he is ready. If this is madness, then he welcomes such insanity. If this is madness, then it is wonderful.

He wants the blend of the two, the beautiful, youthful pout of Nathan mixed with Mary's feminine curves, the new maleness of the boy and the familiar chic elegance of her. He wants to be the object of their desire. They, this beautiful fragile fusion of forms, will, Joseph imagines, produce possibly the strangest threesome a fractured mind could invoke. The kiss is good, better perhaps because at first there is an awkward hesitancy. But Nathan knows what he's doing, knows how to kiss! Then Joseph corrects the thought, *they* he thinks, know what *they* are doing and what *they* want. Feelings not previously understood, coveted, or desired take hold of Joseph. Now it is Nathan and only Nathan that he wants pushing him down onto the mattress. It is Nathan that he covers.

After, lying sated, questions vie for space in Joseph's head: What does it all mean? What makes a person deserving of such privileged attention? What happens now?

Nathan and the wispy, illusory form of Mary mess with his free will. The boy with more reserves of cuteness than a Labrador puppy, is now irresistible to him. His cry and whine a more perfect pitch than any newborn baby can muster. The eyes, with their extraordinary colourless depths, are a seductive laser beam. Joseph feels a beautiful, timeless hug of satisfaction fold about his tired limbs.

The morning inevitably brings embarrassment and regret, believing as he had, that all such carnal feelings had retired within him, all urges dead, or at the very least gone quiescent. Joseph cannot now reconcile the pleasures of last night with the years of obligation sex that had followed Mary's slow and deliberate rejection of him. A history of confusion and deceit is lumped together. Memories of being with Mary, the way she'd assigned love making the same status as all the other household chores she undertook, and the contrasting simplicity and perfection of being with Nathan refuse to fit neatly in his head.

Now he feels both sullied and salubrious, a debauchee and a paragon, wonderful and pained. Unsure still if he is a villain or a victim, he again questions who has seduced whom. Everything is the same and yet nothing will ever be again. He can no longer accept the definition of who he is or even what he is. Certain things he thinks, define us: race, religion, ethnicity, gender, sexuality. And we don't in the cover of one night, change classifications.

He calls Nathan from the bottom of the stairwell, giving him a reminder he will be late for work if he doesn't get a move on. The normally dour-faced boy is all smiles as he descends, his happiness unmistakable, threaded into his swagger, into the care that he has taken in his appearance, and the cheery tune he hums to himself.

"Can you make your own way home?"

"Aye."

Joseph will have the morning at home by himself; Nathan will cycle in to town and back. Joseph marvels at how well their lives fit together.

"Say nothing to anyone."

"Why would Ah?"

"It's just that it's nobody's business but ours. *Evil tongues and lips of treachery and all that, remember?*"

"*Deceit,*" Nathan corrects.

"Whatever. Just give me the same considerations you showed Talia and Lachlan."

"Aye, nae bother."

How strange, he thinks, that they can talk the same way as they have always done. Everything has changed and yet, the necessities of their routines have remained intact—with one notable exception. Mary has yet to appear. Her absence causes Joseph to scan the rooms in search of her, which does not go unnoticed by Nathan.

"What's done is done. Move on." Nathan says, and Joseph is sure he knows something.

"Where is she?"

"In yer heed," he says, and he taps Joseph's temple, the single crafted digit lingering and then slipping into Joseph's hairline. Joseph, feet planted firmly on the floor, his body straight on to Nathan's, arms hanging loose at his sides, lets him get away with it. Intentionally he leaves himself open to Nathan's advances.

"I don't understand," he says.

"Ah know."

"Then explain."

"*Praise Him all His angels, praise Him all His heavenly host.*"

"I still don't understand."

"Have a word whit yersell, Joseph," Nathan says, then kisses him full on the lips and leaves.

Joseph enjoys the silence. He sits at the kitchen table and sips coffee. Pulling up different memories of Nathan's antics, he smiles. It both irritates and amuses him when he tells him to "have a word with himself."

He imagines how a conversation with himself would go. He asks aloud, "What is your problem, Joseph?" And then he lists the answers. Everything has changed, but perhaps for the better. People will talk, and he says aloud, "But do you mind so much?" What will your father think? Who cares. You will never have to see him again, and unless you plug the phone back in, there will be no further conversations.

Then Joseph has the idea that it is not himself that he needs to have a word with. "Come out, come out, wherever you are!" he shouts into the emptiness of the house. "If you're in my head, then I can make you appear."

The wispy image of Mary has yet to manifest even though he stares hard at the empty chair opposite. He pictures her sitting there as she has done many times. He tries hard to recall the image of her as she was in life, and not the faded, fragile version of her that has been skulking about the house.

"We need to talk," he says into the emptiness. "I don't need you, so why are you here? I'm doing fine." The best lies, he thinks, are the ones we tell ourselves.

"You would be shocked how I've changed, but I make a better person now. We would never have parted. We would have ridden out the marriage, believing it was the right thing to do. But... still wrong for both of us."

He sits back against the chair, pictures Mary as she was before the illness, her hair falling in pleasing curls that rest perfectly on her shoulders, soft waves that are the colour of pine straw, hands are folded on the surface of the table, her blouse the grey of Nathan's eyes. He loves the colour and the blouse.

"Did you love me?" he asks. The words hang in the emptiness, and he frowns, looks away, and then back. "I think perhaps you did... in your own way. But why would you?"

He sits forward, placing his hands flat on the table. "Why would you not let me take care of you? Why leave our beautiful home? Why cut me out of it all? Why love someone who could not rightly love you back?" He leaves the questions hanging; there is something else he needs to say.

"I'm sorry that you died. At first it was a big inconvenience, and I lost it there for a while. I'm sorry—for you, for all those things you still wanted to do, dreamed of achieving—but I was also sorry for me. Your absence changed things. Now it's fine. I think now I am... better, a better person. I don't know what you would make of this, of Nathan and, well, that situation."

He now paces the kitchen, aware that his whirling mind, his rambling words and his movement about the room, distil the emptiness and add a sense of excitement to the air.

"Shit," he says, and then laughing loudly, he shouts, "Everyone dies, and that should be the end."

He tugs at his hair, runs a flat hand across the stubble on his chin. He must shave before he leaves for work, he tells himself.

"I am, for the first time, me," he says. The words spill out now, tumbling from his mouth without a thought in an excited burst of honesty.

"Yes." It is the image of his wife, as she was in life, that gives the response. Having willed her into some form of existence, Joseph sees her now exactly as she always was—perfect. He watches her mouth move as she speaks, but her voice does not resonate from her lips but comes from somewhere deep within Joseph's head. Standing with his back now to the Belfast sink, he grips the cold porcelain with firm hands.

"Yes, this is an honest version of you," she adds. At the back of his throat is the acidic taste of a thrilling fear. Joseph can smell her perfume and he can feel once more the air being agitated against its will. The memory of standing in the darkness of the spare room with Nathan vies for space within the chaos of his mind. Mary is as real to him now as she ever was, and he embraces the situation for what it is. He understands that he is experiencing every sense of madness.

"Did you love me?" he asks.

"Yes, and our marriage was everything I wanted. I was not disappointed. I'm sorry if you were."

"At the time I thought it was fine, but now I question it. And why didn't you let me take care of you?"

"You are my husband, not my doctor Joe."

"I'm sorry I was not there to hold your hand when you passed."

"I'm not. Dying was something I would do on my own."

"You were always so independent."

"Still am," she corrects him.

"Yes."

"Why torment me if you were okay with everything?"

"Listen," she says. "Listen… It's all in your head, Joe. All in your head."

There is so much already that he has forgotten. The distance of death has already robbed him of the memory of her voice. Only now does he recall the soft way she rolls her r's, the way she expresses certain words with hand movements. She calls him Joe, the only person ever to do so. He will never be Joe to anyone else, and there is a desperate grief wedded to the realisation.

"I want only to be someone you miss," she says, and in his head the words mix and merge with the sound of his sobbing.

"This is it, isn't it?"

"Yes."

He closes his eyes to ward off the sting of tears. When he opens them Mary is gone. He knows this time the loss is permanent.

"Just so you know, you will always be someone I miss," he says, giving the words life, needing to hear her last wish fill the emptiness.

Chapter 37

A second picture now adorns the stairwell. Nathan nervously tells Joseph, "Dinnae be mad."

"Then stop doing things to make me mad," Joseph says, his tone balanced. It is the only blip in an ocean of calm. The stormy past has been laid to rest, and the future a promise of prosaic quiet.

The new artwork has a simplicity to it that Nathan's previous pieces have not revealed. Pencilled onto the wall, using just twelve lines—Joseph has taken the time to count them—is now a wispy image of Mary. She stands in sunlight cast by the overlarge living room window as it hits that patch of wall perfectly. She looks out across the garden. As the light fades, so does her image, but Joseph knowing that, with enough sunlight, she will be back is no longer tormented. Now she is a true work of art. Finally, she is still.

"Am I to expect more of the same? Perhaps a drawing of you? Intentionally placed between these two?" Joseph asks, wagging his finger at each of the portraits as he speaks.

"Na."

Turning away from the artwork, intrigued by Nathan's offhand answer, Joseph asks, "How no?" He lets his vocabulary slide a little, exposing a new, relaxed version of himself.

"Ah cannae gie the eyes reit. My eyes are weird."

"Yes," Joseph says. "It's your eyes, that's what's weird about you."

At the first ring of the doorbell, Nathan says, "Hide." The sloppy half grin on his face a poor attempt at covering real concern. Descending into domestic bliss has not encouraged either of them to be more sociable. Their life together is simple, and Joseph is protective of this, making sure that work takes second place to downtime. Their jobs less of a priority than leisure—and each other. Daily employment no longer the thing that defines either of them.

The weeks after Mary's final parting have been an aching mix of pleasant and painful moments. Now Joseph dares to believe that they are done with death and drama and that only good times lie ahead. Nathan knows better, and for him, the still unknown visitor on the doorstep is confirmation of more disruption.

"You're a coward," Joseph tells him, sure that nothing can spoil this upturn in events.

"You just dinnae learn," Nathan says, and Joseph, smiling to himself as he opens the front door, is frustrated and amused by Nathan's expectation of doom.

Standing on the doorstep, blocking out any other view, is a man who looks familiar. But for the briefest of moments, context and distance and time conspire and Joseph can't quite place him. He stands several inches shorter than Joseph, his head bald save for a steel grey line of hair running from ear to ear. The dome is burnt dry and red.

"I hate your road," he says. The voice jolts Joseph's memory. "Kenneth!"

There is a moment of awkwardness as Joseph's brother goes to hug him and, unprepared, Joseph first recoils and then accepts the physical contact. Joseph can see a van parked in his driveway and an assortment of people unpack.

"Mum and Dad are here?"

As he says the words, Joseph hears the disbelief in his own voice, and he hopes that his brother will think it's due to excitement rather than panic.

"And Meg and the kids. We all made the trip."

Since ending the call with his father, there has only been one further conversation. Joseph and his brother made small talk without feeling the need to issue further insults. That one call carefully measured, brief but not rude, civil, trite, and succinct. Interestingly Joseph has heard nothing from his father, and he's been fine with the shun.

Now, he is here, and the weight of his father's frailty hits Joseph. He is bent slightly over, his face tanned, the bronzed skin hiding deep lines etched into a hangdog expression.

There was a time not so long ago, somewhere before the storm, Mary's carry-on, and Nathan's arrival when Joseph had longed for his family to visit, longed for their attention. He had hoped that their intervention would stabilise him somehow, bring normality back to his life. Now he recoils at the thought of such an intrusion, *this* intrusion.

"Can we come in?"

Joseph remains in the doorway, blocking the entrance. Embarrassed now at having to be coaxed by his brother to be a good host, he covers his anxiousness with laughter.

"Yes, come in, come in, of course," he says, but all the while the voice inside his head is screaming, "No. Go away! Leave us alone!"

As his father comes closer, he holds out his hand for a formal handshake. Is that how he intends to greet his youngest son after all this time? But copying his brother, Joseph steps into the handshake, hugs his father, and then kisses his cheek. He smells the same, and there is something reassuring in that. The memory of childhood, of their family home, is there ingrained into the scent of his father. Still within the embrace, Joseph whispers into his neck. "It's good to see you."

Moving back from the hug and looking over his father's shoulder, Joseph cannot help but notice that his mother is standing off to the side. She is looking at the garden and not at Joseph, and the lack of eye contact and being surrounded as she is by family members ensures neither of them have to stage any intimate greeting. At least, Joseph thinks, not yet.

Nathan hovers in the hallway, and then as more people file in, disappears into the living room.

"Who's that?" A little girl with a mass of dirty blonde hair pulled into an untidy ponytail, standing belt high to Joseph, hands on hips, asks the question. Joseph bends, putting his hands on his knees to make it easier to hold himself in place and make eye contact.

"More to the point: who are you?" he asks, hoping his question will distract the group because he needs time to think on an answer. How should Nathan be introduced?

"I'm Harper, Uncle Joseph. You know that," she says.

Joseph smiles, puts out his hand to the child, and they shake. "Well, Harper, how lovely to meet you finally. And how old are you now?"

"I'm eight. I had my birthday before and I won't have another one until later. We're on holiday. I should be in school."

The child prattles on, use to the adults in her life valuing what she says. Then, without warning, she takes off and runs down the hallway to stand in front of the pictures on the wall.

"That's naughty. You're not allowed to draw on walls. Did you do this, Uncle Joseph?"

"No."

"Did you draw this one?"

"No."

"Who did? Did you tell them off?"

None of the adults silence her. The parents, it seems to Joseph, aren't interested in doing the parenting thing and telling their daughter to be quiet. Joseph, irked with the little girl's chatter, ignores her questions and turns his attention to the rest of the group.

"Please come into the living room and have a seat. I'll organise drinks. What does everyone want?"

The family, all filing together into the one room, block the doorway, trapping Nathan. Standing in the living room looking like a cornered animal, his eyes flicker wildly about. Joseph's mother stands sandwiched between her son and daughter-in-law, who is struggling with a tired, restless baby. They still present a handy barrier that Joseph is unwilling to subvert. There is a history that he will not gloss over just because his mother is old, and he imagines she will not attempt any loving gestures towards her youngest either. It has, and never will be, he knows, part of her mothering tool kit.

"I can't believe this. I can't believe you're all actually here." The words are rushed, said as Joseph bends to tidy Nathan's drawings and books from the floor and coffee table. He moves shoes from where they are tucked under the side table. He is painfully aware that the house, whilst not dirty, falls a long way short of Mary's standard of orderly. Papers that are not gathered secure in his arms fall and, like autumn leaves, lazily glide to the floor. The pencilled outline of a naked woman, visible now against the deeper grey of the slate tiles face-up, goads a response.

"That's rude," the little girl says, and Joseph has the very real feeling that he is not going to take to this kid.

"Who are you?" she says again to Nathan, who looks to Joseph for help, and a way out. Then, wrapping her arms around Nathan's legs, she looks up at him.

"Take these into the office so we can clear more space here," Joseph says, passing papers and books to Nathan. It is, he hopes, a way of freeing him from the little girl's hold, but nobody tells the child to let go of him. Taking it upon himself, Joseph pries them apart, and then steering Nathan towards the door, he follows him out.

They stand in Joseph's office facing each other, still with armfuls of papers, both unable to find words. Finally, Joseph suggests in a whispered tone full of conspiracy, "Perhaps you should get out of here for a while."

"Where are they staying? Not here?" Nathan's speech stumbles back in time. Joseph has not heard this stuttering, breathy voice in a while, and he is annoyed. This is how his family will see Nathan, as a stammering eejit. He is tempted to shake him and tell him to sort himself out, but the opportunity is missed. Not realising that they have been followed, he is interrupted by the little girl.

"We're staying at the Loch Ness Lodges." She pronounces it "lock" instead of loch, and they both look down at her at the same time.

"How long are they gonnae stay?" Nathan asks, and his question, whilst directed at Joseph, is again answered by the child.

"Three weeks."

Nathan groans and stretches his face out, a clear sign that he is not happy. Joseph feels the first stirrings of anger at the inconvenience and unfairness of it all.

"It will be fine," he says, but there is something in the word "fine" that feels phoney and deceitful. Taking the little girl's hand, he says, "Come, help me get drinks."

"I don't want to," she says. "I want to stay with him." She points at Nathan.

Nodding his head towards the door, Joseph silently tells Nathan to leave while he has the chance. He keeps a firm hold of Harper until he is sure Nathan has gone. Sticky little fingers curl in against his. For a moment the child is silent, and then she says, "You're funny, Uncle Joseph," and she squeezes her hand tightly in his.

They want tea, but neither Joseph nor Nathan drink tea. Mary did occasionally, and so he is sure that there will be some somewhere. Her belongings are still scattered about the house, so why not her teabags?

He finds the tea set, and he rinses matching cups of dust while waiting for the kettle to boil. There is a morgue-like silence in the living room.

"I'm a bit all over the place," Joseph says when he enters, putting down the tray and going back for the teapot. "It's been a while since I've had visitors." The statement is met with more silence, and needing to fill it he adds, "This is great... this is really great."

It is his mother's voice that unexpectedly breaks into the silence. "Isn't that cold in the winter?" she asks, nodding towards the wall of glass.

"No. We... I... There's under-floor heating and the open fire. The house is very warm."

"I'm bored," the little girl says. "When are we going to the park, Granddad?"

"I don't understand," his mother says. "What's the point of it?"

"Point?" Joseph repeats as he looks towards the window. "No point. We just wanted to appreciate the view."

"I'm bored," the child says again, and she pushes herself in between her grandfather's legs, bends her head back, and they share a smile. Joseph, having no memories left of such intimacy himself, feels the instant burn of jealousy.

"We are here to see Uncle Joseph, and we've come a long way to visit. Be good. We can go to the park later," he says.

"Promise?"

"I promise."

Joseph watches as his father bends his head and kisses the little girl's forehead.

He cannot remember there being this many people in his living room before. His mother, sitting with her coat pulled about her chest and hunched forward, stares at the window. Her hair is now dark grey with no hint of the colour that it once was. She looks frail, tired, and cold. She has not aged well. He wants to say something meaningful, worthy of the moment to her. But over-thinking things, instead he settles on a tedious exchange of points regarding her preferences for strong tea, one sugar, and a dash of milk.

"Builder's tea," Joseph says, laughing at his own words. She juggles her handbag and the cup and smiles politely, then looks back at the wall of glass.

Joseph's father says, "It's good to see Joseph again after so long, isn't it?" The question confuses her more than it should.

Frowning, she turns to look at Joseph and says, "This is good tea, strong and hot." Having stepped away from each other's lives for twenty years, they are now strangers to each other.

After making sure that they all have drinks, Joseph takes a seat himself, smiles, and runs damp palms up and down the material of his trousers. He is nervous. He does not know what to say that will not sound trite.

"Have we come at a bad time?" Kenneth's wife asks. She is prettier than Joseph expected, with the same dirty blonde hair as her daughter, long and tied back in a ponytail that is a little neater. Joseph wonders what she sees in his brother. She is not how he'd pictured her, and he wonders what she makes of him. The baby still fusses in her lap, stubby arms and legs flailing about wanting to be anywhere other than where he sits.

"No... no," Joseph says, in answer to her question.

"Only your friend has left. Will he be back in a bit? I told Kenneth that he should phone and let you know we were coming, but he wanted to surprise you."

"It's fine. We were on our way out, but it's fine. Nathan's got things to do, and so he's just away now on his own to sort them. He's fine," Joseph says again, and he wonders how many times he can use the same word in one sentence.

"We can meet him later," Kenneth says, smiling down at the ground and not at Joseph.

Kenneth experienced fatherhood late, Harper being born when he was already fifty. His wife is young, still not thirty. The baby on her lap makes it clear he wants to be down on the floor, and relenting, she places him down so he stands between her legs and she straightens his clothes. This is the way it is, Joseph thinks: the children dictate to the adults. The baby waddles away from her, stands in front of Joseph, points at him and then babbles.

"Does he remind you of anyone?" Kenneth asks.

It's a baby, Joseph thinks. It is like every other baby, only this one seems to have a rather large head that Joseph hopes it will eventually grow into. He keeps his opinions to himself.

"We think you're cut from the same cloth," Kenneth says.

Joseph frowns at his brother. "What?"

"Miserable wee shit. We think he's the living likeness of you when you were a bairn."

Kenneth's wife scolds him in defence of her son. "He has a cold," she says. It has not escaped Joseph's notice that this is a particularly snotty child. Kenneth has yet to interact with his offspring, which is how Joseph remembers his own childhood.

This, he thinks, is our inheritance, our family tradition: ignore, reject, and criticise.

Kenneth's son is just learning to walk. He ambles about, wiping drool-encrusted fingers on Joseph's soft furnishings and woodwork. The mother smiles lovingly while Joseph tries to see traces of himself in the boy, but a baby is a baby and there is nothing about this one that stirs his heart.

"So, Harper tells me you're staying for three weeks," he says, pushing for clarification on what the visit will entail.

"Not all of it here, so don't get too excited. We're away to Aberdeen for two days, then Edinburgh and on to London. Meg has friends and family there."

"That's nice. You'll get to see a bit of Scotland, and… the weather's good."

Joseph lets his brother critique the weather. He compares it to the weather back home, suggesting that what they are currently experiencing is not good.

"This is not warm," he says. "If you want to experience warm, then you need to…"

Two minutes into his brother's address, Joseph interrupts. "Why are you here?"

The question is rude, blunt and direct, but he is already tired of the negativity, the painful silences and the uninvited intrusion into his life.

"Mum and Dad have been talking about a visit for a while now. They have friends and family they want to see, and… well nobody's getting any younger. The timing just seemed right." Kenneth gives a sideways glance at his mother as he speaks. She plays with the teacup, seemingly oblivious to the discussion going on around her.

It does not go unnoticed by Joseph that he is not on the list of reasons given for the visits in his own right, but sits lumped in with the rest as "family."

Chapter 38

Joseph walks them out to the people carrier; their collective footsteps crunch gravel. The visit has been mercifully brief. Kenneth explains, "Travelling has taken it out of us. This is just a quick visit to let you know we're here. Your house is nice enough," his brother says, "but I hate that road."

"Take it slow and you'll be fine," Joseph tells him.

The door to the garage is open, the two cars on show inside.

"I suppose if you drive those, then it's nae bother. But I can't understand why anyone would want to live all the way out here," he says.

They can still salvaged the day, Joseph thinks, if he can find Nathan; and they leave now, then they can go someplace and Joseph can spoil him. He watches his brother make a mess of turning the car in the driveway. Leaning out the window, he is more interested in confirming Joseph's attendance at dinner the following evening than minding the shrubs and one tyre cuts a scar into the edge of the lawn. Joseph will agree to anything just to see them gone. The van bumps its way down the track. His mother sits in the back, squashed between a baby seat and Meg and still clutching her handbag. He thinks that she must be very uncomfortable.

Seconds after they pull out of the driveway, Nathan skids in on his bike, adding to the dust that has been thrown up. Joseph, looking up at the house, says, "We may have to move."

"Why?"

"I rid myself of one ghost and more follow in behind."

"It's terrible tae be so haunted."

"Aye."

"Your life is like the Balbeg bumps, Joseph," Nathan tells him. "All the ups and downs are fun, and then… not so much fun." Joseph notes that the day is jammed with reminders of the past, of childhood, good times and bad. He too rode his bike over the bumps as a lad.

"Where were you?"

Joseph knows Nathan could not have been far away to have known the very moment that his family had left and to return promptly. He must have been nearby and watching the house or road.

"Drinking tea with Lillian."

"Who's Lillian?"

"The neighbour."

"Her name's Lillian?"

"Aye."

"I didn't know you like tea."

"Ah didnae either."

They make it as far as the pub. Joseph watches Lachlan as he helps by collecting empties from the tables. A shinty match has just finished, and both teams are in. Sweaty male bodies talk over each other and jostle for position and space. The atmosphere is charged, the noise just bearable. Nathan seems to know everyone, and he is laughing and smiling, recovered now from any earlier trauma.

"So why are they here?" George asks.

"To visit family and friends before it's too late."

"And they all came!"

"Aye."

"Gonnae be a hellish couple ay weeks."

Joseph laughs, considers George's assessment, studies the glass he holds in his hand looking for answers, then looking back at George, he asks, "Do you remember cycling the Balbeg bumps?"

"Sure. Everyone does the bumps. Why?"

"What are we talking about?" Lachlan asks, placing eight dirty glasses on the bar as he interrupts the conversation.

"Ah'm not sure. The Balbeg bumps, Ah think," George says. Taking the dirty glasses from Lachlan, he looks to Joseph for clarification.

"Do you remember how it felt," Joseph asks, "to pedal so fast and so hard, the fear of coming off, but the exhilaration of speed, losing your stomach and the ground each time you went over the bumps and then hitting the tarmac and trying yer damnedest tae stay on? Knowing that, if you came aff, it was gonnae tae hurt like hell."

"Nae helmet in those days." Lachlan adds.

"Ah still have scars from sliding along the road oan my arse cheeks," George says.

"How old were we then?" Joseph asks.

Lachlan thinks on the answer for a bit before saying, "Thirteen, fourteen mebbe. We were doing the bumps because we waurnae daeing girls."

"Speak for yoursell," George says. Then he asks, "What made you think aboot the bumps?"

"Nathan. He said my life is like riding the bumps. And it made me think about back then when things seemed easy, straightforward." Joseph studies the glass in his hand once more as he speaks, holding it up to the light he swirls the liquid about a little.

"Your memory's playing tricks. It was never easy or straightforward. Back then, it was parents, school, girls, plooks—you name it," George says, and taking the near empty glass from Joseph, he refills it.

"Ah would rather that than ex-wives, divorce lawyers, mortgage payments, and taxes," Lachlan says, giving a summation of his current situation.

Nathan, squeezing himself in between Joseph and Lachlan says, "Ah think Ah'm on the shinty team." His wild blond hair sticks out at all angles, and his normally whitewashed complexion is now pink with excitement.

"Which one?" Lachlan asks.

"Ah dinnae ken."

"You joined a team but you don't know which one?"

"Aye."

George shakes his head at the boy, but smiling says, "We'll sort it," and puts a drink down in front of him and Lachlan. Joseph takes several mouthfuls of his own drink, then turning his attention back to the glass, moves the liquid in circles, watching it roll in waves up the sides. The froth of white horses sticks and then, in its own time, slides back down to become part of the whole again.

"I want to do the bumps one more time before I'm too old," he says.

The unforeseen family reunion, seeing what the years of being apart and the passing of time have done, makes him grieve for the past and for his childhood. He has been reminded of a time when he was not afraid to try and fail. He recollects the many times that the bumps won and he lost, important bits of skin and his pride had taken a bashing. He remembers being teased and ending up the butt of other boys' jokes but being able to brush it off, laugh about it even. The bumps now represent escape, risk taking, a chance of a do-over. The opportunity to try, win or fail. What has been lost, he thinks, might be rediscovered in one carefree folly shared with old friends, and one new one.

"Ah you sure you're nae already?" Lachlan asks. He more than anyone carries his age about him. It causes Joseph to reflect, not just on what Talia sees in Lachlan, who is almost twice her age, but on what Nathan sees in him. He wonders why Nathan would see anything in him. He longs for his youth, but not just in a conceited way. It is no longer just about looking younger but he wants to feel and act it. There is also a deep desire now to shrug off all past adult restraints and responsibility and be carefree, childish. The Balbeg bumps, he believes, are the answer.

"I think we're in danger of becoming old before our time," Joseph tells the group.

"Ah agree," George says, and then pointing at Lachlan, he adds, "and you should want tae stay in good shape for as long as you can."

"Why?"

"Talia. Do you think she's gonnae want an auld man hanging ower her?"

"Love isnae that blind," Nathan says, and Lachlan gives him a gentle swipe to the back of the head for his cheek.

"Think about it," Lachlan says. "First of all you have tae ride up there, then dae the bumps, then you have tae git hame efter. At fourteen, okay, do-able, but the wrong side of forty? Ah Dina think so."

"We have something now that we didnae have back then," Joseph says.

"High blood pressure? Heart disease? Piles? Diabetes?" Lachlan suggests before George interrupts him.

"You have piles?"

"Cars," Joseph says, silencing them both. "We can drive up there with the bikes in the back of our cars, do the bumps, and drive home."

"It's a plan," George concedes.

And Joseph, smiling now as he finishes his drink, relishes the satisfaction of having a plan. This desperate, and probably misguided, attempt to relive better times, do something that is childish and fun, meaningful and scary one more time, excites him. He can picture how the landscape will look in the early morning light, perhaps the verges drying out from a night of light rain and the smell of damp soil mixing with the smell of fermenting mash coming from the distillery.

Nathan is not excluded – he has just not been formally invited to the first of what Joseph imagines will be many family meals. It is Joseph's decision to leave him behind. A day that has dragged now tumbles forward, and Joseph is running late. Nathan walks him to the door. He seems alright about not attending the meal but is less fine with being left alone in the house.

"Don't make a mess."

"Ah willnea."

"I will not be long."

"Ah'm a bit creeped out cos its dark."

"She's gone. She was never here. Just keep the door to that room closed and you'll be fine."

"Aye, awerite."

He is about to leave, but then Joseph thinks of something else. "Where's the bible?"

"Upstairs."

"Go and get it, please."

"Why?"

"Go, now. I'm pushed for time."

Nathan obediently takes the stairs two at a time and can be heard running along the upstairs landing in his stockinged feet to get the book. He is more careful on the way down, the memory of his sprained ankle still raw.

"Put your hand on the cover," Joseph tells him, and the boy does as he's told.

"Swear on the bible that you will not draw on any more of my walls."

Nathan laughs, bows his head, and hunches his shoulders up. "Ah swear Ah will nae draw any pictures oan any of yer walls."

"I won't be long," Joseph tells him as he closes the front door. He hates to leave, hates this unwelcome intrusion into their lives; and having already come through so much, he wonders how much more they can endure.

The drive to the lodge is marred by Joseph's ongoing resentment at having to spend time with his family and not with Nathan. He reasons that he has the rest of his life to spend with Nathan and that this will probably be the last time he sees his parents. That means this time with them should matter more but it doesn't and the resentment has not abated any by the time he parks the car.

The lodge is dated, the linens, décor, and the menu all in need of a serious revamp. Joseph hopes he can use the get-together as an opportunity to reconnect with his estranged family before it's too late. But when he pictured this in his mind as he walked to the door, the setting was much nicer, his family more welcoming, the food more palatable—and somebody else paid the bill.

Kenneth's wife, Meg, has the crying baby in her arms. She is struggling with the infant whilst trying to pull a high-chair out from the table and unfold a puzzle of assorted plastic and wooden parts held together in an impossible contortion of alphabet printed webbing. Joseph offers his help, because nobody else seems inclined to, and is handed the baby. His intention was to deal with the chair. The baby is silenced by this change in events.

"He's still out of sorts," Meg tells him.

Joseph jiggles the child in his arms, pats his back and makes what he hopes are soothing noises. The child coughs in his face.

"Don't drop him," Kenneth says. "We're kind of fond of him now." He thinks he is funny. Joseph has chosen to disremember this trait about his brother, but he is now reminded of a childhood choked with ribbing, teasing, and what would probably be considered bullying now.

"I won't. I know what I'm daein," Joseph says, sounding more confident than he looks.

"I just love your accent," Meg says, and Joseph laughs at the reminder that he has one.

"Watch yursell," Kenneth tells him. "That's how I snagged her."

The meal passes well enough, the conversation lopes from who has died to what buildings have been pulled down and replaced to who has reproduced and with whom. The children predictably get bored and tired and are taken by their mother to bed. Joseph's mother excuses herself at the same time.

"Ah'm tired from all the travelling. Ah think Ah'm still feeling the effects from the journey," she says, and Joseph watches her leave. During the meal, he's noticed her hold her own when recalling the past: reminiscing seems to come easy to her. But he's also watched as his father gently reminds her to eat, encouraging her to finish her meal and to drink up. In the present she appears confused distracted and lost. They may, Joseph thinks, have left the visit too late after all.

Joseph would like to leave at the same time as his mother for a different tiredness hangs about the group and the conversation is hard going. They finish discussing businesses that have closed down and new ones that have opened in their place, and then the silence clogs the space left by the words. It is not a good or comfortable silence, not the sort that old friends can settle into without the need to fill. Finally, Joseph says, "If we're done, I'm heading home."

He has mulled over the words, and whilst they feel right, he leaves the lodge, his family, and the conversation with the very real sense he is leaving something very important that should have been said, but wasn't, behind.

The house is lit up like an airport, and Joseph can hear the backbeat of loud music as he parks the car. Nathan's trousers are in the hallway and his sweatshirt hangs from the banister. Joseph finds him naked save for a baggy pair of underpants; he pirouettes about the living room. With the main lights and the table lights on, the room is awash with crazy shadows from the boy's peppy dancing. He's found a different way to beautify the walls. Aware of Joseph's return, he dances now to his audience of one. The shapes change as their silhouettes combine in shadowy sameness.

"How was it?" Nathan asks, and Joseph has the perfect word ready.

"Fine," he says, and he runs his fingers lightly across the boy's taut stomach. He can feel the butterflies of delight and anticipation under his hand. He folds him in close so that their bodies touch, two-stepping him up the hallway and back. Neither cares that they are slightly adrift of the music.

"Proper dancing," Joseph says, and Nathan laughs, delighted with the intimacy, the movement, and the rhythm. They cast shadows, the same shadows as always, but how can that be when Joseph knows he is changed? There, on the walls of his home, beautiful distortions twist and turn in time to the music.

Unlike Nathan, Joseph is never comfortable naked. In the morning, he will go from the bed to the bathroom and the bathroom back to the bedroom, where he dresses, but that is his limit. Twice he has been downstairs naked, once when alone and unable to sleep and once in the grip of madness, searching for Mary in the darkness. But Nathan is undressing him, the buttons on his shirt, his belt, pulling at the material of his shirt so it comes free from the waistband of his trousers.

"Don't," Joseph says, placing his hands over Nathan's stopping him. "I'm not comfortable with this… with being naked."

"How no?"

"I'm not… not beautiful like you."

"Ah will draw another picture of you, a naked one, and then you'll see."

"No, never. I'll make you swear on the bible. Where is it?"

Nathan's eyes dart to where the book is lying on the side table.

"Ah'm a particular favourite of our Lord's. Ah will swear if you want, but he'll forgive me anything," Nathan tells him.

"The Lord might but Ah willnae. No more pictures, nae oan the walls. And no naked ones anywhere."

He hears it. Being around his family, fighting against their butchered accents, is slurring Joseph's words into a more natural pattern of speech. It's that, he thinks, and possibly Meg's gentle claim to liking it.

Chapter 39

Four times Joseph has dined with them now, four times at the same place, and four times he has had to pick up the bill. He knows the menu well enough now to know there is nothing on it that will not play hell with his insides tomorrow. Each time the conversation returns to the past, a safe subject and the only subject they share, but with every meeting there is less and less to reminisce about, and so the conversation circles. They eat early because of the kids, and Joseph, having come straight from work, is late.

Joseph's last patient of the day was difficult, one of the many "worried well" who frequent his office, concerned that his feelings of being "not quite right" are a symptom of something terminal. The consultation was hard work. Joseph had asked, "Is the problem sleeping, eating, nausea? Do you have a sore throat, any pain, constipated, stressed, dizzy, over-working?" The list had gone on, a no answer to every possible cause.

It's muggy. Joseph runs a finger around the collar of his shirt. The material sticks to his back, and he would like to remove his tie, but he won't. His father is predicting rain and, almost gleeful at the thought of bad weather, his brother nods. Sprawled in the chair, his body language says, "I told you so."

Now alone, just the three of them, the children, his mother and Meg having already gone to bed, Kenneth explains that it has been a long day. They've done a lot of walking, he says, and everyone is tired. In between the long stretches of silence, Joseph wishes his brother had phoned and cancelled. Once more the conversation circles, the topics still safe. But after four attempts at this, there is little left to say. Like the talk Joseph had with his last patient, there is the sense that something more is waiting to be uncovered. Unlike that meeting though, the point here is lost intentionally, hidden and tucked away between banalities, waffle, and guff. Alcohol would help with Joseph's uneasiness, but driving means it's not an option. As Joseph refills his glass with water, Kenneth points out that remaining sober is, "The downside to living so far out the way. Will you move?" he asks.

"No." Joseph says. "Why?"

"Stuck out there on your own…"

"I'm not on my own." The words are out before Joseph realises they have ambushed him, the safe topics of conversation setting a trap that has just been sprung.

"Ah yes, the boy."

Kenneth glances at his father, and the older man nods his encouragement, apparently wanting him to pursue this line of enquiry.

"We thought we might have seen more of him by now."

"Why?"

"Why not? Are you ashamed of him, or maybe of us? Or perhaps…"

"I'm not ashamed. I just thought… I thought it was me that you came all this way to see and spend time with. Am I wrong?"

"No. We have spent time with you," Kenneth says, and he sits back in his chair, placing his fingers together in a steeple, thinking perhaps about the little that has been said so far. "Joseph," he says, after a long pause. "What is this boy to you?"

"His name is Nathan," Joseph says, the first bite of anger clear in the clipped tone of his voice.

"Don't be difficult," his father says, and his words are soft in quality but cutting in delivery, and stir Joseph's resentment further.

"Difficult?" Joseph questions.

Kenneth, perhaps sensing they are digressing, waves his hand about in front of Joseph's face. "I apologise," he says, and then correcting himself, he pursues the question further. "Nathan, what is Nathan to you?"

There is mischief in Kenneth's words. He would never normally apologise, not to Joseph.

"Why the interest? Does it matter who or what he is," Joseph asks.

"Are you homosexual?"

Joseph is looking at Kenneth, who has taken the lead in questioning him so far, but it is his father who asks the question.

"I think the correct term is bisexual," Kenneth says, still looking at Joseph even though he is addressing their father. "Because clearly he likes both," he adds.

"We haven't established that yet," Joseph's father says.

"The correct term is mind your own fucking business," Joseph barks, and half rising in his chair, he's thinking about storming out.

"Joseph, I love you. I have to. You're my brother. But sometimes, mate, you make it real hard to like you. Real hard," Kenneth says.

His father adds, "Sit down," and bizarrely, Joseph does as he's told.

"Does any of this matter?" Joseph then asks, and unable now to look at his father, he fixes his attention on his brother.

"Yes, it matters. I've always thought there was a falseness about you that doesn't fit with your compliance… and the nauseating conformity. Could this be the reason?"

Kenneth, enjoying himself, relaxes, and easing back into his chair, he smiles calmly at Joseph, taking his time over his words. Joseph, in contrast, hunches forward, still ready to leave his seat and the room at any moment.

"It would be nice," Kenneth says, sipping his drink between pauses, "to meet the real you."

"We never felt you suited Mary. I mean she was nice, just… Well, you never seemed…happy… never yourself," Joseph's father says, and he places his hand flat against Joseph's shoulder, pushing him back into his seat.

"I love… loved my wife."

"Right, but what about the boy… Nathan. What is Nathan to you?" he asks.

The conversation has circled.

"This puts me in mind of a patient I was with today just before I left to come here. He couldn't quite put his finger on what was wrong, but he knew that something was not right. There's a long family history of… problems. I think he feels he has to have *something* wrong with him."

"Did you get to the bottom of it?" Kenneth asks.

"No."

"Perhaps you didn't pursue the right course of questioning," his father suggests.

On the defensive once more, Joseph says, "I asked all the right questions." And turning to address his father, he adds, "The timing was wrong, that's all. So I've arranged to revisit the issue at another time."

"Are you suggesting that's what we should do here? Revisit this some other time?" his father asks.

"Yes," Joseph says.

"No," Kenneth says, and he is more emphatic than Joseph or his father. "It's a straightforward and simple question," he adds, clarifying his insistence.

"I don't see what the problem is either," his father offers, encouraged by Kenneth's persistence. Like a tag team, Joseph thinks, they are ganging up on him. Sitting further back in his chair and stretching out his legs to relax a little, Joseph directs his attention once more to his brother.

"I've been spending a lot of time since you arrived thinking about our childhood. How are you enjoying being a family man? Do you think you're suited to it?"

"Don't change the subject. Or is parenting the subject?" Kenneth asks.

"I don't have to answer your questions. I can leave."

Kenneth's face twists into a half grin. "But you won't. Are you attempting to parent Nathan? Is that what you mean?"

Joseph laughs, finding his brother's assessment genuinely amusing. "No, I'm not a substitute father figure."

"Then what?"

Joseph plays with the silence again, which allows his father to flank the question with one of his own,

"Does he make you happy?"

The question is unexpected, but Joseph hears no underlying judgement attached to it, no accusations hidden or otherwise. That fact relaxes him, and thinking on the question, he smiles and nods to himself before he answers.

"Nathan? Yes, he makes me happy."

"And?" his father says, pushing for more.

"I'm with Nathan," Joseph says. It is not the straightforward, honest answer that anyone at the table wants. Joseph is hoping to give only enough of an answer so that the issue will be dropped. He watches his father's face carefully, looking for a reaction.

"Now, Joseph," the old man says, "was that really so hard."

Joseph raps the table loudly with both hands, causing the few other diners still left in the place to turn, puzzled by the interruption. Laughing now, he stares his father down.

"Do you disapprove? Am I a disappointment to you?"

"If you have a sense of anything like that, then those feelings are coming from within you. Don't lay them on your brother or me."

"I lost my wife, and it was the single most heartbreaking thing that I thought could happen. I love her... loved her, not perhaps as I should have, but we had a life together and there was something safe in that. And now... now I have Nathan."

"So, what you're saying is grief turned you gay," Kenneth says, laughing at his own joke and Joseph's attempt at a deep and meaningful explanation. Then he adds, "Bollocks to that. Your whole life right up until this Nathan part was a lie, and the sad part is that you were lying to yerself."

"You can mourn the loss of something, even a lie... a beautiful safe, acceptable lie" Joseph tells him.

In the silence that follows, Joseph takes one more deep breath. His father is building up to something. "He makes you happy, that's what you said, and the details, the why and the wherefores, are of no never mind to me... to us. I've waited a long time to hear you say that. To hear it, see it, and believe it," he says, and sitting back in his seat, he nods first at Joseph, and then at Kenneth, and then once more to himself.

Joseph, his throat too dry to speak anyway, has no more words. And his internal voice the one that would normally proof his response, is too busy relaying over and over what is now the single most significant sentence he has ever heard. He wants to hear it said again, wants and needs to hear more, but his father is done.

Standing up from the table, he says, "Well now, it's late and I'm old, so I'm away to my bed."

Kenneth stands as well. Looking at his father and perhaps seeing something in the old man's face, he does not continue the conversation. Instead he says, "I'll walk with you. Good night, Joseph."

He practises his words in the car, getting them right for Nathan, saying out loud into the darkness everything that has so far gone unsaid. He uses his father's phrasing: the details, the why and the wherefores, are of no never mind to me. He likes the way it sounds. He likes it just as much now in his own voice as when his father had said it earlier. This he thinks, this is a precious memory that he has now laid down in his mind to recall from time to time and savour. He says, "I love you," out loud into the darkness of the car over and over, feeling validated. Stupid as it is, he realises that his father's response, although his approval was never wanted or sought, still holds much meaning and weight. He hopes that by using the same words Nathan will experience the same feelings and he will finally understand.

Only one light is on. After four evenings of this, Nathan is used to being in the house alone now. Scattered about the living room floor are fresh drawings of Joseph. Nathan has stopped short of sketching him naked, but some of the pictures leave little to the imagination.

"How are you?" Joseph asks him.

"No bad. Yer sell?"

"Aye. No bad."

Joseph slumps into a chair, unable to think of how to start such a meaningful conversation. The words have dried up, squandered perhaps in the darkness on the drive home and now he has nothing left.

"How was it?" Nathan asks.

"Wonderful."

"That's good. Ah was worried you were nae enjoying their visit."

"Do you see me as a father figure?"

"Lord, no. Amen."

Pulling himself out of the chair, feeling weighted now with regret for what has and hasn't been said and for all that still needs to be explained, Joseph pours a drink, hoping alcohol will loosen his tongue. He's keenly aware that Nathan is watching his every move.

"Dae you see me as your son or somehin then?"

"Hell, no."

"Amen."

Renewed embarrassment for what he has blabbed to his father and brother and what he has yet to say to Nathan dissolves the last remnants of the validation he felt earlier. The memory of his father's words are already losing their lustre, replaced now by the more usual feelings of inadequacy, regret and self-loathing. Once more Joseph feels ashamed, but now he has a new source of shame to add to the usual list—self-hatred. He hates his old self and there are parts of that person loitering in this new version tainting his joy. His old self lied, and worse he had believed and lived the lies. He lied about who and what he was and everyone had seen through it—everyone but Joseph. The ghost of that lie was there in his marriage. Mary might be gone but the lie has not.

Both might have felt abused, wounded by their fathers. Nathan's injuries are evident, whilst Joseph's own scars, left by a perceived emotional neglect, would always be the hardest to see or prove. The wounds for both nevertheless cut deep. Crushed by the realisation that he has expressed feelings for Nathan to those that do not matter but not to the boy himself, Joseph ponders his next move.

Chapter 40

As Joseph settles back in the chair, Nathan rummages in the drawers of the coffee table. In the past those drawers only held a small amount of loose change, the TV remote-control, and some spare batteries that may or may not be any good. Now Nathan has them crammed with rubbish.

"Do you know what makes me happy?" Joseph asks him, struggling still to find a way to connect and continue the conversation he has just walked away from with his father and brother.

"Ah havnae a fucking clue," Nathan says, concentrating more on continuing his search than on anything Joseph has to say. "Ah'm still trying tae work out what sends you mental," Nathan adds as he leaves one drawer and opens another.

"Leaving drawers open with stuff spilling out of them is one thing," Joseph tells him.

"Then dinnae move stuff so Ah cannae find it."

"I don't move stuff. I put stuff away. There's a difference. What are you doing anyway? What have you lost?"

"My bible pencils. I ken how to sort the problem wit my weird eyes. Ah jist need my bible pencils then Ah'm all set."

"I take it back. Your eyes aren't weird. I love your eyes."

"Yer such a girl sometimes, Joseph."

"Use the pencils on the floor."

"Ah cannae. They're nae the reit ones."

Scattered in amongst the many drawings that Nathan has produced whilst Joseph has been away are his new pencils. They are incredibly expensive. Nathan insisted that no other pencils would do. Now he is saying they are no good and he needs his old ones.

"Do you know what makes you happy?" Joseph asks him.

"Aye. And that makes me smarter than anyone else on this earth."

"What makes you happy?"

"Everything that makes me happy is reit here," Nathan says, but he does not indicate further what he means by "right here." He does not point or offer any clarification and his answer is too big for Joseph, too unwieldy for him to make sense of.

He says, "Explain." And then he adds, "Explain what you mean by everything's right here?"

Nathan sighs. Giving time to both the search and Joseph's questions requires energy that he does not have. The silence stretches, and Joseph considers filling it with suggestions of his own. Then Nathan says, "What? You want a list or somehin?"

"Yeah a list of the things that make you happy."

"Okay. Sleeping next tae you every night, waking up next tae you every morning, coming home tae you efter work, drawing, my faith—God. All that stuff makes me happy."

"I make you happy?"

"Aye, but not when you move my stuff."

"What do you like about me, Nathan? Say something nice."

"Found it," Nathan says, and to drive home his point, he holds up the stub of a thick black pencil. Doing a little victory dance, he says, "Yer'll need tae bring yer drink and follow me if yer want tae keep blathering."

Stretching over Joseph, he takes the bottle of whisky from the side table, then tucking one of the sofa cushions under his arm, he leaves the room. Turning on lights as he goes illuminating the hallway and spoiling the darkness. His thin summer shirt is open and flaps as he walks. His feet are bare and the top bottom of his worn jeans is undone with the zip slightly down. Standing, Joseph follows him into the hallway.

"Sit," Nathan says, and he points to the sofa cushion that is now on the floor up against the far wall. He has placed the bottle of whisky beside it.

"Why are we out here?" Joseph asks as he takes the seat.

"Ah tauld you, Ah ken how to fix the problem whit my eyes." As Nathan speaks, he moves to the other side of the hallway, and in the gap between the portraits of Mary and Joseph, he draws a thick dark black line onto the wall.

"Christ help us," Joseph says. "Holy fucking hell, Nathan, you promised, and you swore oan the bible as well."

"Amen, amen, amen, amen," Nathan says, and then using the side of the palm of his left hand, he smudges the black line further into the wall so that it leaves a horrible shadowy blemish. "What was the question again?" he asks. Then in answer to his own question, he says, "Oh aye, what dae Ah like about you. Ah like your hair," he says. Then he adds another dark black line above the first one.

"My hair?" Joseph questions. Given the state of his father and brother's heads, he is just happy to have hair on his head at all and the condition and style of it has never been a factor.

"Aye, and Ah like yer wobbly bits, the bits you try tae hide from me. And Ah like it when you go mental, when you get all out of sorts about something silly but then ignore the big stuff like sinkholes and viruses."

"We live on the side of a mountain so sinkholes are nae gonnae be a problem, and Ah've told you, wash your hands more often and you'll no get flu, any kind of flu. And Ah don't think destroying my walls is going mental about silly stuff."

"Want tae ken what Ah love about you?" Nathan asks as he turns for the first time to look back at Joseph. There are now a lot of marks on the wall, some are smudged, some are thick and black, and others are wispy fine grey smears. It has not occurred to Joseph that Nathan would see love and like as two different concepts.

"Okay," Joseph says, and he pours himself another drink.

"Ah love your breath, and Ah love yer age…"

"My age?"

"Yeah, it makes you interesting, and Ah love sex with you. Yer right. It's lots more fun with someone and nae oan yer own all the time. Ah love all that lovely Joseph-ness."

"God Lord."

"Amen."

"So everything I hate about mysell, that's what you like…"

"Like and love, there's a difference."

Nathan, the untouchable genius, is an artist in the midst of creating a masterpiece. His talent has freed him. As he talks, he draws. Lines merge, the summer shirt flaps with each new movement.

"Ah told them, my father and brother, that Ah'm with you," Joseph says. The words are rushed and slurred and said too loudly. The sound of them echoes inside his head.

"Because they asked or because you wanted tae."

"They asked… and asked and asked," Joseph says, fighting now to find the right pitch.

"Didnae kick the shit out of you, did they?"

"No, worse than that. They seemed awerite with it. Even made out they knew all along."

"Shit, that's terrible," Nathan says, and then laughing at his own forced sincerity, he drops to the floor to start on a different part of his masterpiece. Now that he is no longer blocking the view, Joseph can see hair that needs a cut flying out from the top of the portrait. There is still no face, but one arm stretches out with the fingers angled as if trying to reach the portrait of Joseph. The other arm extends in the other direction, reaching out to Mary. The portrait of Joseph, perfectly positioned as it is, smiles and looks to be about to stand and move away from the tree—it's as if one portrait wants to join the other. Mary, now able to manifest in the bright lights from the hallway, her face turned away, looks like she will at any minute notice what is happening further on down the wall. Joseph imagines her then turning slowly and touching the hand that is reaching out to her, Nathan's hand. Would she like Nathan? Joseph thinks she would. She would enjoy watching him dance and carry on, but she would not join in. Mary would stand at the side, content to just watch. Joseph is sure of this, but even so, he thinks, she would find something about Nathan "amusing."

The new portrait is still without features, but Joseph knows Nathan is in the grip of making his first self-portrait. The picture of Joseph is poised, Mary's is still, and Nathan's is a riot of movement and energy. Now adorning the wall not as a shadow but as a life-size version of himself, the boy is dancing. In every line of the drawing there is pace, in every smudge rhythm. The hips seem to sway, the fingers to waggle, and the feet feeling the beat are drawn ready for action.

"Dae yer think they're reit, that they did ken something was aff with you?"

"Kenneth described me as phoney and false."

"Harsh. Spot on, but still harsh."

"Nathan, when I go, will I be someone you miss?"

"Where you gonnae gae?"

"When Ah die."

For a moment Nathan's hand is still. He looks at the wall and then briefly at the floor, but not at Joseph. Fussing with a line, he rubs at it, fading the mark perfectly into the bigger picture, then he says, "Aye, of course. Ah would be devastated. But knowing that naethin lasts, that's what makes it mean so much. Losing Mary made you love her more. There's a lesson in that. Ah ken at some point Ah'm gonnae lose you, so Ah make the most of you now, no matter how much of a tit you are."

Leaning his head back, Joseph closes his eyes briefly, smiles, and then looking back at Nathan, he says, "Finish the picture."

The portrait of Nathan is in the throes of turning, perfecting a spin. One bare foot balances on tiptoes and the other is tucked into the calf of the opposite leg. Drawn true to life, the figure is wearing the same clothes as Nathan. The shirt flaps out at the sides, exposing a bare midriff and ribs. The material of the jeans clings at the thigh but bags out loosely at the feet. Joseph is impatient. He wants to see the face. How, he wonders, is it possible to see oneself clearly enough to draw a true likeness? Standing up, Nathan blocks the view again and Joseph thinks it's a tease. So using the cushion to slide, he scoots on his bum and moves further down the hallway. Careful to bring the whisky bottle with him, he is now side on to the drawing. He watches as Nathan smiles to himself, jiggles his hold on the pencil, and moves in closer to the picture. The face, breathtakingly beautiful, appears. The eyes look to the ground, so are mostly obscured. The lips are slightly parted, the head tilted at an angle, straining to hear the music from the other room. Joseph has danced with this version of Nathan many times, and now he has it forever captured in pencil in the hallway of a home, which is changed for the better.

It is finished. Nathan stands back to admire his work. "What dae yer think?"

"Ah think it's the best yet," Joseph says. And then, "Want tae dance?"

He knows, as he moves forward and stands, that he is mirroring the portrait of himself coming out of his camouflaged hiding place into the light. "Found at last," he thinks.

"Always." Nathan says, and he takes the glass from Joseph's hand, downs the contents, and shimmies away down the hall.

Chapter 41

On the bar in front of Joseph are four drinks, but the owners are scattered. Nathan and Talia are at the far end, feeding coins into the jukebox. The events of last night—Nathan and the new portrait on the wall, the dancing—have left Joseph wrestling with contradictions. A contented, confused disquiet has attached itself to his life.

"So, what's new?" George asks, and Joseph smiles at the question.

"Everything, and then at the same time, no much."

"Ah love those moments in life," George says, and Joseph smiles, appreciating the fact that George understands.

"Yeah, good times," he says.

"Your boy needs to raise his eyes," George says, and he has one eye on Nathan, who has both eyes on Talia, mostly her chest.

"Do you mind so much about Lachlan and her?" Joseph asks.

"No, because Ah'm wise tae the ways of love."

"Oh."

"Yer aff yer heid if yer think you have a choice in who tae fall in love with."

With his head bowed sideways, Joseph looks along the bar at the young pair. They are now dancing.

"That boy of yours sure loves tae move," George says.

"Aye."

Big and little Scott McPhee and Liam, whose surname, if Joseph ever knew it, he's forgotten, are playing pool. Seeing Talia and Nathan dancing, little Scott and Liam team up and copy their moves. Big Scott, without a dancing partner, uses his pool cue instead, and he skids and slides his way around the pool table. Behind the bar, George, liking what he sees, gets into some serious dad dancing of his own. Joseph won't leave his seat, but when Talia is sidetracked by Lachlan, he allows Nathan to stand behind him and put his hands into his. The boy grinds to the music.

"Have I walked into the musical version of yer life?" Kenneth asks as he takes the seat next to Joseph. Caught up in the action, Joseph had not seen him come in.

"What do you want?" he asks.

"A pint, ta very much," Kenneth says, choosing to ignore Joseph's rudeness and wrangle a drink instead.

George, ever the peacekeeper, places the requested drink in front of Kenneth, saying, "It's oan me. It's guid tae see you. It's been tae long."

"Aye," Kenneth says, and forgetting about Joseph for the moment, busies himself catching up with George.

Joseph watches as Nathan works his facial muscles into an expression of distrust. He remains standing just to the side. An uneasy feeling settles in the pit of his stomach as two parts of his life come together.

"Where shall we eat?" he says, wanting an out, and he turns to address Nathan, and only Nathan.

"Lets gae haem,"

"Haem!" Kenneth says. "Ah have jist got shot of the family for a wee while tae spend time with my wee brother and his pals. Dinnae gae hame."

"Where are they all?" Nathan asks, and Joseph is surprised that he would voluntarily interact with Kenneth.

"Shopping. My wife loves tae shop, and she's determined to buy every piece of tartan crap she can find. Lord knows how she thinks we're gonnae get it all back hame."

"Amen," Nathan says, and he is smiling at Kenneth as Lachlan and Talia join the group. Kenneth is then sidetracked again, catching up with Lachlan and expressing his disbelief at how Talia has changed. He is not shy in telling her how beautiful she is.

"Wheesht," she says. And then in a modest effort to get Kenneth to stop listing her attributes, she asks, "What's the plan fur tae-morrow?"

"Meet at six," Nathan says before Joseph can intercept the conversation and change the subject.

"In the a.m.?" George questions.

"Aye," Nathan says again, "there's nae much traffic that early."

"Aye, rite, and fur a reason," George says, he is not a morning person, and although he wants to be part of the outing, he would like it to be more on his terms.

"What's going on?" Kenneth asks, his nose getting the better of him.

"Nothing," Joseph says, and he stands, making clear he wants to leave. Nathan, ignoring the obvious signal, again answers the question.

"We're away tae dae the Balbeg bumps."

"Why?" Kenneth asks, and he turns fully around on his bar stool so he is addressing Nathan, and only Nathan, with the question, but it is George who answers.

"Because they're there and we still can... or we think we still can," he says.

"Ah'm in. Have you a bike Ah can borrow?"

This time Nathan answers. "Sure, you can borrow Mary's bike. She's deid so she willnae mind, will she?" The question is directed at Joseph, but it is rhetorical. "It's pink but that willnae bother you, rite?" he adds, and if Kenneth is surprised at the boy's blunt way of speaking about Joseph's wife, he hides it well.

"Pick me up at quarter tae … no ten tae. Ah'll stand outside and wait."

It has rained hard all night, and puddles trim the edges of the road. After much thought, Joseph has chosen golf trousers, hoping that they will not chafe as much as jeans. Transporting three bikes requires the fitting of the bike rack, which took most of the evening to achieve. He has been out cycling a couple of time with Nathan in preparation for today, but he insisted on flat ground and straight lines on these outings. Today was always going to be a challenge, but now there is the added inconvenience of Kenneth, and Joseph feels the first niggle of regret at having suggested such a foolish venture.

Kenneth, true to his word, is outside the lodge waiting. Joseph had been hoping that the enthusiasm of yesterday might have worn off at the sound of the alarm and he would be a no show.

"Should I get in the back?" Nathan asks as Joseph pulls the car to the curb.

"No. Stay where you are. He's fine in the back."

"Raining," Kenneth says as he struggles with the seat belt.

"Perfect," Joseph says.

"Aye, well it was this or drive our mother to Skye for the day, and Ah would rather do this any day ay the week. I tault her, mother I said, there is nothing in Skye, but she's insisting there's some wee tea shop over there she wants tae see. It's probably been closed down for ten years, but there's no telling her."

"You'll mebbe have time efter," Nathan offers, helpfully. "It's gonnae still be early."

"Nae chance. Ah tault them Ah was whit you all day."

"Lucky us," Joseph says, and Kenneth laughs off his brother's sarcasm.

Talia and Lachlan are organised and have already unpacked their bikes. Lachlan is wobbling slowly up and down the road adjusting gears and causing the chain to clank and slip.

"There's something wrang whit this bike. Just so you know. If Ah dinnae make it, it's because of the bike."

"There's nothing wrang with the bike," Talia tells him.

"Woman, am Ah tae expect nae support from you?" he snipes back, and then he smiles at her as he cycles past and she smiles back.

George and his bike are both still in the car, parked on the opposite side of the road. He is drinking coffee, trying to get his own gears working. Kenneth has his eye on Nathan's bike.

"Why can't I ride that one?" he asks.

"It's Nathan's," Joseph tells him.

"Where'd he get it?"

"He built it himself."

"Very good."

George stretches as he gets out of the car. He opens the back door and drags his bike out. Clattering it onto the tarmac, he lets it fall from his hands.

"Let's get this ower with," he says.

They stand in a line, each surveying the eight bumps that make up Balbeg. The highest is the point at which they are starting and will be ending. The other seven bumps are more or less the same in height and length. Joseph remembers the secret is to get off to a good start, get your speed up on the first downward slope and use it to carry you over the other seven. Out, as they say, is "nae bother." Coming back is the hard part. There is no high starting point on the way back, and so your speed is entirely self-generated. Already tired legs must work harder than ever so that enough momentum can be found for the last and highest part.

Talia's fancy lady's bike, with its wicker basket on the front, will bring up the rear, and Lachlan, because he sees himself as a gentleman with gear and chain issues, has already decided he will stay with her.

"It's not a race," he says.

"Aye rite," George shouts, and he's away, disappearing over the edge of the first bump before anyone else has agreed they're ready. Nathan, taking the challenge and with the madness of youth, launches himself after George, leg muscles straining to get the bike going from a standing start. It is in fact a race, Lachlan's assertion aside.

Joseph takes off a second ahead of Kenneth, determined to keep Nathan in his sights. Kenneth, just as resolute, catches and keeps pace with him. Gravity does its job for the long drop and the slight upward hump, the riders losing the ground at the highest point of the bump and then finding it again at the perfect point of the next downward slope. One after another, the bumps slide past; one after another the riders rise and fall and rise again.

George is whooping and shouting at the end of the eight. The wind has caught his hair and pushed it back from his face, leaving the rugged redness of his cheeks framed by the white of his forehead. Nathan, his bike turned to the side, is quick to greet Joseph with a cautious smile.

"Okay?" he asks, and Joseph, still needing all his breath, as he pedals, nods and smiles back.

Talia and Lachlan are not that far behind the rest of the group. Like silly teenagers, they are laughing and teasing each other. They find enough breath to grade each other's performance. Stepping back into childhood, the cobwebbed memories of the past scuttle out from the darkest corners of Joseph's mind. The smell of early morning and damp ground mixing with the blur of passing scenery reminds him of his childhood walk to school. The sound of bicycle chains and tyres on gravel puts him in mind of school holidays, outdoors, and freedom. The feel of the wind tussling at his hair and clothing, dishevelling him, reminds him of a past self, a boy with scuffed shoes and trousers that no longer sit at his ankles but that his mother says are good enough to play in. His breathing steadies and falls back into a more regular pattern. Muscles that have not been used in years protest. Stretching out first one leg and then the other, Joseph tries to work the ache and stiffness away. A longing for that younger, fitter, more resilient self mars an otherwise perfect moment.

"You cannae coast oan the way back," Nathan tells him. "Push hard all the way. Dinnae stop pedalling no matter how fast yer going or you'll nae make it up the other side."

Joseph nods and looks at the endpoint. "Let's go," he says, stealing George's idea, and side by side they take off. Nathan whoops and shouts, "Keep going!"

Leg muscles screaming, lungs burning, eyes watering, Joseph grips at the handlebars with every bit of strength he has.

"Pedal," Nathan shouts, and if he could, if he had the spare air to waste, Joseph would shout back, "Ah am." But there is only energy enough to pump the pedals and stay balanced on the bike.

As he thumps to a stop, the momentum keeps Joseph's bike moving sideways on him and it is only Nathan putting out a hand and grabbing the handlebars that keeps him and the bike upright. Bent over, head down, gulping in air, Joseph smiles at the sight of the others covering the distance at a more sedate pace.

"Sit up," Nathan says, and he pulls at Joseph's shirt so he is upright. Joseph manages a breathy laugh. George, coming to a stop just ahead of Talia and Lachlan, staggers from his bike, letting it fall to the road. Lying in the wet grass, he groans and rolls from side to side.

"Doc," he says, "Ah am having a heart attack, mebbe, or a stroke."

"What's the difference?" Lachlan asks, sounding genuine in his interest, if not his concern.

Nathan is the only one of the group who shows genuine concern, and with a lot more care for his own bike and Joseph's car, he rests it against the bike rack. Standing over his fallen comrade, he asks, "Ah you gonnae be awerite?"

"Help," George says, and then rolling to his left, he farts. His flatulence, taking him and everyone else by surprise, goes on for far longer than anyone would like.

"Jeee-suss," Kenneth says.

"Amen," Nathan says, and he moves upwind.

"Doc, stand down," George says, even though Joseph has yet to move or comment on his condition.

"Ah think it's just trapped wind."

"Really?" Joseph says, lowering his own bike down to rest gently on the ground before stepping over it and wobbling his way to his car.

With recovery comes self-praise, the recognition of what they have achieved, the relief that it is over, and the childlike joy that comes from unencumbered playtime. Memories of past misdemeanours, adventures, and mishaps trip and tumble in fragmented pieces from each of them in turn. Facts and the truth are fudged as they each slice together bits of the past, putting their own unique spin on things. Good natured arguments ensue, mixed with laughter and teasing. The years fall away, Joseph glimpsing again just for a moment, how things once were.

Perhaps, Nathan's age means he is still too close to childhood to need to immerse himself in memories, and choosing not to get involved, he takes himself away from the group along the edge of the road. Joseph watches as he finds a small lumpy pack of ground overlooking the fields. Highland cattle and sheep mingle in happy co-existence.

Stretching out his arms, legs and feet tight together, face turned skywards, Nathan waggles his fingertips, testing the air. He is crucifying himself, Joseph thinks, before others have a chance to, and then he watches as Nathan shouts into the haze-blurred skyline, "*Cause me tae hear thy loving kindness in the morning; for in thee do Ah trust: Cause me tae know the way wherein Ah should walk; for Ah lift up my soul unto thee.*"

Nathan's words, his stance, his very existence there on the side of the road, silence the group.

"Amen," he says. Then throwing back his head, he fills his lungs and sings, "Aaaaaaaaamen. Aaaaaaamen. Aaaaaamen." He stretches out the single word, breaking the stillness, filling the landscape.

Joseph loves him. The realisation throws him forward, back to the here and now. Finally, he understands. In Nathan's act of not giving a fuck, of showing his love for God's work, and being content in his own skin, Joseph knows he loves him.

"What the...?" Kenneth says, taken aback by Nathan's excited behaviour.

George, now with his where-with-all back, says, "Mind," and the simple one word of warning is enough to make Kenneth take heed and go silent once more.

Nathan, turning back to face them again, says, "Ah'm away."

Standing is difficult. Joseph's legs are already stiffening. He shuffles as he walks, closing the distance between them.

"But we're going for breakfast."

"Ah need tae spend some time with our Lord." Nathan, ignoring the puddles, the road, the fields of sheep and cattle, the prone form of George and the others, walks into Joseph's arms, folding himself in against Joseph in a show of intimacy they have not revealed in public before.

"Later I'll be away home to die on the sofa. Come check on me, okay?" Joseph says.

"Aye," Nathan says, and looking at Joseph, and only him, he adds, "*Because your steadfast love is better than life, my lips will praise you.*"

"Bible?" Joseph asks.

"Aye."

"Beautiful."

With Nathan in his arms, he can forget. He presses his nose into the boy's hair line. They are a perfect fit. Disregarding the others, he puts his mouth against Nathan's cheek—it's as good as a kiss. The boy smiles, and that's all that Joseph wants or needs.

Chapter 42

They push their way into an already crowded café , the breakfast is good, but sitting crammed together at an end table and close to the door, the chill of early morning seeps into Joseph's tired limbs. The food only goes partway to making up for the location of the table.

"So you're happy," Kenneth says. He waits until the others are distracted before asking. Laughing at the statement, Joseph is reminded that he asked the same question of Nathan the evening before, he uses Nathan's answer as his own.

"Yes. Everything Ah need and want in my life Ah have. Ah'm happy."

"You mean Nathan."

Joseph lowers his voice, sighs, looks away across the already busy café, and says, "This is me."

"You've changed," his brother says. Then he adds, "In a good way."

"Aye. Today Ah did the Balbeg bumps, and last night I danced naked in my living room with a beautiful blonde in my arms. Who knows what I'll get up tae tomorrow."

"I'm glad we came tae visit. It's a pain in the arse and hellish expensive, but for Mum and Dad, and seeing you and catching up, I'm glad Ah bothered."

"Mum is…" Joseph says, but then he struggles to find the right word to finish what he wants to say. He could pluck some medical term from his memory banks, but this is their mother and it needs something more personal.

"Aye, she's losing it. We cannae talk about it. Dad is pure insistent that we don't mention it. She comes and goes."

"How long has she been like that?"

"A year, maybe longer. There never seemed a good time to mention it tae you. You're one drama after another. I thought you had enough to deal with."

"Thanks," Joseph says.

"Your boy, Nathan," Kenneth says, standing up and stretching out sore and tired limbs.

"Yes."

"Ah like him. He's as wired as fuck, and those eyes… are strange, but Ah like him."

"Me too," Joseph says, and standing he puts enough money on the table to cover the cost of both breakfasts.

"So what will we do now? Ah'm in hiding all day so you have to think of something," Kenneth says, pushing his chair in, turning from the table, and waiting on Joseph to come up with a plan. As an afterthought, he adds, "Tomorrow we're eating at five. Sunday roast. Bring him."

"No."

"Bring him. Harper wants to see him again before we leave. Ah think she's sweet on him. And Ah want him tae give me those words, steadfast love all that stuff he was saying. It will come in handy if Ah mess up with the wife."

"They're in The Bible. You can find them there yourself."

"Good… Lord," Kenneth says, at the thought of having to trawl through The Bible to find the right part.

"Amen."

"Where shall we go?" Kenneth asks again.

"There's a farmer's market on in Dingwall."

"Aye. Okay, that will do."

Nathan's delighted with the invite. Joseph goes to great lengths to explain how awful it will be, but it doesn't put him off. Arriving last means places are already assigned. Nathan is seated between Joseph's mother and Harper, leaving Joseph no choice but to sit between his brother and father. Now seated directly opposite Nathan, he smiles, holds eye contact with him, and prays. There is plenty of opportunity for awkward silence. Sitting up on her knees, Harper empties a carton of coloured pencils onto the table and demands that Nathan do colouring in with her.

"Ah dinnae want tae," he tells her.

Never understanding the colouring pencils and paper thing at meal tables, Joseph's glad Nathan is not interested in pandering to the little girl. Then she looks up with big brown empty eyes and spreads her tacky hands.

"What, then?" she says, and she's kind of cute, innocent—very persuasive.

"Ah will draw something and you guess what it is," Nathan tells her, and he takes all the pencils from her and sorts them into his left hand.

Joseph, looking across at Meg, watches as her eyes lower and her lips relax into a flirty little smile as she looks at Nathan. His mother has turned her chair as well and now sitting at a better angle, Jospeh sees her face is composed, but her eyes dance about and then also settle on Nathan. She frowns at him, perhaps not remembering their introductions, Joseph thinks. With no encouragement, Harper crawls onto Nathan's lap. He moves just enough to accommodate the dirty blonde head of hair in his eye line as he draws. He ignores Harper's constant questioning, keeping her and everyone else guessing. Grandmother, mother, and child are all equally engaged. Kenneth, sitting back from the table, feeding breadsticks to his son, ignores the rest of the table. The bloody-minded part of Joseph is happy with the silence. But Nathan has softened his resolve, and yesterday's venture back into childhood has quieted the worst of his demons.

"Do you still enjoy a game of golf?" he asks his father.

"When I get the chance."

"I'm still a member. Nathan and I play occasionally. Perhaps we could make a four before you leave?"

He has not asked Kenneth, but glancing quickly over, he sees him smile and nod.

"I would like that," his father says, and Joseph stills for a moment, letting his thoughts carry him away to an idyllic round of golf, of finding the perfect swing, perhaps even getting a rare win. Harper scars his musings, letting out a squeal followed by a shout. "It's me!"

Looking back at the little girl who is crowded now by her mother and grandmother, Joseph sees the finished picture in her hand.

"Look, Granddad," she says, holding the picture, so it faces out towards the group. "It's me. I'm a rainbow."

Nathan has used all the colours available to draw her. Harper now runs forward out of the paper, arms spread wide, eyes bright, and laughing. Her hair falls in red folds over orange arms. Yellow, brown, and green blur and run together to make her skirt and top. He has done the background in shades of violet and midnight blue. The little girl is now a bright light emerging from a shadowy landscape.

"Awesome," Kenneth says, his words caught and lost in the group's general appreciation. Joseph's mother presses in closer to Nathan.

"How did you do that, Joseph?" she asks, and Nathan stumbles and stutters his words.

"Ah jist colour it," he says, but he looks to Joseph for an explanation, why has she called him by the wrong name?

"No lines!" she says. "Ah never knew you could draw, Joseph, how clever."

"No lines," Nathan repeats. "Ah jist blur and smudge it all taegether."

Nobody offers to correct the situation. Here is the real story, and Joseph gets it. His father is also coping with the loss of his wife. They should be able to share this platform of grief, but they won't.

"Look," his mother says, pointing at the picture Harper still holds. Her smile is genuine. "Look. Isn't Joseph clever."

"Joseph *is* clever," his father says, and he smiles at his wife, holds her gaze and avoids looking at anyone else.

His mother is lost to to him. A mother, who never attempted to recognise or acknowledge her son's actual accomplishments praises now those of an imposter. She will never know or understand this version of him, the choice taken from both their hands. The truth of a lie that had hurt and damaged them both in different ways is being played out. Harm that was done a lifetime ago is forgotten in favour of the sad failings of a mind and body that are winding down and giving up. Here is another ending, Joseph thinks, and he appreciates the journey his father is about to take. He allows the confusion and loss to go unchallenged.

"It's fine," he says. The words said loud enough for anyone to hear, but meant only for himself.

Nathan's a con. A beautiful con but a con nonetheless. Joseph has seen this performance played out many times before, and been the willing recipient of this act on many occasions. The boy stutters and stammers his answers and wins over the family members one by one. What's not to like, Joseph thinks. what's not to love.

At the end of the meal, they say their goodbyes. There will be a few more before the final one, and Joseph is already preparing for that moment.

Opening the front door, there is a safe sense of returning home. The sparse light of late evening changes the colours of the walls. Joseph's vision is smoke-blurred. Everything is the same; but it all feels different. Needing to sort the silence, Nathan skips past fragments of songs on his playlist until he finds what he likes.

"You want tae dance?" he asks.

"Always," Joseph says, copying Nathan's answer from yesterday. He likes the word better than "fine." "But first, a drink," he says.

Finding a reason to stay connected, Nathan runs the flat of his hand across Joseph's shoulders.

"Your maw's lost it a bit there," he says. "Ah didnae ken what tae do when she called me Joseph."

"It's sad, but I guess it's to be expected at her age," Joseph says, and anticipating a wave of hurt, he is confused that he feels nothing.

"What was she like before?"

"Distant." Joseph says. He has not thought about how to describe his mother, but then, nobody has ever asked him to. The single word seems to fit her well enough. Recalling the woman that she was, the memory of waiting at the school gate to collect his brother comes to mind. It is, he thinks, his earliest memory. Too young to go to school himself, the highlight of his day is holding his mother's hand and walking to and from the school to collect his brother. She allows him to run along the fence line and look in at the children playing. When his brother comes out of school, he walks ahead of them on his own, but Joseph must hold his mother's hand again and stay at her side. The memory links with other later memories of coming home late and his mother's wrath, of being grounded and thinking she was unnecessarily harsh and cruel. "Difficult," his father would say to him. "Joseph, why do you have to be so difficult?"

"Do you think I'm difficult?" Joseph asks Nathan, trying to anchor the version he has of himself in the past to the person he is now.

"Aye, most of the time you're bloody impossible."

Hurt by Nathan's words, Joseph snaps. "Then why stay?"

"Free bed and digs," Nathan says, and dancing away from Joseph, he grinds his hips in time to the music and hums to himself.

"Why was your maw distant?"

"I think she wanted more from her life, only she did nothing about it. Also, I don't think she ever got over the disappointment of not having a girl."

"You're kinda a girl."

"When you say things like that, I have to question why we are even together."

"You need tae lighten up. Ah'm with you cos Ah love you." Still humming in between his words, Nathan grinds his way back to Joseph.

"Did you give Kenneth the piece of paper?" Joseph asks, ignoring his attempt to smoothing things over.

"Aye."

"Did he tell you why he wanted it?"

"Aye, he said he was going tae use the words oan his wife when he needed tae come up with something special because they are the most beautiful words he's heard. But he didnae want to have tae read the whole bloody bible to find them."

"Did he say anything else?"

"Aye, he said he never thought he'd see you with a blonde."

"You work hard," Joseph tells him.

"Aye. Ah have tae. You're hard work."

"No rules? No lines," Joseph says. "Do you really love me?"

"Aye."

"When did you know?

Nathan, using his mouth on Joseph's neck, says nothing, and waits.

It has turned out to be a good day. Things being as they are and as they have always been is, he thinks, well, fine, and sometimes fine will do. Not everything can be sorted or fixed. The past, unlike his dreams, is what it is. He cannot correct or re-wright, or put right any part of it. Here and now and the future is where his focus should be, he tells himself.

"It was spring," Nathan says, breaking the silence. "Ah was sitting at the bottom of yer garden on a bucket, Ah wisnae looking my best. Ah watched you walk out onto the decking, shielding your eyes from the glare of the sun. Ah waved, and you walked across the garden and come down tae where Ah was sitting—it was then," he says, and moving gently in time with the music, he catches Joseph's hand, pulling him in closer.

"Then!" Joseph says.

"Then."

And Joseph smiles. It feels every bit as good as the smile drawn by Nathan on the portrait in the hallway. He has looked at that portrait's face many times now. In it he has seen a truth. Like a childish game of hide and seek, Nathan found him, dug him out of his hiding place where he was trapped, in his own lies. We all need to be found, Joseph thinks.

He says to himself, "Come out, come out wherever you are."

Finally he has been found out, he thinks, and the lie that haunted him laid to rest, as all good ghosts should be.

About the Author

Michelle Graham-Taylor was born in 1967 in Tidworth Hampshire. She works as a local social worker and lives with her family and an assortment of animals in the Highlands of Scotland over looking Loch Ness. The Ghost of a Lie is her first novel.

Printed in Great Britain
by Amazon

65823708R00187